The COST of LIVING

Also

by

David Dorsey

■

THE FORCE

The COST of LIVING

David Dorsey

VIKING

VIKING
Published by the Penguin Group
Penguin Books USA Inc., 375 Hudson Street,
New York, New York 10014, U.S.A.
Penguin Books Ltd, 27 Wrights Lane,
London W8 5TZ, England
Penguin Books Australia Ltd, Ringwood,
Victoria, Australia
Penguin Books Canada Ltd, 10 Alcorn Avenue,
Toronto, Ontario, Canada M4V 3B2
Penguin Books (N.Z.) Ltd, 182–190 Wairau Road,
Auckland 10, New Zealand

Penguin Books Ltd, Registered Offices:
Harmondsworth, Middlesex, England

First published in 1997 by Viking Penguin,
a division of Penguin Books USA Inc.

1 3 5 7 9 10 8 6 4 2

Grateful acknowledgment is made for permission to reprint an excerpt from "Cross Road Blues" by Robert Johnson. Copyright © (1978), 1990, 1991 King of Spades Music. All rights reserved. Used by permission.

PUBLISHER'S NOTE
This is a work of fiction. Names, characters, places, and incidents either are the product of the author's imagination or are used fictitiously, and any resemblance to actual persons, living or dead, events, or locales is entirely coincidental.

LIBRARY OF CONGRESS CATALOGING-IN-PUBLICATION DATA
Dorsey, David
The cost of living / David Dorsey.
p. cm.
ISBN 0-670-87471-X (alk. paper)
I. Title.
PS3554.0715C67 1997 96-52419
813'.54—dc21

This book is printed on acid-free paper.
∞

Printed in the United States of America
Set in Janson
Designed by Kathryn Parise

F
o
r

RICHARD TODD

Dramatis Personae

RICHARD CAHILL	Account executive at a mid-size advertising agency in Rochester, New York
MEG CAHILL	His wife, owns an art gallery
DANA	Their teenage daughter
ALEC	Their twelve-year-old son

■

JIMMY	*Jimmy Sorley*, Cahill's best friend from college, a writer and account manager for Veritex, the agency's largest client
VINCE	*Vince Stringer*, employed by Veritex as a marketing-communications manager, controls money that comes to the agency from Veritex
TISH	*Tish Anderson*, newly appointed as Stringer's boss at Veritex

JENNIFER	*Jennifer Dewinter*, secretary and receptionist
PENNY	Cahill's employer, agency's owner, *Penny McKee*
WES	Cahill's best friend, *Wes Mercer*, a star writer at the agency
WHIT	Cahill's superior, *Whit Sutherland*, head of client services
GREGG	*Gregg Corcoran*, Meg Cahill's business associate

■

BOGARDUS	An investigator for the county, *Frank "Fuzzy" Bogardus*
WILL	*Will "T-Boy" Breedlove*, a gang member, in his teens
PAULETTE	*Paulette Breedlove*, Will's older sister
CLYTEMNESTRA	*Clytemnestra "Clytie" Breedlove*, mother of Will and Paulette
DEWITT	*Calvin "The Benz" DeWitt*, an older gang member
GP	*Eugene "GP" Price*, a powerful drug dealer in upstate New York
FATHER GREGOR	A Russian Orthodox monk

The COST of LIVING

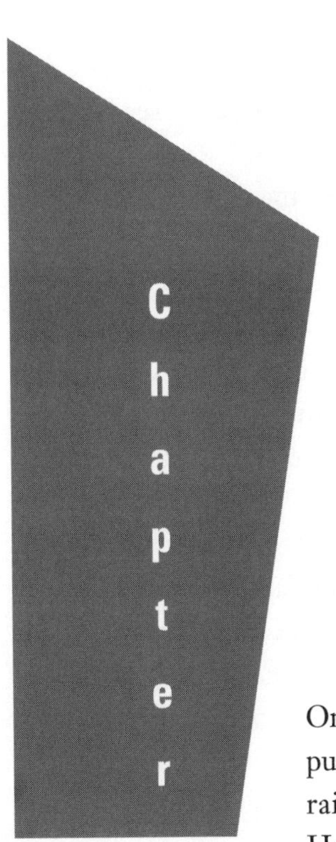

Chapter 1

I'm standin' at the crossroad, babe,
I believe I'm sinkin' down.
—*Robert Johnson*

On the highway, I drink my coffee and push my luck with the speed limit. It rains over Syracuse and Utica and Herkimer. I take the off-ramp and drive up the winding roads into the green Adirondacks as sunlight and blue sky break through the clouds.

When I pull around the last turn, the little Orthodox chapel glows in the sun; everything looks vivid and crisp against the green grass. Every little corner of wall and roof folds into another surface at a slightly different angle, every slate-blue shingle so steep it's almost vertical, every peak pointed and crowned with an onion dome, shiny and golden, like a huge Hershey's Kiss. It makes me feel guilty just looking at this place—everything trimmed and raked, polished and scrubbed. My own newly seeded lawn could use a good weeding.

I park in front of the church, near the flower beds full of blooming white peonies. I finish my coffee and toss my Starbucks go-cup into the Escort. Nine years and counting with this car. Maybe *next* year I'll buy a new one, if we can get over the hump on our bills. A monk in his dark habit pauses and tilts his head in my direction as if he thinks I belong on the thirteenth hole somewhere, draining a thirty-foot putt. Hold that thought, brother. I don't plan to be here long.

"Can I help?" he asks.

"I'm here to pick up something from Father Gregor?"

He looks me over, as if he has indeed heard of my species for years without ever seeing an actual specimen. Then I follow him up the steps as he leads me into the dormitory, where a man I assume is Gregor sits at his desk, working at a computer. He's scribbling something on a notepad beside his old electronic relic from a decade when the *hardware* was known as a word processor. The other monk nods and leaves the room.

Gregor turns around and then stands up quickly, as if he feels he's been impolite by not greeting me already. His long beard hangs down over his collar; he looks muscular, as if he's usually one of the people out in the fields in October, leading the harvest. He's alert, calm, completely aware of everything around him, unhurried, undistracted. He looks strikingly happy. I wonder what Web page *he* was on.

"Richard?" he asked.

"Hi," I say, shaking his hand.

"At last," he says, grinning. "Can I get you some tea?"

"No, I'm fine," I say.

I scan the bookshelves for volumes in English, the peculiar musty scent of old books tangled up with something else, like the scent of cinnamon. Father Gregor watches me. I want to walk around and run my fingertips over the circular tea stains on the wooden surface of the desk, the spectacles resting on a torn sheet of paper, the old rotary-dial telephone under the desk lamp beside that computer with its dark screen and bright green letters. It all looks simple and backward and trustworthy. Nothing in my own house looks as real as the scuffed old workboots in the corner, the scratchy woolen scarf hanging on a peg since the March ice storm, or the photograph of an old woman, her head in a babushka, her eyes closed, the background a blur. We both sit, and he sips his tea, watching me. I imagine a samovar kept in a closet somewhere, beside a yellowed photograph of the Tsar.

"How was your drive?"

"It's beautiful up here. I can see why my mother loved this place," I say.

"Isn't much of an escape. If that's what you're thinking."

"No. Just slower, maybe. Nicer."

"Your mother felt at home here."

"I'm just here for the money."

"Why didn't you want it before?"

"I thought you guys could use it. I know she would have been happy if I'd given it to you. When you said no, I came up with an alternative."

"Besides spending it, you mean?"

"I don't want it for myself."

"Ah—" he says.

"I figured you people would *need* the money," I say. "You aren't exactly rolling in the big bucks up here."

"I was always under the impression *you* people needed it more than we do. Correct me if I'm wrong, but did *you* take a vow of poverty?"

"So, do I have to sign something?"

"Forgive me for prying. But can you tell me what you intend to do with it?"

"Does that make a difference?" I ask.

"I'd like to know. That's all."

"There's someone who needs it," I say.

"More than you do."

"Yes."

"It's a lot of money to give away," he says. "I have no idea what your income is like, of course."

"Trust me. It's never enough," I say.

He reaches into a locked drawer and removes a wooden cigar box with the words *Benedit Cigars* burned into the side. He unlatches the little brass hasp and opens the lid and holds the box out to me: I reach for the check made out to me for the balance of a money market account at a bank in Utica: $22,543. I recognize my mother's signature at the bottom. Then I place the check back into the box, and he sets it on his desk.

"So can you tell me about it?"

He's good. He's *very* good. He should be working as an interrogator for the county. Investigative reporter. IRS auditor. Get him a shave. Good pair of shoes. He's already got the killer curiosity.

I begin at the moment of the crime, the *first* crime. I'm not sure what good it does. I've reached the awkward age when it's clear that if you add things up—beautiful wife, intelligent children, nice home in the suburbs, and a solid career—all the things you might say about your life will never clarify how hard it is to face the murky way it feels. It's just that at some point you realize there *is* such a thing as the truth. And you realize, in some small way, you have to surrender to it.

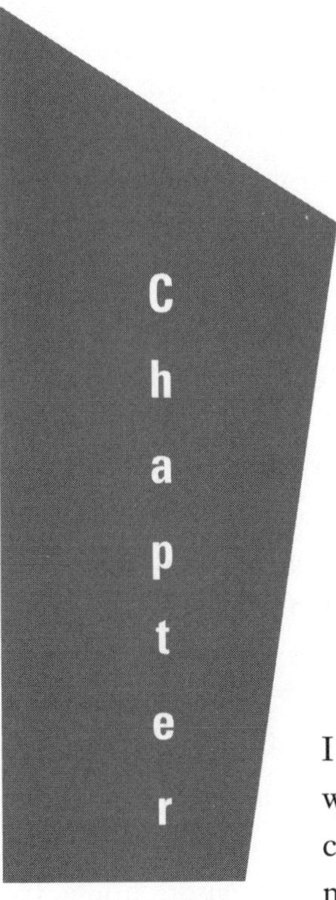

2

I wasn't watching when it happened. I was waiting my turn in line when they came into the McDonald's. I didn't notice them at first, even though the tall one had a Mercedes hood ornament hanging around his neck, with his head shaved around a patch of hair buzzed into a White Sox logo. I glanced around long enough to see untucked Polo shirts under hooded sweats, black stocking caps, and Oakley sunglasses, and then I turned back to the menu.

Outside, it was still snowing. A winter in upstate New York turns the sky a shade of gray worthy of some fogbound prospect in Seattle or Copenhagen, but the Lake Ontario ceiling didn't bother me, not when I was about to embark on the single most productive Saturday of my life. I wanted to get in and get out, and then put in five hours at the office. I'd had three cups of coffee before leaving home: I might as well have been floating a foot off the ground. My brain was lighting up my retinas from behind. I was ready to take on anything.

I checked out the Saab where I'd parked it diagonally across two slots, though it was hardly big enough to fill one. I'd angled it beside a platinum BMW with a black man sitting behind the wheel, reading the business page. When I got out of the Saab, he glanced at me, and our eyes connected for a second, and then he looked away. I hesitated, wondering if I should leave Alec alone, but then I headed inside the restaurant. I could see Alec, a little pink blotch moving behind the Saab's fogged rear window. He was in a rush to sign up for a winter CYO basketball camp. Alec was twelve, and he weighed about as much as a racing dog, but he was convinced he had serious business to conduct someday with the National Basketball Association, and these ambitions took seniority over all other considerations in life. He had big, happy eyes and a haircut called a fade—on a white kid, it looked like a bowl of brown hair with a little stubble around the ears and neck. He looked like a cross between a Benedictine monk and the Little Dutch Boy.

As usual, I gravitated to the slowest line. The kid at the counter reminded me of myself: eager, dutiful, and too observant of what other people wanted. I actually went through a period in college when I hid for hours in the stacks, studying books of manners so I wouldn't make a fool of myself when everyone else knew which fork to use. I took out student loans and worked a trick shift at the brewery's loading dock to keep from starving, though you'd never guess it to look at me now. I could pass for just another J. Crew suburban dad, as if I hadn't grown up in a broken home and labored almost full-time since the age of nineteen and got married and had my first child the year I was graduated from college.

When I saw those two black kids rubbernecking in the next line, the older one, with the Benz medallion, stared at me through his sunglasses for about five seconds. It was like hitting a dead key on a piano. I looked away, but my heart was pounding, and then I cut another quick peek and saw the younger one staring at me. His skin looked familiar, but I couldn't remember why. It was *sierra*, exactly the shade I'd seen on a carpet sample with that ridiculous name—our realtor showed it to us. We ruled it out as a possibility for the house we were planning to build.

As I turned back toward the menu, the Benz produced a gun and fired a single round into the ceiling. I was falling to the floor before I realized what was happening. I had time to act, but not to feel frightened. It was as if every last one of us had been doing it all our lives: pick up dry cleaning, get lunch at McDonald's, drop and crawl during gunfire, and then try to salvage the rest of our Saturday. I turned my head just enough to see they'd pulled ski caps down over their faces.

"Come on, come on," the Benz shouted at the cashier. "T-Boy. Keep an eye on them they's over on the floor."

"God *damn*, what I tell you?" the younger one shouted. "No names."

The room smelled like the Fourth of July. Suddenly it got quiet. Then I heard the cashier's muffled sobs and the jingling till and clean sneakers squeaking on the tiles, circling around behind me. The shoes came into view, a pair of unlaced white Converse All Stars, and when I looked up, I could see it was the one called T-Boy, with that sierra-colored skin around the eyes and lips I could see through the holes in the stocking cap.

"Keep you head down," T-Boy said, almost confidentially, as

if the two of us might otherwise have been terrific friends. "Stay still."

I was grateful for this little aside, and, as usual, I struggled without success to come up with a clever response. I wanted to act as if I'd been through this sort of thing a hundred times, if only to make him relax and get it over with. The older one said something to the girl behind the counter that cracked me up: *And a Big Mac.* I imagined shouting my own order, with my face pasted to the floor: *Count me in for a Happy Meal down here, would ya?*

"Move!"

"Come on!" the Benz shouted across the room at T-Boy, standing near me. Outside, the BMW pulled up to the door. "Get you ass in gear, Home."

As T-Boy started to get up, he leaned his hand against my spine, and my billfold slid out of the pocket. I knew I was losing everything: my cash, my plastic, a list of everybody's birthdays and sizes (including my own), my driver's license, my Social Security card, and my pocket calendar with my appointments for the month and the little notes I'd jotted to myself in the back. Gone, all the crib sheets and crutches I needed to live my life with order and decency, including the fifteen To Do items I'd assigned myself for the rest of the day. There was no way I'd remember them without the list. He picked it up and flopped it open across the back of his thumb.

"Richard Cahill," he said quietly.

"Nice meeting you," I said.

He wasn't amused.

I figured everything would work out if I just did nothing. I knew how to look the other way as other people did things I wouldn't think of doing myself. I was sure if anyone was going to get hurt, they would have gotten hurt already. I felt strangely safe.

Slowly I lifted my head up, until my eyes were high enough to see the door. I had to look between T-Boy's legs, but he was too busy watching what the others were doing at the counter to notice. The windows were low enough to let me see Alec's head as he got out of the Saab. Why was he getting out? It could have been anything: the time I was taking, a change in his order, a quick trip to the men's room. As I saw him shut the car door, I kept praying he would change his mind and go back. I kept repeating the words in my mind: *Turn around, turn around, don't come in, just don't come in.* The girl at the counter was fumbling with the money, spilling coins on the floor, as the Benz got louder with her: *Hand it over, bitch. Come on, come on!* Alec was reaching for the door.

It was all I could do to stay down, watching my little boy's face coming up to the glass, pulling the door with his skinny arm. I watched him come through the door and realize the McDonald's seemed to have emptied out as he saw all of us stretched out on the floor. You could see the creepiness of it rushing through him. He spotted me almost immediately and started in my direction, as if he could sneak across the restaurant and curl up beside me on the floor without anyone's noticing, but I kept waving him away with one hand, just moving my hand and mouthing the words: "Get out!" But he kept coming.

The rest seemed to happen in slow, disjointed flashes. As Alec got halfway across the floor, he slid into a puddle of spilled soda, with a gravel of crushed ice spread across it. As I watched him slip, I squeezed my eyes shut, and without even realizing I was doing it I began whispering the Orthodox prayer my mother taught me as a child: *Have mercy, have mercy, have mercy.* When I opened my eyes, he was already falling.

"Dad!" Alec shouted.

"Go, go!" I yelled at him, exactly the words I used whenever I waved him past third base in Little League, but in this case, he'd already started his slide.

"God *damn*," T-Boy said, turning around and spotting Alec as he hit the floor.

He landed on his hip, and the impact knocked a little squeal out of him. He never whined, so I knew he was in trouble. His Michigan cap twisted sideways, and he was clutching himself, all doubled up, with his knees pulled to his chest. I looked up again, and watched through the window as the third man got out of the idling BMW, the man I'd seen with the business page. He approached the door, and he had a ski cap over his face now, too. As he came in, he looked over toward Alec and then walked slowly across the floor, finally standing over him, and looking at me, as if he knew I was the unstable element in that room. He was a big, almost calming presence, arriving to take charge of this mess. I was frantic, but stunned—I wanted him to see I wasn't going to try anything. Alec groaned, and the tall one with the Mercedes ornament around his neck backed away from the counter, slowly making his way toward the door, stepping over people, until he stood beside the driver.

"Let's go," the driver said quietly. "Now!"

T-Boy hopped across all the spread-eagled customers and, as he caught up with the others, he paused over Alec's body. Alec stayed curled into a ball, his eyes shut tight in pain. I imagined rib fragments prodding his lungs and heart. The driver shoved backward through the door and shouted: "I said *now!*"

As T-Boy reached down and twisted Alec's cap so the visor pointed backward, turning it into a rally cap, I pushed myself up. Before I realized he was trying to do something *for* Alec rather than *to* him, I yelled: "Hands off, T-Boy! Who you guys think you are?"

I was shaking. After I shouted those words, they kept looping in my mind: *think you are, think you are, think you are.* I never shouted in public, except at a Bills game. I had no idea what I was doing. If only I'd handled myself the way I normally did on any other day of my life, if only I'd kept quiet, then nothing else would have happened quite the way it did. But something clicked into place, and I entered one of those zones where fear melts into something else just as ungovernable. When I look back at it now, I realize the moment I shouted that kid's street name was the beginning of everything that has happened in my life since then.

The driver looked at me steadily, pulling his head back an inch, so his chin seemed to sink into his neck. He looked surprised and puzzled, almost smiling at my audacity, as if he wasn't sure whether he ought to shoot me or ask me if I needed a lift. He had the presence of mind, and the sense of leisure in the middle of all this, to find me *interesting*. He came over slowly, and hunkered down beside my head, almost whispering in my ear: "What did you say?"

I lay as still as possible, not looking up, not knowing if he had a gun, not knowing what he was going to do. When I didn't answer, he got up, moved away again, and as I looked up, I saw him grab T-Boy by the collar and yank him outside. The third one, the Benz, was biting into his complimentary Big Mac as they scrambled into the BMW.

I flew across the room and bent down over Alec.

"Can you move?" I asked.

"It hurts. Right here. My leg."

"Jerks," I said, looking up, my eyes filling with tears. "Animals."

"I think something broke," he said.

"I'm going to carry you to the car, kiddo. You ready?"

He nodded.

"Hang on to me tight. Easy. Hold on."

"Let's just get out of here," he said.

I took Alec into my arms, slowly lifting him from the floor, and he started to cry. He dug his nails into my neck as I kissed him on the head, as if he were five years old and on his way to bed after *The Wizard of Oz.* I carried him out through the door, and the cold wind fired snowflakes into my teeth. My feet didn't seem to belong to the rest of my body.

The roads were tricky. You couldn't see the black ice coming on the interstate. A big eighteen-wheeler jackknifed near the interchange, and I was almost off the highway behind it, but I managed to pull out of the skid and swerve away from the oncoming cars. I kept glancing over at Alec, and he had himself curled up, trying to brace himself against the little jolts and shimmies of the road. I reached over to comfort him by touching his arm, his shoulder, his face.

At Strong Memorial, I rushed in, told them what had happened, and they sent a wheelchair out to the car and brought him in. The hot air in the emergency room pounded our faces as the doors slid open. It was take-a-number and take-a-seat. I couldn't believe they would make us sit there along with everyone else with their complaints of dizziness and aching stomachs and twisted ankles. The place seemed crammed with refugees, all reading magazines. None of them seemed to be in pain.

I eased Alec into one of the few vacant seats, beside the dented snack machine, and I headed around the corner to the pay phone. My hands were shaking so badly I could hardly get the coins into the slots. The phone swallowed four of my quarters, and then, on my fifth, it pitied me with a dial tone. I could have avoided all this by using the cellular phone I'd installed in the Saab, but I never remembered it was there when I needed it.

"I'm at Strong Memorial," I said when Meg answered.

"Why?" she asked.

"Alec fell."

"At the tryouts?"

"At McDonald's," I said.

"At Mc—"

"I lost my wallet. I had everything listed in there. The things he's allergic to and everything. I can't even remember if *I've* had chicken pox. They want to know."

"Is Alec all right?" she asked.

"It's his leg. He must have broken something. Take the back streets. Highway's a mess."

I expected her to hang up, but instead, I heard her put her hand over the phone. Then she came back on.

"Who's there?" I asked.

"Gregg stopped by on his way over to the new office complex. He just offered to drop me off at the hospital."

"Tell Gregg we've got two cars," I said.

"I'll be right there."

With Alec to worry about, it was easier to ignore the queasy feeling I got every time she mentioned Gregg Corcoran's name.

When Meg arrived, I waved at her from beside the front desk, but she was looking for our son, and then Gregg came through the door, trailing about ten feet behind her, looking concerned, keeping his distance, with his little hoop earring and his Vandyke beard and his ponytail. Meg was shorter than I was, and I was a couple of inches shy of six feet, yet she had the arresting profile of a model. With her blond hair parted on the side, she was still as beautiful as when I'd dated her in college. She handed me her purse with a worried look.

"You all right? Where is he?" she asked.

"Over there."

She headed for Alec as I fished for the information I needed and signed the forms and then glanced back at Gregg, who leaned forward and held out his hand.

"Is there anything I can do?" he asked.

"I can take it from here, Gregg," I said, giving his hand a single, perfunctory shake. "Thanks for giving Meg a lift."

"Sure I can't help?"

"This is going to take a while. Thanks, though."

He craned his neck until Meg looked up and gave him a little wave, and he smiled, lifting his head to answer the wave, and then turned and left. I joined Meg and Alec by the vending machine. She was talking with him quietly, and he seemed to have regained his usual good humor, despite the pain, managing to smile at a few things she was telling him. I couldn't hear a word of it. The caffeine was wearing off, and I was feeling weak with hunger, but I didn't even glance at the candy. I kept looking at the front desk, fighting the urge to go over and start interrogating the woman. Finally, I walked across the room and stared at her as she took information from an older couple. I could hear the man wheezing, but I didn't care.

"Can I help you?" she asked.

"You see that little boy over there?" I asked the woman at the desk.

"Sir? Someone will be with you in—"

"He needs attention. Look at him!"

"What is it you want me to see?" she asked.

"He's in *pain.*"

"Everyone here needs attention," she said. "Please be patient."

"Tell that to *him,*" I said.

When I went back across the waiting room to where they were seated, Meg had her arm around Alec. My heart was thumping again, and I felt angrier than ever.

"How is it now, honey?" Meg asked.

"It won't stop hurting," Alec said, the tears drying on his cheeks.

"They'll take care of it."

"You think we can get out of here in time?" Alec asked, looking up at me.

"It doesn't matter," I said. "We don't have to get there today. They'll sign you up the first day of practice."

His eyes filled with tears, and his mouth crumpled. He looked down, but he didn't make a sound. He wanted to be one of the starters, one of the All Stars. I could see him falling behind the others, loitering in a doorway somewhere while his friends piled into a bus together, leaving him with the sunlight weighing on his face.

"They really have a gun on you?" Meg asked. "Alec told me."

"Not *on* me."

"God."

"What? I'm practically deaf in this ear," I said. "Where's Dana?"

"She's bagging today at the supermarket. I couldn't get through to her. I left her a note," Meg said. "The way she works, I don't know how she keeps up her grades."

I went over to the front desk and asked the nurse to take another look at my son's face and then tell me we'd have to wait another half hour to get some attention. She told me someone would be with us shortly. Another nurse came up, with a pair of Advils and a cup of water, and wheeled Alec into a room. Almost half an hour later, the intern arrived.

"You Alec?" he asked, probing the injured hip. Alec winced and nodded.

"So. What happened?" he asked.

"He slipped on some—"

The intern held up his hand, and I stopped.

"He's a big guy," the intern said. It didn't take me long to figure it out. If a kid showed up injured, even if the parents were there, get a story from the one who was hurt, not from the potential assailants. I wondered how long it would take for the intern to realize he was the world's most annoying twit. I couldn't wait to see the truth rise into his face.

"I was at the McDonald's," Alec said.

"Uh-huh," the intern said. "Does this hurt?"

"Yes! Ow!" Alec said, flinching. "And I slipped."

"Tell me about that, uh, Alec," the intern said, having to glance at the form to remind himself.

"On the ice."

"What ice?" the intern asked.

"On the floor. They spilled it. They had a gun, so I wasn't looking, and I fell."

"Gun?" he asked, glancing up at me. I glared at him.

"Everybody was, like, on the floor?" Alec said, his eyes filling with tears again. "It really hurts."

The intern glanced sheepishly at me and then at Meg.

"What's he talking about?" he asked.

"I told them at the front desk. I walked into a McDonald's just before it was held up," I said. "Alec fell in the middle of it."

"Can we speed this up?" Meg asked.

The intern went back to work, probing Alec's hip with his fingertips, manipulating the leg a few times again, making Alec yelp, and finally he decided on X rays. *Gee, tough call. Who would have guessed?* After a two-hour trip to radiology and back, with Alec on a gurney, the intern walked into the little room where Meg and I waited, saying nothing to each other. He had the X rays in hand, and they flapped, making a sort of tongue-clucking sound. He looked as if he'd never been more delighted.

"See that?" he asked. "That little cap of bone on top?"

"Where?"

He pointed to the joint, but I wasn't listening. You could hold Alec's pelvis in your palm almost, with the backbone above and the dog bone of his leg below. The skeleton was so thin, it looked as if I could have folded it up and carried it away in a gym bag. I imagined his little heart making a fist, over and over. Looking at the X ray, I wondered if he'd ever make another jump shot or if he'd end up like his father, a midlevel managerial type in a midsize advertising agency, trying to provide for himself and his family, feeling the weight of it get heavier every year.

"See how it's out of line, compared to the other leg? See? That little line, there, right there, that's where the cap's going to fuse with the rest of the femur."

"So what's all this mean?"

"The bone's coming apart at the growth plate. It hasn't broken away yet, that's where he's lucky. But when he fell on his hip, it got knocked loose," he said. He sounded thrilled. A find like this one, it was a good night for him. "It's pure textbook. It's called a slipped femoral capital epiphysis. It's not really common. You wouldn't mind if I show it around later, would you? Only place I've ever seen it's in the classroom. Usually, if you see it at all, it's in overweight adolescent black males."

"Is this permanent? Will this affect the way he walks?" I said. "Will he be able to play basketball?"

"He'd better go easy on that for a while. That's the bad news," he said. "He'll be up and walking around in no time. But no team play for a while."

"The good news?"

"This isn't routine surgery but it isn't high-risk either. It's a small incision. We use a pin to hold the bone together until it fuses. I can wheel him into surgery tonight, you sign a couple forms," the intern said. "OR's got some downtime. Work him right in. Get him home tomorrow."

We talked with the surgeon for a couple minutes as the nurses wheeled Alec down the hall and out of sight. I felt paralyzed, just watching it all happen, unable to touch him, to be there with him. He was already half unconscious from the IV, and when we hugged him goodbye, I'm not sure he even knew we were there. I wanted to be there, holding on to him, so he'd feel my hand on his arm even when he was asleep.

I glanced compulsively at my watch, and realized I'd spent my Saturday in the hospital rather than at work. I knew exactly what awaited me at the office. I had a marketing-communications plan to complete, as the centerpiece of a new business pitch I was doing in addition to five brochures, a speech, a sales-training video, and billboards I was handling for one of our other account executives, away on vacation. We were still so behind the curve, we didn't have the proposal's sample copy done, even though I had tickets in my desk for a flight to New York on Friday, when we were going to pitch the idea at the new client's corporate headquarters. I felt my children's future rested on it: Get that account, then get the raise, then start a college fund with my broker, start building the nest egg to help keep Dana and Alec out of debt, give them the edge I didn't have at their age. And I'd only just paid off my own college loans a few months before.

Meg and I took the elevator down to the hospital's empty lobby, where they told us we could wait through the surgery.

"Did you talk to the mortgage guy at all?" I asked on the way down, though I was in no mood to hear about it.

"I'll tell you about it later," she said.

I'd intended to drop Alec off at home after signing him up for basketball, and then head to work for a few hours before joining Meg and the housing developer to discuss our application with our mortgage rep, Lloyd Tubbs. We wanted to build a new house in Fairfield, an older suburb where we already lived, which meant we had to put up the smallest house the development would allow, on one of the few remaining available tracts in our town.

We'd started talking about it a year earlier, after we'd pumped three feet of water out of the cellar and discovered an infestation of bats in our roof.

Our house had old-fashioned street appeal, with its yellow stucco walls and dark brown trim and the tight net of ivy holding up the cracked chimney, but once you went inside, the charm faded. We'd bought the place before the children were born, and it was a little over a thousand square feet, if you didn't include my attic study, which could have served as a storage refrigerator in the winter. Living in that house had come to feel like a sort of punishment. On the second floor, we had three tiny bedrooms and a shared bath—the only bath, the only toilet, in the house. Our bedroom had such a small closet, we kept half of our clothes, sometimes even the clothes we needed for the current season, on a long dowel I'd hung between two walls in the attic. In the winter, you could see your breath up there. The roof was insulated, but the old windows were so leaky, there was no way to keep the attic comfortable when the mercury dropped below twenty. I was worried my little Macintosh would freeze up: I mean, *literally*. Dana had enough room for a double bed, a dresser, and a chair, but not enough for a desk. Alec's room had only enough space for his bed and a dresser. The headboard pressed against one wall with twelve inches between the opposite wall and the foot of the bed.

The bats were the worst, with their pointy ears and the claws on their elbows. They lived under the roof, crawling down between the joists when the weather warmed up, burrowing out at dusk to feed on insects. Occasionally they found an opening into the house itself. The night Meg found three of them—two circling in a holding pattern just under our bedroom ceiling, another huddled on the bathtub drain—was the night we vowed to move out.

I wanted my children, for at least a few years, to live in a new house, a house with enough room to invite their friends for sleep-overs, a house that kept us warm in the winter, and where everything worked the way it was supposed to. I wanted to live the way we'd been raised to believe we *could* live, if only we worked hard enough and saved scrupulously enough. I could imagine the sunlight flashing from yellow leaves in October, the smell of marigolds a dog's pelt brings in from outside, the clinking of dishes from a neighbor's open kitchen window.

We'd looked at a few older homes, though the only one Meg liked was completely renovated and out of our range, hardly less expensive than the new ones. We'd be right back in the same spot as before: replacing the furnace, putting in copper plumbing, pumping out the wet basement in April, patching holes in the roof to keep out the squirrels and bats, and taping clear sheets of plastic over all the windows to keep out the winter draft. Inside, our current house looked like an oxygen tent by the time snowflakes started falling in November.

Once we'd settled in the lobby, I gazed at Meg's face as she closed her eyes and rested her head against the cushion behind her. She'd done some shoots for a small-time modeling agency out in Webster, run by a fellow who used to say things like: *The celadon in that divan and the hunter green in those shades, well, they fight.* Or, when he talked about someone who'd died: *He's gone to room temperature.* Those sessions covered tuition for her degree in art history. Now she ran a little gallery in the basement of a Cambridge Street apartment building, flying off to New York every three or four months to meet with dealers in SoHo and on Fifty-seventh Street, trying to get better representation for her Rochester clients. A year earlier, she'd teamed up with Gregg Corcoran, an artist who'd become an agent and then the dealmaker of the two. Together, they'd tripled her gallery's revenues. Gregg had helped Meg get three big contracts with commercial real estate developers, who bought hundreds of works from her artists, all bundled together in the deals. It was a new way of selling art for her—in bulk—and it made her uneasy, but we'd both come to rely on the money.

"I hate this," I said.

"It hasn't been that long. He'll be fine."

"Why can't we be there when he wakes up?" I asked. "That's what pisses me off. Why's he have to be by himself when he wakes up?"

"Let's talk about something else," she said. "Okay?"

"He's going to open his eyes and not know where the hell he is and you know he'll just—"

"I mean it. We're just going to get all worked up. Talk about something else," she said. "You all right? You look—"

"I'm fine. You talk to Lloyd?"

"He called. He said, and I quote, we're all set to rock and roll."

"It bothers me we won't have money for anything else. We're really out on the edge with this," I said.

"Actually, he said the payments would be a little less than we thought. We covered everything on the phone."

"Dana's going to be in debt up to her ears for college," I said.

"With your raise and this new deal I'm hoping to close, we can start putting away some real money. Gregg said he talked with the Kestler brothers a few days ago and he thinks it's just about in the bag."

"What about that other art dealer? The one from Toronto?" I asked.

"Gregg's going to put a bug in their ear about the stuff getting hung up for weeks in customs. It happens, I guess," she said.

"Are the Kestlers returning his calls?"

"They're out of town or something. We'll know better in a week."

"That Canadian dealer's bid was a lot lower than yours, though, right?" I asked.

"Let me handle it, okay?"

I sighed and said, to no one in particular, "God, why can't they come down here and tell us how it's going up there?"

Meg finally got through to Dana. She'd just gotten home from work. Dana said she could stay the night at a friend's house, and her friend's parents would drop her off at the hospital in the morning. I closed my eyes, and two hours later, woke up and went looking for the earliest edition of the morning paper. The robbery made the front page, below the fold. The BMW, on its way out of the parking lot, had clipped a pedestrian and knocked him onto the sidewalk, where he cracked his skull. They found the car—the "drop car," as they called it, which had been stolen from the South Avenue Garage two hours earlier—abandoned in a parking lot. The old man was in guarded condition at Rochester General, unconscious but stable. The robbery netted only three hundred dollars. Someday, somebody would stab each of them eighteen times with an ice pick, and I wouldn't shed a tear.

"Jerks," Meg said, tossing the newspaper onto the table.

The guard at the front desk called to us: "Mr. and Mrs. Cahill? You can go up now."

We found Alec, out cold, in a circular suite of rooms. The air stank of stale coffee and peppermint antiseptic, the aromas drifting in from the nurses' station. It *was* slow around there. Alec had a semiprivate room all to himself. I went straight to his side and put my hand against his cheek, but he was totally knocked out—he didn't even shift. I pulled up a chair and stayed there, resting my hand on his shoulder, waiting for him to open his eyes, asking the nurses, whenever they came in, how long it would take for him to come around. Eventually, the foot traffic quieted down and I found myself dozing in my chair.

The sun woke me in time to see Dana walk in, dressed in her strategically torn jeans and her barn coat and one of my own wool sweaters with the tail of her flannel shirt hanging below, her blond hair in a ponytail. She was one of the thinnest girls in her class, and she was shy about it. She'd reached an age where, half the time, her greatest ambition seemed to be to pitch a tent at The Gap and live out her teens there, emerging only for a latte at the nearest Starbucks. She would obsess for days about finding a barn coat as close as possible to the color of the Stadium Court at the U.S. Open in Flushing Meadows, New York—a sort of dull grayish olive. She drank milk shakes, but they didn't take, and she wore flared jeans to cover her skinny legs when other girls wore shorts. Meg told her to rent a couple of Audrey Hepburn movies and imagine the possibilities; ever since, she'd been circling Hepburn's name in the television schedule, watching *Breakfast at Tiffany's* with the door closed. It made me want to hug her, if only because she'd acted on something we suggested.

"Did you thank Jesse's parents for the ride?" Meg asked.

"Of course," Dana said, without looking at her mother. She'd reached the age when every encounter with her mother could generate friction, and every spark might give off little flames.

"How was work?" I asked.

"Boring. I hate that job."

"Welcome to the club," I said.

"How's Alec?"

"He's been through a hell of a lot," I said. "They say he's going to be fine. I'm still worried about this leg, though."

As Dana moved around the bed, I realized the hospital room was so bright, the light hurt my eyes. Alec was stirring, groggy and sullen and disoriented. I went to the bed, and Meg stationed herself on the other side, and we each took one of his hands—or, rather, Meg held one hand and I rested my fingers on his other arm. I didn't think he'd want to wake up holding hands with his father.

"My head," he said, moaning, pressing his hand to his temple.

"How's your leg feel?" I asked.

"Still aches. But not as much."

"The doctor said it should heal up just fine. You just have to give it a rest," I said.

He looked drawn and pale, as if he'd aged while he was under. You could spot everything he was thinking and feeling right there in his face. Dana reached into the deep pocket of her coat and handed Alec a biography of Shaquille O'Neal.

"Still remember how to read?" she asked.

"That was almost funny," he said, and then looked at the book. "All right!"

"You're such a wigger, Alec."

"What's a wigger?" I asked.

"White kid who wants to be black," she said.

"And you're a poser and a half," Alec said to Dana.

"You want anything?" I asked. "You thirsty?"

"Some orange juice?" he asked.

"You bet, kiddo," I said, leaning over and kissing him on the forehead. "I'll ask them for some Tylenol or something, too."

When I headed out of the room, to ask the people at the desk for orange juice and where I could get a cup of coffee for myself, Meg followed me.

"You coming right back?" she asked.

"Yeah. You want some coffee?"

"How about a hug?"

I put my arms around her and felt a little twinge.

"It's been a while," I said.

"Too long," she said. "We never even have time for a hug anymore."

Maybe this is what it took. As a last resort, if we wanted to get together as a family, one of us could always decide to be hospitalized.

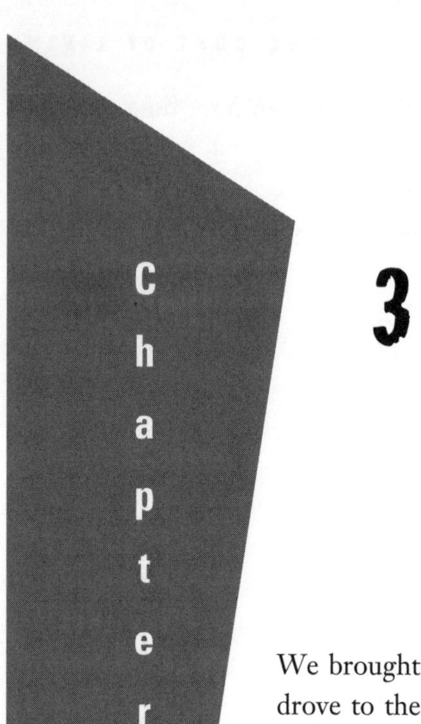

Chapter 3

We brought Alec home later that day. I drove to the office, picked up a stack of job jackets, and brought them home. In between helping Alec get used to his crutches—reinventing a game where he attempted to hit me with a Nerf football and defend himself against my own throws with both crutches, which allowed him to compete without moving around much on his feet—I reviewed brochure copy, two speeches, and a video script for several of my own clients, not to mention the one I was handling for our vacationing account executive. The entire day became a constantly alternating current of attention—half an hour playing games or watching television with Alec, followed by half an hour of voice mail, e-mail, copyediting and Day-Timer scheduling, while he watched ESPN or listened to the Bills on AM radio—the telecast was blacked out once again, for lack of ticket sales. By evening, Alec was walking around, hardly limping despite the ache in his bones, and I was almost caught up with my work.

That night, when the kids were in their rooms, on the phone or listening to CDs or whatever else they did with the door closed, I found Meg in the kitchen, papers spread around on the little table, including a printout spreadsheet for her gallery. I came up behind her quietly and gently squeezed her shoulders.

"So when are we getting together?" I asked, bending over and speaking softly into her ear.

"That hurts. Not so hard," she said, shrugging off my hands.

"Sorry," I said, wrapping my arms around her.

"I'm trying to concentrate," she said. "I'm really tired is all."

I let go and moved around the table, leaning back against the counter, with the dishwasher going behind me, feeling the heat, the pleasant vibration, against the back of my legs, getting a faint, sobering whiff of detergent.

"What happened to the mood?" I asked. "I seem to remember a hug at the hospital."

"Gregg is still having trouble getting the Kestlers to return his calls."

"I thought they were out of town," I said.

"Until now that hasn't stopped them from checking their voice mail and calling."

"We aren't going to die if you don't land that deal."

"It's a lot of money, Rich," she said. "It would be our Future Fund. Without that deal, we're spending everything we make."

Our Future Fund is what we called the cushion we needed to feel comfortable buying the house. We knew we could afford the new house, but only by pinching almost everything else in our lives: vacations, saving for the kids' college, a new car, and extra money put away for our retirement. My raise and Meg's deal with the Kestler brothers were supposed to give us a solid start on our Future Fund. So far it amounted to only a couple thousand dollars.

"I'm still hoping for a raise," I said.

"Nobody's told you how much it will be, have they?" she asked.

"Is this your way of telling me you don't want to get together tonight?"

"You have to admit this has been a rough weekend," she said. "Aren't you exhausted? You've been working all day. Playing with Alec. Doesn't that wear you out?"

"No way. You get energy off Alec, just standing within a thirty-foot radius of him."

"Maybe tomorrow," she said.

I leaned over and kissed her, and she put her hand around the back of my neck and pulled me down for a second kiss.

"I'm getting twinges."

"I'm just worn out," she said. "You kiss like you mean it, too."

"I *do.*"

After everyone had gone to bed, and I was channel-surfing aimlessly, unable to get sleepy, I went up to the attic to check my e-mail and found the light blinking on my home office answering machine. I was surprised, because the house was small enough to let me hear whatever calls I got on the separate line in the attic. I pressed the PLAY key without paying much attention and scrolled down the e-mail list. The voice, as calm as the voice of my own boss: *Yo Cuz. Don't no man think he get away with it, but I do. Except you, Cuz, don't get away with it, do you? Got to change all that.* He laughed. *We see to that.* A little snort of a laugh. Click.

I turned away from the keyboard and faced the answering machine, waiting for more, but it whined as it rewound itself and the light quit blinking. I listened to the voice again, and then again. My fingertips felt as if somebody'd taken acid to them.

On Monday morning, feeling as if I owed myself at least a few minutes of relief, I took the long way into the office. I often dragged this trip out, giving myself a break from the pressures of the job, refusing to use the cell phone. Yet, much as I wanted to extend my drive time, it was no luxury cruise in the Escort. I hated that car. I'd been driving it for eight years, and sometimes on my way home I detoured past the Mitsubishi dealer to look at the new line of Eclipse coupes, something with enough horsepower to be fun on a winding road. I was proud of having abstained from buying myself a dream car: first came the Christmas list, a new house, the college fund—if we could ever get one started. I was determined to drive the Escort into the ground. The steering wheel vibrated whenever I got above forty, the air conditioner hadn't worked for four years, the stereo picked up only half the FM stations I wanted, and this car had rattles from regions too deep for any mechanic to reach.

On my way into work, I popped a motivational tape into the cassette player and waited for the rich bass tones of the speaker's voice. I was down on myself, as I often was on a Monday morning. The man on the tape assured me nothing was impossible if I trained all my energy and hunger on achieving it. I didn't believe him. But I kept listening. It helped, somehow, to hear him say it.

His picture was on the box; it was a demographically perfect face, right in the middle of the spectrum, brown hair, brown eyes, big phony smile, and perfect teeth. This was a man who, among other things, taught you to walk on hot coals in your bare feet (there was even a line in an R.E.M. song about it), presumably as a way of learning how to work up enough courage and personal energy to write more effective memos and say no to your mother-in-law as if you really meant it, not to speak of unlocking spiritual reserves of Initiative and Drive, and all those other good free-market virtues, the better to dig that new swimming pool or rule a small Indonesian state, if that happened to be on your To Do list. At first, I'd laughed at these tapes. Then I started listening without laughing. Finally I played them so much I had to hide them whenever one of the guys climbed into the car for a ride to lunch. *You have within you reservoirs of energy and imagination so explosive, you can become anything you want to become* . . . and what might *that* be exactly? That was the tough part.

I usually drifted off as he was getting to the instructional material, where you had to *do* something. I had too many things to do already. I wrote reminders on the inside of my cuffs. I didn't have time for another list. All I wanted was to listen to the sound of his voice without having to decide whether or not I believed in what the voice was telling me. The *sound* of his words, with all those octaves of success and satisfaction rumbling through it was usually enough to make me feel a little better about facing the dozen unfinished jobs awaiting me on my desk.

It was good to see the Rochester skyline. I never got into the city anymore. Most of us had jobs at office parks in the suburbs. We shopped at the malls. From the highway, Rochester looked as small as a city could get without being called a town. People from out of state assumed we were a suburb of the Big Apple, some kind of phonetic hybrid of New Rochelle and Westchester, yet it took seven hours to drive to New York City, a tough commute. And though we never seemed to appear on New York State Thruway destination-mileage signs between the listings for Buffalo and Syracuse, we weren't a speck on the map. We were the origin or at least a temporary sojourn to a few notable things and people: Frederick Douglass, Susan B. Anthony, John Ashbery, the 1995 Ryder Cup, Walter Hagen, Ron Shelton, Louise Brooks, Cab Calloway, Son House, Lou Gramm, Jeff Sluman, Nicholson Baker, Ted Bundy, Wendell Castle, Albert Paley, Cal Ripken, Mad Dog Sullivan, Norman O. Brown, the Boston Strangler, Eugene Genovese, Anthony Hecht, George Eastman, Xerox copiers, Ray-Ban sunglasses, French's mustard, as well as the time-release technology in Contac cold capsules and Black Beauty amphetamines. And, not to leave anything out, Rod Serling died here. In other words, Rochester was easily more impressive than, say, Toledo. I kept track of these things in a compulsively defensive way, and I even knew books and movies where Rochester gets mentioned—*Spellbound*, *It's a Wonderful Life*, and one episode of *Seinfield.*

A few big corporate high-rises dominated all the two-story-high wards sprawling away from midtown in all directions toward the suburbs, but it wasn't a dazzling skyline. Rochester seemed to have donated much of its vitality to other places when, years ago, several of our biggest companies folded or took their headquarters out of state, to escape New York taxes. We were a *mature* city. Living in Rochester was like living comfortably into middle age with the same wife you married in your twenties. As a town, we weren't going anywhere interesting anymore, even though most of us had no desire to leave.

The atrium at McKee Communications knocked you out, the first time you saw it, all polished white oak and glass and track lights and spiral staircase and a fresh bouquet of lilies on the receptionist's desk every day, dusting the counter with yellow pollen. Overhead, three stories up, the skylights in the roof of this old, converted warehouse were surrounded by duct work and pipes and I-beams, painted lavender and apricot and plum. It was exactly the look you'd expect in a place where art directors ruled.

We talked a lot about long-range marketing and demographics and international reach, but clients judged things mostly by how they looked. Half the time, they wanted pretty pictures, which we called "glamour" shots, of electronic equipment. No one at McKee was overweight. No plain brown wrappers. Most of our people were female, young, well-educated, fresh-faced, genuinely good-natured, and severely ethical.

Working in advertising and public relations on this scale doesn't mean writing the next national Kodak Moment commercial. It's closer to designing the next sales brochure to help some rep sell a new microfiche reader to the Fargo Public Library. It isn't a matter of doing spin control for the *Exxon Valdez* oil spill so much as organizing a grand opening for the new Caldor's, where monster trucks attempt wheelies in the parking lot, or designing a booth for the next annual convention of the Association for Document Management. We were more an extension of our corporate clients than a separate business, almost totally dependent on a handful of huge accounts.

We were an overgrown boutique agency, not much by Madison Avenue standards. Penny McKee had started it a decade ago, at first working alone out of a converted Penn Central dining car parked along some old tracks out in Penfield, then moving into bigger quarters every couple years as she hired more people. It bored me to describe the work, let alone produce it, but I knew the pitch by heart. We could grind out low-cost work, ahead of deadline, with hip design and sharp writing. We didn't win awards but we got results. I enjoyed doing a good job, when that was possible, even though the work itself meant almost nothing to me. It wasn't a calling or even a fulfilling vocation, so much as a game you played to win.

When I arrived, Penny's secretary, Jennifer Dewinter, was sitting in for our receptionist. She was almost thirty and expecting her third child, yet she still had the levitating hair of a mall girl and the manner of a woman unaccustomed to taking crap from anyone. She'd pulled a little Watchman television out of her drawer and was studying it while managing the switchboard and paging people. Some of us fantasized regularly about what our lives would be like now if we'd run into Jennifer in our single days. We joked about bedridden weekends of having to suffer through recitals of *Soap Opera Digest* and marathon performances of Bon Jovi and Van Halen while eating Chinese takeout, in exchange for the privilege of learning things about functions of the human body we'd never be able to put into words. She seemed to like me a lot more than she liked Jimmy Sorley—which I tried to point out to Jimmy at every opportunity—probably because she knew it was safe to tease me. Jimmy would interpret anything so much as a hello as an invitation to pioneering erotic mischief.

"You're late," she said.

"Fashionably."

"Look at you. Can't you have Meg buy your ties?" she asked.

"I've had this tie for a year. Where've *you* been?"

"All I know is, it isn't my turn to babysit you," she said, smiling. "How's the new house coming?"

"All depends on the New York pitch."

"Penny's been wanting to talk to you about you-know-who and that copy he's supposed to be writing for the New York pitch," she said. "She said she may have to sic Whit Sutherland on both of you."

"Hey, Whit and I are like this," I said, crossing my fingers. "We're flying out together Friday. We intend to kick some butt in Manhattan."

"I'll believe *that* when I see it," she said.

"Whit's my personal hero."

"Whit's a stiff."

"Jimmy'll have that copy for me. He promised," I said.

"You'll believe anything."

"Is he in yet?" I asked.

"I go all day trying to avoid that slimeball. I make a point of *not* knowing where he is."

"Jimmy would be gratified to know you have these feelings for him," I said. "I know I am."

"Want to hear the latest? Why is Jimmy Sorley's love life like a hockey game?"

"I don't know. Why?"

"A lot of motion and noise, but not much scoring," she said.

"Jimmy's got the life all of us wanted when we were sixteen," I said. "That's why we love him. He lives the dream."

"Jimmy's got the attention span of a gerbil is what I hear," she said. "Shoo. *Good Morning America* is back on."

My work area was private, tucked into the end of a long hall lined with offices for a couple of writers and the other account executives. I had a desk, a computer table, a filing cabinet, a chair, and two plants: a diseased ficus and a palm tree stuck into a pot of rancid soil. When I signed onto my computer, I went quickly through my e-mail. Apparently I wasn't the only one who'd worked through the weekend.

To: RCahill
From: WhitSuth

A few reminders. The voice-over for the video needs to be at SGI. Where's it stand? The brochure copy is at what stage? I saw the latest take on the speeches. Let's discuss the openings. And the prototype stuff for the pitch in New York—I'm in a fog. Shed light, please.

ASAP. And how was *your* weekend? See? I can make small talk.

To: RCahill
From: PMcKee
Got a minute for me this morning?

To: RCahill
From: Wes
What was the name of the clown on Letterman? The original Letterman? I want to use him in a spot I'm doing for Genesee. Sitting at a bar, bitching about his wages, having a Michael Shea's. Like we talked about. A long shot, but what the hell. Can't be too expensive to get rights to use the character, can it? I'll make the calls.

To: RCahill
From: JS
What's with Penny? She been snooping around about costs on the Veritex work. Whit the Twit, too. What's up? I'll have that brochure copy to you soon, by the way. The trip's Friday, right?

I deleted the messages and typed out my answers.

To: WhitSuth
From: RCahill
The sound track for the video is wonderful. I can't believe we can just send a script to this guy in Alaska and he records it in his log cabin or his igloo or whatever and just FedExes it

back to us with a bill for ten thousand. What a life. What a voice! But guess what. The SGI mixing guys have gone totally digital. Digital tape or CD-ROM is all they take. Nobody tells me this until the eleventh hour. Know anybody with a digital audio recorder? The guys at SGI are drawing the line: they refuse to transfer from analog to digital. It ties up their equipment. Can you believe this? (Behind schedule.) We're on the eleventh draft of the brochures. Major nightmare. Contemplating ritual suicide. Please suggest instruments to use. They want us to recycle verbiage from previously approved brochures. Our writer is off her lithium again, in case you haven't noticed. She looked catatonic at the last client meeting. Help! I'm thinking of handing it off to Wes. (Behind schedule.) Ready to talk about those speeches whenever. (Almost on the timeline.) Jimmy says he'll have the copy for our New York pitch ``soon.'' (Way behind schedule.) I'll get specific with him. Wes is on top of the brewery spots, as always. My weekend was a working one. Personal complications Saturday. Don't ask.

To: PMcKee
From: RCahill
Anytime you say. I'll be around all morning.

To: Wes
From: RCahill
I can't remember the Late Night Clown's name. Go ahead and see if you can get permission. You going to be around this morning?

To: JS
From: RCahill
I have no clue what's up with Penny and Whit. What are they bugging you about? Whit's dying for the copy for the trip. What's ``soon'' mean? Think maybe you could dry out long enough to work your magic and get me off your back?

He owed me copy for two mock-up brochures to accompany the marketing-communications plan I'd written up for the prospective clients in New York. I claimed Penny McKee was holding back a raise she'd promised me until I got the copy back from him. We needed to edit, typeset, and print it in a couple days if we had any hope of having everything ready in time for the flight.

Just as I sent off the batch of mail, Penny McKee came in and seated herself across the desk from me without a word. When she entered a room, it was like the moment before a thunderstorm when you smell something significant about to happen. Dark suit, a red silk scarf knotted at her throat, and black hair in a French knot. She was tall and thin, and had a husky voice, from smoking constantly in her office with the door closed, even though no one else was allowed to smoke anywhere in the building. She was beautiful, despite the most subtle signs of aging, but there wasn't even a hint of sensuality in that face. The job had baked certain pleasures out of her. She'd divorced her husband years ago, and no one knew if she even dated anymore. I never saw deeper than an inch into Penny's life, and she wanted it that way.

"Check your voice mail much?" she asked, smiling. "Mr. Cahill."

"That was next on my list."

"How's life?" she asked.

"I'm surviving."

"The stuff for the pitch is right on the money. You're really on top of this thing, except for Jimmy."

"I've been bugging him."

"Should've had the brochure copy done last week," she said.

"Jimmy needs to grow up," I said.

"We were hoping you'd set an example."

"I need to grow up?" I asked.

"You need to *move* up."

She was trying to coax me into a promotion I'd been resisting for months. In these circumstances, almost anyone in his right mind would have considered himself one of the chosen few. But once you went into management, you could never do a U-turn and become the nice guy you'd tried to be before the promotion. *All ye who enter here, abandon all hope of not being the royal pain they're paying you to be.* It would be a total desk job, hounding other account executives, staying indoors rather than roaming the world, bringing in new business, working directly with the writers and art directors. I wanted to stay out in the field, have a hand in the art and the copy—produce something I could hold in my hand.

"I'm just a suit. I'm no manager," I said.

"Not yet."

"I'm going to bring in a huge account when Whit and I fly to New York. It'll be a full-time job for five people. Just watch."

"Let's see how it goes," she said. "Meanwhile, we need your help."

"What's up?"

"Veritex."

"Jimmy's got a lock on it, doesn't he?" I asked. Isn't he pretty much empowered to do whatever he wants?"

"I think we're calling time-out on that. Jimmy's letting costs get way out of line. We want you to step in."

So that's what she and Whit were sniffing out. The Expenses. I knew all about where that was headed from when I'd handled Veritex. I was glad to let go of the account, considering the way Vince Stringer was wasting his company's money, but Jimmy didn't mind. With Jimmy, whatever the client asked, the client got.

"He just does what Stringer wants. They play hard when they go out of town," I said. "He likes to eat well. He likes to be entertained."

"Tell Jimmy he needs to detail how he and Vince have been using the expense budget."

"Vince is the one who calls the shots," I said. "Jimmy just does what he's told. You know that's the way it works. If Vince wants to blow a thousand on dinner in Chicago, Jimmy puts it on the cards and bills Veritex for it. You should see the bar tab those guys rack up."

"Just have him put that down on paper. Exactly that sort of detail. For the last three months," she said. "And tell him to get up to speed on the copy he owes you. He's been playing catch-up for months now."

"But when he hands in the work, it's great," I said.

"He knows it *better* be," she said. "Tell him my trigger finger is starting to itch, big-time."

I worked for three hours trying to catch up on all my other jobs, bugging people in print production for corrections on bluelines, checking on all the work Whit had asked me about. We were behind the timelines on everything, and everything was going to cost more than we'd estimated. Nothing was ever under budget or on time. Which is why it didn't strike me as odd, and seemed a little less than world-shaking, that Jimmy wasn't up to speed, or under budget, even though we *did* need to put the whole proposal to bed for the trip to New York.

Finally, late in the morning, I checked my voice mail. My first message was dead silence followed by a dial tone. Next, I heard from a stockbroker whose entire destiny seemed to ride on my having his work sheet on asset allocation. I knew all I needed to know about asset allocation: phone bill, power bill, mortgage, groceries, car repairs, Visa, MasterCard, orthodontist, school loans. My third message, from Jimmy himself, invited me to The Office, his favorite bar, after work. The fourth served up nothing but the rustle and thud of the receiver and then the sound of a Craig Mack remix video in the background and, finally, the voice: *Got a little clue for you, Cuz. I'm gone read you this little article say past three years wages—for bitches like you—have continued to fall while productivity, profits, and stock prices have soared. See, me, my profits been soaring. You and I need to get to know each other little better.* Click.

The adrenaline chilled my arms and weakened my legs. The same voice as before. The message and the voice felt the way one of my professors told me a bad death and a great poem were supposed to feel: unexpected but inevitable, and impossible to ignore. I saved the message and forwarded it to Wes Mercer's extension, with my own comment attached to it: *What do you make of this?* Then I got up and went down to his office and stood in his doorway, watching him download icons onto his computer from a Monty Python CD.

Wes had a computer rigged for fun. If you pressed the tab key, you heard the imprisoned black man from *Raising Arizona* describe to the members of his therapy group, in his deep Barry White bass, when he first discovered he was a woman trapped in a man's body: *Sometimes ah get the menstrual cramps real hawd.* If you hit the return key, you heard Albert Brooks doing his lounge singer's audition for the new National Anthem: *You know Vegas is a great place, an exciting place, but originally I come from a much quieter place, a place up north, out west, a place I call Portland.* If you copied a disk, you heard a woman moaning with far more authenticity than Meg Ryan's rendition in *When Harry Met Sally*.

Wes Mercer was an intellectual oasis for me. Sitting in his office, I could always escape the encroaching Spanish Inquisition of life by having fifteen minutes of semi-intelligent conversation. His office was about as austere as one of the less-lived-in cells at Attica: a desk, a chair, a long table, and a white bookshelf. The only thing on the walls, was a framed close-up of a flat tire, with Dick Trickle's signature in the lower corner. Wes wouldn't tell anyone how he'd fooled the NASCAR driver into signing this gag photograph at Watkins Glen. Whatever happened, Wes took it and didn't whine. And he was totally honest.

"You seen Jolie lately?"

"She still have a pulse?" he asked.

"How long's she been off her meds?"

"Who knows. More than a month, by my count," he said.

"Any way you could finish the brochures she's been writing? They've been through about a thousand drafts. The client just wants us to recycle verbiage from previous brochures."

"God. I'm already getting slimed on three other jobs," he said. "Can you give me until the end of the week?"

"I'll see what I can do," I said. "You read about the holdup at McDonald's?"

"It was about a mile from our house," he said. "Wish I'd been there."

"I was."

He turned around to face me: "What?"

"Alec slipped and fell right in the middle of it."

"You were *there?*"

"I had to take him to the hospital. Surgery, the whole bit. We were up all night," I said.

"Is he all right?"

"He'll be fine. Thing is, listen to your voice mail," I said.

He dialed up his messages. I could tell when my message came on because he raised his eyes and stared directly at me as he listened, shaking his head faintly by the end of the message.

"Is that true? Is the economy in that much of an upswing?" he asked.

"Very funny. Can you believe this? They must've gotten my number from my Day-Timer."

"Probably Stringer, crushed on kamikazes with Jimmy. Remember that time he called you pretending to be some mob guy you owed money?" he asked.

"This isn't Vince. Think I should call somebody?"

"Like who?" he asked.

"The police," I said.

"Good luck. They'll get there in time to zip you into the bag," he said. "Remember that night we had on our street? Showed up about an hour after it was over. Coffee cups in their hands."

"They can trace calls, can't they?"

"Phone company can tell you who's calling. Get caller ID. We've got it," he said. "You sign a statement?"

"Uh-uh. I was in a rush. With Alec and all," I said.

"This guy knows you got a good look at him, right? Lie low."

"I intend to," I said. "I mean, what else do I ever do? You know what this is about? I yelled at them, when they were leaving."

"You yelled at them?"

"*Who you think you are?* I mean, I even used the kid's name. I heard them say it before the shooting started. Smart, huh?"

Wes's eyes narrowed.

"It was so stupid," I said. "He seems to think I was actually asking a question."

"God, what were you thinking?"

"I *wasn't* thinking. That's the problem."

"It was only a robbery, right?" Wes asked. "They'll cool off."

"They knocked out some old guy on their way out, remember?"

"He still alive?"

"Far as I know," I said.

"Man."

"Meanwhile, I've got Sorley jerking me around on that story. Penny enlarges my ear about him this morning. Alec can't play ball. Now this," I said. "Everything falls apart at once."

"All I know is, I'm hoping death isn't the big letdown I expect it to be. Last night, eight-year-old rerun of Letterman on cable. The Late Night Clown was on."

"And?"

"Flunky."

"God. Right! Why couldn't we remember that?" I asked.

"Orange wig. Chain-smoked. Bitched about wages. Gets up to leave and Letterman tells him how pleasant it was to have him on. *Yeah, sure*, he says. He's walking off. *Yeah, sure*. Doesn't even turn around. He's perfect for the beer spot."

"Where the hell's Jimmy, anyway?"

If I called Jimmy at home, would he be in the process of discovering something verifiably female from his own species in bed with him? Would he be smoking a cigarette already, squinting through the kinky blond hair in his eyes, letting the Merit hang on his lip, wearing a pair of boxer shorts and his Eat The Worm T-shirt? He was only a few years past thirty, but on most mornings he acted, as Wes put it, hungover-the-hill.

Jimmy's father had taught him, by example, that he had to do two things with skill in order to consider himself a man: first, in a single sitting, be able to drink many times the amount of whiskey required to induce cardiac arrest in a small lab animal; and second, sleep with as many women as possible. My own father hadn't taught me a thing, except that if you want your children to despise you, the best thing to do would be to run off when they are so young they won't even remember what you look like. I still remembered the day I found his Luger in a sock drawer.

In the abstract, Jimmy wasn't the sort of guy I'd ever expect to be friends with now, considering how we'd drifted apart since college. I was married and had a family. He'd been engaged for about three months in his twenties, and now he considered himself the most untamed member of our ex-fraternity group. The others all went on to live settled lives. One became a computer expert, another a local news reporter, yet another invented laser optical devices for arthroscopic surgery, and most of the others landed the usual jobs: dentistry, electrical engineering, software. Jimmy refused to undergo the usual morph from fraternity prankster to somber, responsible adult with mutual funds and an in-ground sprinkler system and a living will and a governing sense of integrity. I kept waiting and watching, half of me hoping to see him grow out of it, the other half smiling at how amused he managed to keep himself. He was a lout, but he didn't seem to be harming anybody but himself.

Wes glanced over my shoulder, and by the time I'd turned around, Jimmy had already shut the door and pressed his back up against it. He hadn't changed much since college, except now he tucked in his shirttail. He looked like a doctored photo. His hair and face didn't belong above that crisp new suit and tie.

He lifted a finger to his lips: "Penny's got a hard-on about that copy I owe you."

"She'll be using it on me if she doesn't find that story on her desk tomorrow morning," I said. "Why're you doing this to me?"

"*Irresistible impulse. I can't help myself.* That'll get you out of anything these days," Sorley said. "Like at McDonald's over the weekend. You see that in the paper? This country's out of control, man. That's the movie we ought to make. O.J. with his pitching wedge. That says it all."

"I was *at* that McDonald's."

He stared at me. The words didn't add up.

"One of them ordered a Big Mac right in the middle of the thing. Now *that* was funny."

"You mean, you were there when—"

"And now he's getting threatening phone calls," Wes chimed in.

"Are you serious?" Jimmy asked, standing up straighter. He was like a dog, right after the squirrel hops into view.

"Never mind," I said.

"You say the word, I'll go down there with you. I've still got my dad's service revolver from when I was living in New York. Used to keep it under my mattress. I'll make sure it's self-defense," he said.

"Jimmy, tell you what. How about you protect me from Penny? I need that copy."

"What's this guy saying on the phone?" he asked.

"Nothing. Don't give *her* the copy. Let *me* give it to her," I said. "And she's bugging me for details on Veritex expenses. Vince's fun money."

"Whit's been sniffing around, too," Jimmy said. "I'll get the copy done in time. Get tough with them. And that money—they know I don't keep receipts. Vince doesn't require it."

"Get tough with *them?*" I said, laughing.

"Hell, she loves you. Type up a conference report every time you pick your nose," he said.

I laughed, too, but not as enthusiastically as Wes and Jimmy.

"I need that copy. And I need a memo on the expenses. Give me all the detail you can. Without getting him into trouble. By tomorrow morning," I said.

"Hey, I'll see what I can do, if you're *that* scared of Penny," he said, coming across the room and placing both his hands on my shoulders, giving me a brotherly squeeze. I wriggled free and stood to face him.

"You're the one who should be scared of Penny. Not me."

"Tomorrow morning, for sure. It'll be in your box."

When I got back to my own office, I checked my voice mail again, and held my breath as I listened to the first message: *Mr. Cahill, please give me a call. I need to speak with you. My name's Frank Bogardus. I'm an investigator for the sheriff's department. I have something I think you may want back.*

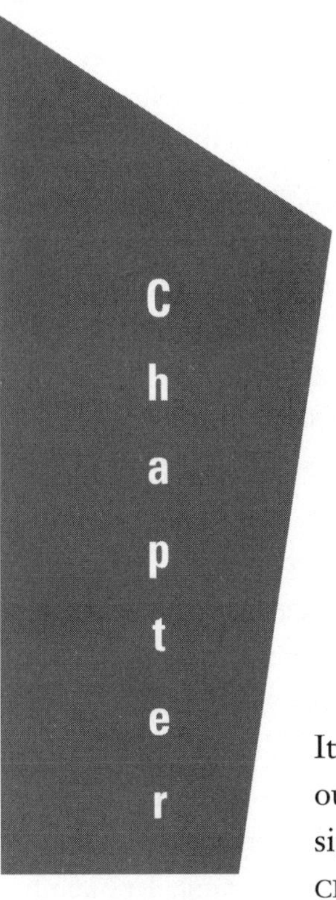

Chapter 4

It was already dark when I pulled onto our street. I smiled at the town-limit sign: WELCOME TO FAIRFIELD. DISCHARGE OF FIREARMS PROHIBITED BY TOWN ORDINANCE. It struck me as a far more cynical, sophisticated motto than Webster's: WELCOME TO WEBSTER, WHERE LIFE IS WORTH LIVING. In Fairfield, life might not be worth living, but at least people would think twice before they put you out of your misery.

Fairfield was the area's most highly taxed bedroom community, even though it was more an extension of the city than an actual suburb. It didn't look wealthy, except in one small section along East Avenue, where there probably wasn't a single home under a million dollars. Ours was one of the oldest neighborhoods, with a lot of heat-inefficient stucco and modest Federal homes built of stone, all of it backed by a small forest of shade trees and a couple country-club golf courses. Typically, the homes were older, Depression-era or pre–World War II colonials. Everything, except that tax bill, was quaint in Fairfield. It was an old village, with a lot of new money and a certain multicultural mix: across the street from us were Orthodox Jews who'd moved here from Tel Aviv, along with the Romanian family four houses down, and on the next street over, several black professional families, including Jackson Parsells, a professor I'd had at the University of Rochester.

We lived on one of the less expensive streets, only a few houses away from the commercial district on Durand Avenue. We were within walking distance of almost anything we needed: a six-pack of Bud Light and the 7-Eleven, a haircut at Supercuts, or a gallon of semigloss latex from the Sherwin-Williams outlet. With so many things so easily within reach, some children in Fairfield grew up feeling the world owed them everything. I remember once taking Alec to a Little League preseason gathering, where the leaders of Fairfield Baseball handed out books of raffle tickets each Little Leaguer needed to sell. Alec was sitting beside one of his wealthier friends from school looking at all the prizes that would go to the kids who sold the most tickets: a baseball glove, an aluminum bat, a Sony Discman, a boom box, a 13-inch cable-ready color television with remote, and a 64-bit Nintendo entertainment center. The boy sitting on the other side of Alec leaned over and said, "I've already got all that stuff." Presumably he'd been hoping for the Mercedes one of the fathers parked outside in the turnaround.

As a child, I'd dreamed of living in a neighborhood like this. My early years I remembered as a series of drawn curtains in a little yellow duplex on Laburnum Crescent, my mother in bed for three weeks after my father abandoned us, the white sheets twisted into fists under her chin. I walked home with my books, made her peanut-butter sandwiches, macaroni and cheese, and she'd take three bites and fall back asleep in that room that smelled like burned toast and sour milk. Only days after my father left, two bored and sullen men showed up, grinding their cigarettes under their heels on our stoop—*he owes big money to Jay because Jay's a good guy he's giving him time and now Jay, he says time's up so tell that weasel time's up*—and a week later we found all the windows broken in the Toyota, a dead ferret in the driver's seat, and all the tires punctured with ice picks.

Once my mother's sick time ran out, she crawled out of bed and returned to her job in the dark film production lines at Kodak, going through the motions, eating, sleeping, smiling, talking, but she wasn't alive. She was animatronic, a little gap in everything she did, living through an act of will, a sort of heavy oil in every gesture I could feel seeping into my own life. She started spending weekends on retreat, at a monastery in the Adirondack foothills, three hours away, leaving me. When she was gone, I stayed out with friends, smoking, listening to music she wouldn't allow in the house—*Music from Big Pink*, *After Bathing at Baxter's*, *Déjà Vu*, *Wheels of Fire*, *Electric Ladyland*—dreaming of owning a guitar and a little Fender Super Reverb studio amp. All while my mother spent her weekend in her Eastern Orthodox escape, giving in to her own mother's Armenian faith. She told me I could come with her, stay in homes of friends she made there, members of the monastery's little church, but I refused, waiting out the years until college, when I could make my own life, start over, become the person I wanted to become. Or the person my mother feared I would become, like my father.

■

When I got home, Meg was in the kitchen, stabbing a fork into a white box of take-out sesame chicken, and as I came up to her to give her a kiss on the cheek, she said, "You've got a visitor."

"Who?" I asked.

"We in trouble? Maybe you should've stayed until the police got there," Dana asked, sitting on one of the stools squeezed between the butcher block table and the dishwasher. Her lovely face looked alert and almost pale as she lowered her voice and came closer.

"I don't think he's a real cop. He doesn't have a gun," Alec said.

He was standing near the doorway, positioning himself to eavesdrop, holding his new basketball between his wrist and his hip. I'd bought it for him the day before the robbery, and he'd been carrying it around with him, dribbling it all over the house as he moved from one room to another, feeling useless, trying to hide his limp.

"His name's Bogardus. You know him? He says he called you," Meg said.

"This is *just* what I need."

I folded my jacket across the back of a kitchen chair and went into the living room. The sheets of clear plastic taped over the leaky windows seemed to inhale slightly as I came into the room—every little breeze outside made them swell. As Bogardus got up from the couch, he winced, pressing the heel of his palm into his back. His eyes, squinty with curiosity, crinkled at the corners from smiling too much. He looked a decade older than I was. He had on a wrinkled olive raincoat, chinos, and a pair of cheap loafers. Under a covering of fuzz remotely resembling human hair, his face had a softened doughy consistency, like something perishable left out overnight. He looked like a man who never took a vacation, who kept maps on his basement wall showing all phases of the Civil War.

■

"Mr. Cahill. I'm Frank Bogardus, with the county sheriff?" he said. "I'm real sorry about barging in here at the dinner hour."

"What's the problem?" I asked, my heart pounding. I wondered how serious a crime it was for a witness to leave the scene of a crime.

"I know this is going to be a chore, but I'd like you to make a quick trip downtown with me to the civic center," he said. "I have your billfold, and I just have to have you fill out a little paperwork."

"Tonight?"

"If that's all right. I understand why you left the scene of the holdup at McDonald's, with your boy getting hurt and all," he said. "Is he okay?"

"Yeah, he's fine. But how did you know I was there?"

"Guy in narcotics spotted your wallet. Under the tailpipe of an old Pinto out front. No money. Plastic's still in there. Fine piece of leather," he said. "One of the witnesses recognized you from the picture on your driver's license. She said you were the one whose boy slipped."

At the edge of my vision I spotted Alec as he appeared in the doorway, staring at me. Once again, if only I'd done what I normally would have done in a situation like this, if only I'd denied everything and kept quiet, maybe nothing would have happened the way it did. Yet Alec kept staring, and I was getting to the age where I paid attention to the sound of his laughter when I walked out of a room. I felt Bogardus sizing me up. It probably looked soft from his perspective: the house, the family, the career. But then there was all that plastic on the windows.

"Yeah. I was there," I said.

Bogardus was looking at Alec.

"You the boy took a fall?"

Alec nodded.

"What's *your* name?" Bogardus asked.

"Alec."

Bogardus pointed to the basketball.

"You play?"

"Not this year," he said. "I'm doing Hot Shots."

"Since when?" I asked.

"Coach said it would be okay," Alec said, looking at me.

"What's Hot Shots?" Bogardus asked.

"You stand on different spots and try to make the most shots in a minute," Alec said. "I did it last year."

"You any good?" Bogardus asked.

"I was okay."

Meg wandered into the living room, leaning one shoulder against the wall, listening. No way was I going downtown. I wanted to get all of them out of the living room, especially this investigator, and then I'd be able to change clothes and eat dinner with my family around me for an hour before I needed to go back into the office for an evening of catch-up work.

"I play," Bogardus said.

"Where?"

"County jail," he said. "Bunch of us guys from the sheriff's department and the city. Us against the crews. The blacks."

"They good?" Alec asked.

"We stay in their face."

"Cool," Alec said.

"Alec," I said. "Go help your mom."

"See ya," Bogardus said.

"Yeah," Alec said as he left the room with Meg, who waited a little longer, as if she wasn't about to be dismissed that easily. Then she left. If she didn't like it, she could always call Gregg and whine.

"Like I said, I didn't really see anything," I said. "The ski masks and all."

Alec stuck his head back in the room long enough to say, "Not when they came in."

He disappeared as soon as he'd said it. Bogardus glanced quickly at me, but he didn't push it.

"By the time the whole thing happened, they had the masks on. I don't think I'd recognize anybody," I said.

"Woman who was there, one who identified you from your license, let's see," Bogardus said, pulling a little spiral notebook from his shirt pocket and thumbing through it. "She said the father of the boy who was hurt shouted—that would be you, I guess—let me see . . . here it is. *He shouted out the guy's name. The man with the mask was bending over the little boy, and the boy's father shouted out the name.*"

"They were in line next to me," I said. "I overheard them talking. I heard them use the name."

"They were standing in line talking? Wearing the ski masks?" he asked.

"No. But, I mean, I didn't see so I would remember them. I *heard* them. You know, they were talking."

"You heard them, but you didn't see them," he said.

Alec showed up again in the doorway, watching Bogardus, not me. My life had none of the clean, graceful magic of a perfect shot from center court. Nothing I did had that kind of hold on him. Nothing in my life had that kind of hold on *me*. Now my life was interesting. Alec kept coming back, looking for a lump in the guy's coat covering the gun that wasn't there.

"Alec," I said. "You heard me. Go on."

He disappeared again, looking disappointed.

"But you knew the name." He riffled through his notebook, looking for the name.

"Yeah. T-Boy."

"Right," he said quietly. "But you didn't see him."

"Not for long. I mean before they pulled the masks down. But I couldn't really describe him for you."

He shut his notebook. He looked as if he'd gotten what he came for.

"So can you spare an hour, hour and a half?" he asked. "Just a quick trip, little paperwork to fill out. I'm afraid you'll have to."

He took the off-ramp past a couple old Victorian gingerbread homes with little Historical Society placards out front, and then he turned onto Main Street. I had my window rolled down halfway, to generate some air, and it smelled like spring again, the scent of wet grass and moist blacktop, with big pewter clouds clearing Lincoln Tower and the statue of Mercury on the Lawyers' Cooperative building. The light slanted into the windows of a paper company, and a woman rose from her desk and gazed up into the thunderheads, but I could see only a lozenge of shadow on her shoulders. In fifty years, she would be gone, the building would disappear, the clouds cruising the way they did when the ice cap reached Mexico. I was a waste of air, a shadow bruising the pavement. I had no place to put my arms and legs in this car. The wind sifted my hair. The light wouldn't stay put in my head. I grabbed the door handle, knowing at least my body would gather onlookers if I jumped. At least the pattern of my broken bones on a sidewalk might amount to something new in the world.

In his office, Bogardus had tournament golf trophies, and in a vase on his desk a Monroe County flag, beside a motto framed behind glass: *Lord, make my words tender today, because tomorrow I may have to eat them.* First, I needed to give my statement. He brought out a tape recorder and had me repeat everything I'd said earlier. Then he wanted to give me a quick tour of the jail. He wanted to put a scare into the kid who had me on the floor, the one I remembered as T-Boy. Will Breedlove was his name. Bogardus knew the boy's mother, Clytemnestra Breedlove, from her days as the wife of his former partner, before his partner was killed. He was white, she was black.

"So you're going to arrest him?"

"We've already arrested him. He's downstairs in the holding pen," he said. "I just want to scare him. That scene at the McDonald's was Will getting quoted."

"What's 'quoted'?" I asked.

"Initiated. Wants into the hardest crew on the street. Eugene Price. Got a sheet out of state long as my leg. He's the big dog. The other two, they were supposed to hurt somebody while they were there. Will and this other numbnuts, Calvin DeWitt. He's the one shot the round into the ceiling. Will doesn't have a clue what he's into."

"This his first arrest?"

"Once before," he said. "But no charges. Shoplifts half the clothes he wears."

I sat there, waiting for details.

"Will needs some coach at Ignatius see him play."

"This basketball thing's the biggest lie of all," I said.

"But it would keep him busy."

"I don't know . . ."

"You don't think it's your problem," he said, "but white kids from outside the city are getting into these crews."

"Not *my* kids," I said.

"Here's your wallet," he said, handing it across the desk. The credit cards were still inside, along with my driver's license. Everything was in place except for the cash, which was gone.

"Can't we just skip the tour?" I asked.

"Won't take long," he said.

■

In the jail's gymnasium, on the gleaming hardwood court, two teams of black players were toying with the ball. A lot of long, overhand bomber passes from one end of the court to the other, with a player stationed for an easy layup, nobody guarding him, nobody breaking a sweat, nobody getting winded. Each of the players looked lean and powerful, not an ounce of fat, their buffed muscles shining under the lights. Some wore regular shoes, others wore Converse All Stars.

"The All Stars crack me up," I said. "Will had them."

"State-issue shoes. Means they're from the pen. Guy over there's from Attica. What they all wear up there. They're back here on other charges. Will wears them to make it look like he's been in the pen."

He led me out of the gym as the basketball game broke up and the prisoners huddled near another door, ready to be herded back to the cell block. As Bogardus led me down the hall, I realized we were headed toward the same elevator as the prisoners. One of the guards held them back, behind a wire-mesh door, and I could hear them hush one another as I walked up with Bogardus. I felt their eyes on my oxford shirt, my cordovan loafers. Feet shuffled. Somebody sniffed. We waited. Finally, inside the elevator, I realized I'd been holding my breath.

Bogardus took me to the cell block. Along the surrounding catwalk, two tiers of cells opened into a larger communal area, also surrounded by bars. Some of the inmates washed their clothes in a stainless-steel slop sink in one corner, and others draped their socks and T-shirts through the bars, letting them dry. A boom box played at the other end of the cell block.

"These guys wash their own uniforms. Lay those pants out under their mattresses. Get up in the morning, got a nice crisp pair of creases."

"My wife never irons my shirts," I said.

"Welcome to stay *here*," Bogardus said.

I could see into each cell, no two rooms alike, each one individualized with posters, news clippings, photographs. Bogardus pointed into a dark room for solitary confinement. Nothing on the walls, nothing on the floor but a cot and a stainless-steel commode, one little window in the door, a square foot of view. I couldn't get my mother out of my mind. She would have felt right at home here. A cell to call home. The dark path and the light path both leading to the same renunciation, maybe even the same sort of awakening. Saint Anthony and Malcolm X. I remembered lines from college, the words of William Blake: *Damn braces, bless relaxes.* Except these guys all looked pretty damned relaxed to me.

Upstairs, we entered an older part of the building and turned a corner. Bogardus led me into a long, narrow room with a large window, which offered a view of a larger room where there was a long, black line of tape on the floor. The room we could see through the window was brightly lit. In the room where we stood, there was a battered file cabinet, a few folding chairs, and a television with a VCR on a portable stand. After getting us each a mug of coffee from down the hall, Bogardus nudged a videotape into the VCR's slot and hit the PLAY button. He didn't say a word as the gray images glided across the screen, a soundless composite of violence photographed from the ceilings of all-night convenience stores.

A thin blond white woman walks through the door, steps up to the counter, pulls a pistol from her purse, fires three times into the clerk's chest and then reaches around to steal from the till and leaves as the clerk dies on the floor. Two blacks with do-rags, Jheri curls and rifles slung over their arms climb over the counter, force a clerk onto the floor and pick up the cash register, smashing it beside their captive's head until it shatters and spills currency everywhere. A tall white man with a scarf around his mouth shoves a shotgun into a clerk's neck and says three words.

I close my eyes until I'm sure this one is finished, and when I look again, two teenage boys of uncertain race stuff money into their pockets as the clerk hands it over. When they're done, they both start to walk away; then one of them turns, takes three steps back up to the counter, fires two shots into the clerk's face.

"Some pipehead doesn't know his own name will do anything. Anything. Tape's nothing. You should see it live."

"Turn it off," I said.

He touched a button on the remote. I felt the chill creeping up from my toes, the heart-pounding rush of helplessness.

"And that's where Will's headed. Either he'll end up like one of those pieces of shit you saw on tape, or he'll be setting them loose on the rest of us by feeding their habit. It's a no-win deal. Almost nobody comes through alive."

"How does somebody like that live with himself?" I asked.

He dragged on his cigarette and looked at me.

"I've gotten phone calls since the robbery," I said.

"What kind?"

"Strange. They aren't threatening, exactly. But I know it's one of them. From McDonald's," I said.

"What do they say?"

"I've never actually talked to him. He leaves messages. I know this sounds strange, but he leaves messages about the way things are. These days. Little commentary sort of things," I said. "Could you arrest somebody for that?"

"If he threatens you," he said. "Doesn't sound like he is. You sure it's one of them? Sounds like a telemarketing thing to me."

"I mean, if it's harassment, couldn't you stop them? If it's this Will kid, maybe he'll cut it out after you scare him."

"I'll see what I can do about the calls," he said. "If you'll do something for me."

"What?"

"Just tell me if you see Will in the next room, would you?"

When I looked up, six men were filing into the other room. Will was the fourth to enter. I recognized him immediately. He looked completely out of place. There were two other black men, two whites, and one who was a little hard to pin down. They were all comically dressed in untucked thick Pendletons, baggy pants, unlaced Converse All Stars (some black, some red, two white), and a couple of them had extra ornamentation shaved into their hair. Each of the bogus suspects stepped forward to the black line, turned right, turned left, and then moved back to the wall, mixing up the order: number two, five, one, and then Will, followed by six and three. I knew they couldn't see me, but I headed for the door. Bogardus put out his hand.

"Wait," he said.

"I don't believe this," I said. "I can't believe you just brought me in here."

"I just need to know for sure. If you recognize him."

"Take me home," I said.

"You saw him, didn't you?"

"It's obvious, isn't it?" I asked.

"What?"

"Others look like some white guy's idea of a Spike Lee joint."

Bogardus didn't say a thing for a beat. He didn't want to coach me.

"He's the fourth from the right," I said.

"Your right?" he asked. "Or their right?"

"My right. Can we go now?"

As they turned to leave the room, Will looked up. He gazed directly into the glass. It was a mirror on his side. He couldn't see me, but it was as if I could feel his gaze on my skin. Then he moved on.

"They can't see in here, right?" I asked.

"Nope," Bogardus said. "You did good."

"I want those phone calls stopped."

"I think we can manage that," he said. "You're doing the right thing."

On my way back to my house, we made a quick detour. As he took corners in his government-issue black Gran Fury, stacks of papers tumbled in the backseat and sloshed onto the floor. The fabric of his cheap blotched seat covers gave off the scent of cloves and cigar ash, and a little jagged tree-shaped air freshener swinging from the mirror tried to stand up to all the other odors with a faint whiff of pine. Bogardus himself reeked of cigarettes and English Leather cologne. He had a sticker on the dashboard, above the holster for his cellular phone, that announced: *ONCE YOU GO BLACK, YOU NEVER GO BACK.* Someone had filled in every *O* with black ink, giving them jagged edges to look like bullet holes. It seemed that he'd tried to peel it off, but hadn't been able to scrape away more than the corners. He'd been talking nonstop since I stepped into the car in the garage under the Civic Center: "With Will it's Penn State or the state pen. He's at a crossroads. Kid's a hell of a player. Your son would be amazed. Floats over the paint, you give him an inch. His mother? She's teaching full-time and both her kids—that's the crazy part of it—her kids ought to worship her. She's over on the West Side teaching these welfare mothers how to pass their GEDs. But those kids, they look at the house and the neighborhood. They know it doesn't add up. She'll never get ahead."

He pulled up to a small Cape Cod off Jefferson Avenue, one of the toughest parts of the city—he called it Thug Central—and he swung the Gran Fury around back and parked beside a black Honda Civic del Sol. The little house had a side door into the kitchen off the driveway, with a tulip bed, the jonquil leaves poking halfway out of the ground. In the backyard, a bird feeder hung from an old laundry pole. The place looked immaculate, a new coat of pale blue paint on the siding, new gutters, and a flower box with yellow crocus petals halfway open under the kitchen window. It was an image of old-fashioned decency, scrubbed, everything in order.

I stayed in the car and watched him go up to the door. A black woman appeared, wearing a dark blue sweatshirt with a hood, a pair of black jeans, and sneakers. Her face looked rounded, strong, and she was slimmer than I thought she'd be, considering the shape of her face. She looked up at Bogardus as he stood in the doorway—she was several inches shorter—and he spoke quietly to her. Twice she glanced over toward the car, but quickly, as if she didn't want me to notice.

Then Bogardus went into the house, and a young woman came through the door. At first, I thought she was white. She had the skin tone of a woman at McKee who spent two hours every week at the tanning parlor throughout the winter. Straight black hair, cut level with her chin. She wore black jeans, tight all the way up, and a down-filled sport vest over a turtleneck. No matter how hard I stared at her, she wouldn't look away. Her lips were a perfect, full oval, her skin smooth, the color of cappuccino, and she walked the way hawks ride thermals, no exertion, just gliding. It was as if her body fell into a walk as a state of restfulness.

She still had her eyes on me when she opened the door of the del Sol and looked away only as she ducked into the car. As she turned on the ignition, she rolled down her window and stared at me.

"Y'all afraid that car gone roll right here in the drive?" she asked.

I looked down and realized I still had my shoulder strap on.

"He still in there?" I asked.

"Yeah. Talk about this nappy little Jamaican with one eye my mom date. She always give Frank the latest."

"Why's he here?" I asked.

"Can I ask you a question?"

"Uh-huh."

"You work out a lot?" she asked, rising up in her seat, the better to see the rest of me. "Look like it."

She had my son's emotional transparency. You could see everything she felt in her eyes, her face. She looked as if her body could conduct emotion directly into the fingertips of anyone who touched her.

"I used to run."

"Isn't what I mean."

"Who *are* you?" I asked.

"Dog! Never you mind! I s'pose now you want my zip code," she said, shifting her car into first gear. She drove a stick. Any woman, when she drove a stick, suddenly became twice as interesting.

She started to pull out. As she passed the side door, Bogardus emerged, and without slowing down, she shouted through her window: "He a lot cuter than you made him sound!"

He was smiling a slightly troubled smile when he got back into the driver's seat.

"Doesn't waste any time," I said.

"Doesn't know what delayed gratification means, if that's what you're saying."

"What a face."

"What a package," he said, looking at me. "And that's the last I'm going to say on that topic. I've known her since she was a baby. I'm practically her godfather."

"It hurts to look at her. I didn't realize she was black until she got into her car."

"That's because her father was white," he said, as he backed out of the drive. "That's Paulette. I was telling her mother how we're all set down at County. Won't be long before her son's back home, if it all works out. And it will."

After he dropped me off at my door, I finished the cold sesame chicken Meg had left on the counter and went up to the attic to check my e-mail. On the second floor I could hear the televisions going behind all the closed bedroom doors, Meg and Dana and Alec each tuned to a different channel.

Soon the kids came looking for me. I had the space heater on, and it was almost comfortable, as long as you didn't stand too near a window. Alec had on a hooded flannel shirt now, and he turned on my little portable color television, sitting on the futon I'd doubled up on the floor in the corner. While he waited for Chipper Jones to step up to the plate, I typed a conference report on my computer, and answered a string of e-mails from Whit Sutherland. Every time I tried to open my word-processing program, the computer told me I didn't have enough memory. I had to close one program before opening another. You'd think if Penny wanted me to work twenty-four hours a day, she'd spring for upgrading my laptop.

Dana appeared at the top of the stairs in her longjohns and an oversize plaid pajama top. She played on the high school girls' JV basketball team. She was at that age when she still wanted us to notice her, still wanted to read her writing assignments aloud to us in the kitchen. Everybody wanted to be watched. Except me—I wanted to watch more than *be* watched. I liked to think of my role as the concerned observer, a man on the sidelines trying to distinguish the penalties, cheering when the right thing got done. Alec was surfing channels, stopping at MTV.

"Who is this?" Dana asked.

"Tori Amos."

"She's so weird," she said, stretching out on the bed. "Is this the one—"

"Oh. Oh yeah. The one where Butthead goes, *No cleavage sucks*," Alec said, grinning.

"Turn it off. Pretty soon they'll have snakes or bugs or something all over her. Ugh. Turn it off," she said. "What're you working on?"

"Just checking e-mail," I said. "Where's the crutches, Alec?"

"Downstairs," he said, going through the motions of dribbling a basketball and releasing it above his head with a loose wrist, but not *too* loose.

"How's the hip?"

"Hardly hurts," he said. "Mom drove me to sign up."

"She did, huh," I said.

"How come you aren't going back to the office?" he asked.

"I'm too tired. Besides, I'd rather be here with you," I said, getting up, starting to move toward him in a crouch, like a professional wrestler. "Giving you the old—"

I leaped into the air above him as he started giggling and stretched out sideways on the futon, covering his grinning face. I came down on my elbows and knees, without actually pressing hard against him.

"*—body slam!*"

Dana moved back out of the way, picked up the remote, scanning to see what was on as Alec and I pretended to toss each other around the room. I lifted him into the air and came down with him onto the futon, cushioning the fall with my own body, but we both pretended I'd given him a crushing blow. Then I let him pretend to kick-box me with his good leg, until we were both out of breath, tumbling onto the futon together. Meg would have yelled at both of us to be careful of his hip.

"How about you?" I asked Dana.

"You guys are such losers. Sucks to be you," she said.

"No," Alec said, "Sucks to be *you.*"

"Oh, what a diss."

I panted, catching my breath.

"I guess that hip *is* in good shape," I said, and then turned to Dana. "So how was the job tonight, sweetie?"

"Boring. I only need a couple hundred more for the down payment on the Neon."

"Are you really making enough every week to make the payments?"

"More than enough," she said.

"You could always put the money away for college and keep sharing the Escort."

"When are the cars ever available? You guys are always at work."

"What's your mother doing?"

"Resting, I guess," Dana said. "She's still got the door shut."

I glanced at the phone. I fought the urge to pick it up quietly and see if she had Gregg on the line again. Then footsteps creaked up the stairs, and Meg's head appeared over the banister. She was wearing black stirrup pants and a baggy purple sweater, one of her most appealing outfits. She was smiling.

"Bedtime," she said.

"Ah, come on," I said. "Can't I stay up another hour? The Braves are winning!"

"Very funny," she said.

"It's only nine-thirty," Alec said.

"Go on. Turn on your own television if you want."

Slowly the kids wandered down the stairs and into their rooms. I clicked off the television.

"Admit it. I look nice," she said.

"You look nice," I said, without looking up.

"So when are we going to get together?" she asked.

"I thought you were too tired," I said.

"That was last night," she said. "How'd it go downtown? Did he give you back your wallet?"

"Yep. He had me identify the kid—the one I shouted at—in a lineup. He says he just wants to scare him. They aren't going to prosecute him."

"You mean you actually saw the kid? You remembered him?"

"Yeah. Bogardus tricked me into it. I think he needed me to do that in order to hold the kid for more than a night, which appears to be the big idea."

"And that's it?" she asked.

"That's it," I said, thinking about the drive to the house on Jefferson after the lineup, the young woman who emerged from the house and got into the car beside me. The look of her face, her hips, her waist, the way she moved. Just thinking about Paulette, I felt the heat flare inside me, the desire starting to stir things up again, the pressure, the old feel of things mobilizing.

Then we both heard it: the scraping, scratching sound that moved slowly across the ceiling. It was one of the bats coming in from outside. Just the thought of that little animal inside our walls turned my stomach.

"I hate this house," I said.

I heard the sound of Alec's portable television tuned to ESPN, and when I was sure he'd fallen asleep, I ventured down from the attic and opened his door. His room was a shrine to competitive team sports and alternative entertainment: posters of Barry Bonds, Shawn Kemp, Michael Jordan, Nirvana, Green Day, with rows of major league baseball caps on nails over his headboard, his bookshelves filled with miniature plastic baseball helmets, video games, baseball and basketball trophies, *Sports Illustrateds*, and an Atlanta Braves good-luck troll doll. He was half outside his covers, his injured leg hanging over the edge of the bed, as if he hoped someone would collect it and replace it with a healed one before morning. I went into his tiny room, turned off the television, and pulled the covers up to his neck; I opened his window a crack to let in some of the fresh spring air, and then I went back out in the hall. Meg was in the bathroom.

The small bedside lamps lit our room with a warm glow: the waterbed, the brass bedstead, the painting of Nantucket above the pillows, the distressed dark wood of the dresser, and the ultramarine quilt. On one wall hung Meg's photographs from college, strips of dust showing along the tops of the black frames: vineyards in France, stones in Britain, fogbound streets at night in Syracuse. I hadn't stopped to glance at them in years. In college, when she wanted to be a photographer, and I fantasized about becoming a newspaper reporter, we'd drive around the city taking shots of old railroad spurs and abandoned factories, sit in her car until a homeless man forgot we were there so she could get him candidly on film with her telephoto lens, then sneak up onto the roof of Lincoln First to capture a lone woman through the open window of her office across the street, a scene from Hopper. We were mysteries to each other then: she'd pick my brain for quotes from *The Palm at the End of the Mind* or *Samson Agonistes*, lines I'd memorized for midterms, and she was amazed I could commit so much to memory and then discard it. I asked her about the sort of country-club life she'd known as a child outside Cincinnati, where her father started as a brand manager for Procter & Gamble and rose quickly through the ranks. It was like some fabulous middle-class fiefdom in my imagination, as if she were reciting poetry about jousts and quests.

Now, after all these years, we hardly read books anymore, let alone felt the tug of something mysterious and charmed in our lives. I sat on the bed, leaning back against the pillow shams, with one foot planted on the floor, like somebody in an old sitcom.

The bathroom door opened and Meg emerged, wearing a short black silk chemise. She'd brushed her blond hair over one eye, and she was smiling, looking five years younger, her lips, eyes, profile, all perfect.

She still had one of those faces worth trademarking, as if her eyes and lips and nose formed some kind of connect-the-dots facial equivalent of the shape of cartoon hearts found on Valentine's Day cards. Her nose reminded me of Suzy Parker's in old photographs. I could always detect some kind of interesting, indecisive conflict going on between what was erotic in her mouth and what was perky and engaging in her eyes. I was helpless to contend with the shape of her silhouette at certain angles, and sometimes there seemed to be no limit to how far that helplessness would get us.

She approached the bed, wasting no time, gathering up her nightgown, straddling me, pulling her leg up underneath her, taking my face into her hands. Always, the more resolute she was about her needs, the fewer words she used. Fabric parted and slid off. It used to take us half an hour to get to this stage, after I'd nibbled her shoulders from behind, slowly moving my tongue and teeth down her back, making her wait before she even rolled over onto her back and I went to work with my tongue on the *other* side, and by the time I penetrated her she was close to the edge, almost starting to come, and then I'd stop, making her frantic, until she'd push me up into the air and I'd hung there above her, hardly moving, letting her bring herself to the brink by pumping against me, and when I pushed her to the bed and started to thrust she would sob for me to stop because she thought she'd pass out. Now it was all routine, and always the same. We positioned ourselves so she could stroke herself as we made love, side by side, and I held back until she was ready. This time, I had to be as patient as ever. She masturbated for a while, as I gently moved inside her, careful to avoid bumping up against her circling fingers, and when she opened her eyes and looked toward the ceiling, and started to move her head back and forth, I started in a little too fast, my eyes shut, surprised to realize I was thinking of Paulette getting into her car. It was over sooner than usual, without the familiar chain reaction between us.

"You cut me off," she said.

"It's hard to tell what you want me to do," I said.

"I've got so much on my mind," she said. "God, my head hurts. I'm sorry."

"If you want, we could wait a little while and . . ."

"I think we need to get away. No kids. No work."

She sighed and closed her eyes, and a few minutes later I could tell she was masturbating again, quietly, the muslin sheet moving over her knuckles. I leaned down and mouthed her breast, and her entire body went stiff: she bit her lip to stay quiet, gazing at the ceiling, then she closed her eyes and rolled sideways, without another word. I wondered who *she'd* been fantasizing about.

I lay in bed an hour. Then I went back up to the attic to watch Letterman, and saw the light blinking on my machine again. I went over to it slowly, and pressed PLAY. *Yo Cuz, I guess you*—I pressed PAUSE. Everything turned smooth and numb to the touch as I pried the little cassette out of the machine and replaced it with a blank. Down in my throat little blades revolved, level with my heart, making their incisions in time with my pulse. My knees fizzed. Downstairs, I hid the tape in my billfold's money pocket, on the dresser. The message it contained made everything else in my wallet seem futile and weak and ridiculously *white*.

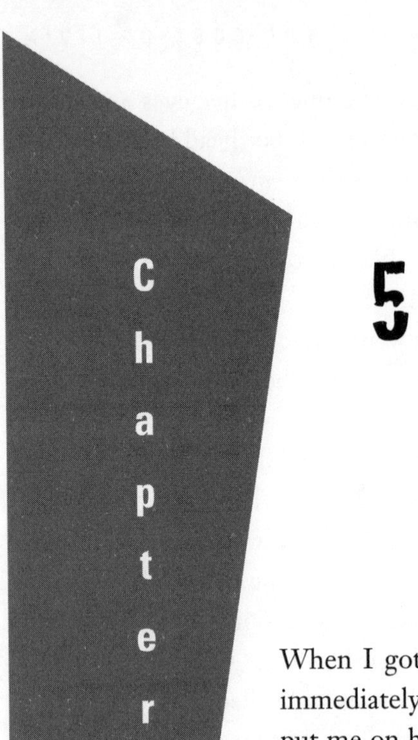

When I got to work, I called Bogardus immediately. The sheriff's department put me on hold for twenty minutes. Jennifer Dewinter showed up in my doorway and smiled, wearing one of her red dresses. She warned me Whit wanted to talk to me about Jimmy's brochure copy, and would be coming to my office in about three minutes.

"Where's Jimmy?" I asked, putting my hand over the phone.

"No idea," Jennifer said.

I considered locking myself in the utility closet with a full pot of French vanilla coffee and a copy of *Advertising Age* and a cellular phone. With the phone wedged between my shoulder and my ear, I took the cassette from my home answering machine out of my wallet; I found a tape recorder in one of my drawers, snapped in the casette, and rewound it to the beginning.

I sorted through the stack of mail I'd collected from my box downstairs on the way up. In the middle was a memo from Jimmy.

TO: Cahill, Sutherland, McKee
FROM: Sorley
I`m trying to track down expenses for the past three months on Veritex, but I haven't held on to receipts at all. It will be pretty much from memory. I'll try to have some kind of report to you in a couple days. A lot of this money, as you well know, went into garter belts. I don't know how that would fly with his new boss. I think we should just say he blew it on drinks and dinners.

I wrote an e-mail to him.

TO: JS
FROM: RCahill
Use your judgment. All I know is, I've got Whit breathing down my neck already this morning. I'm the one who's going to be in trouble if you don't come up with a breakdown on how Vince used his expense account. Come through for me, man.

As I was wondering if my spiral phone cord would stretch far enough to let me refresh my coffee at the corridor sink without having to hang up, Whit Sutherland appeared. He wore a dark, double-breasted flannel suit with a striped shirt and a silk tie knotted against his throat. His wavy blond hair looked as flawless as the plastic coif on a Big Boy. He was tall, thin, bony, with a liberal arts degree, useless to him now except that it was from Yale. He always seemed unperturbed, in his rep ties, his starched shirts and tasseled loafers, and I liked to imagine him coming home to his living room, where his Junior League wife had turned their grand piano into nothing more than a staging area for the gin martini she stirred for him every afternoon. He seemed to have been beamed into my office out of some urbane black-and-white comedy of manners from another era called *The Rochester Story*. It was hard to believe people could still live this way.

"You on hold?" Whit asked.

I nodded. I had certain kinds of eye contact, certain tones of voice, I used only with Whit, who had a way of standing me at the edge of his inner circle. He liked to share two or three little asides at lunch, about some minor screwup or lunchroom dispute. These confidences felt privileged enough to establish the illusion of a secret understanding. I believed Whit was preparing me to move up because he genuinely liked me. But then, he seemed to like everyone. With me, he seemed to be saying that if I'd had the breaks he'd had, if I'd had his family, I could have been there at Yale with him. He never appeared to sweat. He was never wrinkled, never drunk in a damaged or damaging way, never at a loss for the correct change at a tollbooth. He was the managerial equivalent of a centerfold.

"Can you talk?" he asked.

"Sure," I said, my palm cupped over the mouthpiece.

He handed me a printout of Jimmy's copy. I braced myself.

"Brilliant stuff," he said.

"Really?"

"That isn't *your* impression?" he asked.

"I just didn't expect to hear it from you."

"We need to get him out of this mess. Why so late with the copy? Did he say?"

I lifted my hand to silence him as a voice came on the line at the sheriff's department. "Mr. Bogardus? Can you hang on?"

"Make it quick. I'm—"

"Great," I said, holding my palm over the phone and turning back toward Whit to listen.

"Let's get together my place tonight. Five-thirtyish. We'll talk about where to go next with Jimmy and Veritex," Sutherland said. "And I want to talk about your future here. By the way, he'd better get serious about the Veritex expenses. That memo was a little too cavalier."

"Fine," I said.

"Can you talk to him today?"

"I'll try."

It was about time somebody wanted to talk about my future. I wondered if he would tell me how much I'd be getting for my next raise. As usual, he was going to make me wait all day to hear the details. As Whit left the room, the air thinned, the sharp edges grew blunt.

"Cahill? You there?" Bogardus was shouting into the phone now.

"Listen to this," I said as I held the tape recorder up to the telephone. I replayed the whole message for him, the deep voice, the crisp syllables, the imposing sense of ease and amusement at the other end. Bogardus waited a beat when the tape was finished.

"It's got to be that kid," I said. "That Will Breedlove kid."

"He couldn't have made that call. He was busy having a long talk with us after you left last night."

"Then who is it?" I asked.

"Maybe it's one of the others at the holdup. I wouldn't sweat it."

"You said you'd do something about these calls," I said.

"You aren't a threat to these guys. You're an embarrassment. You're getting dissed is all. You know the term?"

"You know this guy, don't you? Tell him to cut it out."

Bogardus chuckled. "Gee, why didn't I think of that? If I knew where he was, he'd be down here with Will. But he has resources Will doesn't have."

"What does that mean?"

"Means he's a lot harder to pin down," Bogardus said.

"I've got the guy on tape for you."

"Listen. I'll do what I can," he said. "I'd like to come by tomorrow. Nothing official. Just stop in for a few minutes. You can give me the tape then. Would that be all right?"

"Long as you can tell me you've made progress."

I rushed Jimmy's copy over to print production, skipping the proofreader, begging our print-production supervisor to get a stat of the pages over to Whit as soon as the typeset copy was camera-ready. On the way, I scanned through the copy. Whit was right. Jimmy never ceased to amaze me, once he got around to doing the work. He could pack more meaning into three sentences than anybody else, except maybe Wes, could get into three paragraphs. All the while, I kept moving the time I'd allocated to my other clients down in my pocket calendar until they finally appeared after the dinner hour—further down than the grid reached—right after my planned visit to Alec's first basketball session. I figured I could show up long enough for him to see my face, but not so long that I'd get behind on the six different jobs I had going at work.

I called Jimmy at home twelve times. I left each of the messages blank, hanging on to the phone for about five seconds without saying a thing. I figured that might trouble him more than anything I could have said. Then I sent him seven identical e-mails: *Please see me immediately about the Veritex thing.* I cut in on Jennifer's phone conversations at the switchboard to ask her if Jimmy'd shown up yet. She said he'd called in earlier to say he'd be at Veritex all day, meeting with Stringer. I called Vince Stringer's number at Veritex, but always got a busy signal or his secretary, telling Vince and Jimmy were in a meeting and couldn't be disturbed. I'd been through this before.

Vince worked at the Veritex headquarters, a rambling, nondescript, one-story facility out near East Rochester. It was a typical software company. The CEO, a guy not yet thirty, a college dropout, had hair down over his collar, a big house alone on a hill in Canandaigua, and a place in Barbados. The surreal demographics of high-tech were like ancient history: kids ruling empires. In ten years, he'd grown the company into an international presence. It was a miracle he remained at the helm. Most people his age, with his talents, got pushed out in favor of professional managers. He was hanging on, making big promises to the press, talking about going public, doing the Chinese fire drill with his top staff every couple years—it was amazing that somehow Stringer had managed to defend his turf.

When the magazine prototype was complete and the copies were being printed up, Stringer returned one of my calls.

"Jimmy there?" I asked.

"Yeah."

"Put him on," I said.

"Easy, tiger. He isn't right here. In my office."

"They're starting to sniff around about how you spend money when you're out of town, Vince," I said. "Jimmy needs to get me some kind of accounting on it. Maybe you can help."

"We don't leave a paper trail."

"I see you haven't changed," I said. "It's serious this time. Least, that's the way it looks."

"Spoken like a true ball-buster," Stringer said, then laughed. "How are ya, Rich? Still trying to break a hundred? Shot a seventy-eight three weeks ago with orange balls. I was unconscious."

"Yeah? Kinda cold for golf, wasn't it? A seventy-eight? God. Is that with Mulligans?"

"I was clockin' the ball. Hole after hole. Click, click, click."

"I have to admit my passion for the game has fallen off," I said.

He laughed. "You'll believe anything. Wish I could see your face. Shit, I'll never shoot a seventy-eight. I can't stand to play anymore. The wheels come off on the tenth or eleventh hole, every time. I end up bending a club around some little staked tree that isn't even in my way."

"Tell Sorley I'm going to wring his neck."

"They on your ass?" he asked.

"No. I'm on *his* ass."

"You're becoming one of them," Stringer said.

"Just have Jimmy call."

"We've been putting together a whole new campaign. I see money earmarked for you. I foresee many evenings out of town. You should join us."

"You get out too much, as it is," I said.

"God, I hate this place."

"I thought you thrived over there," I said.

"I've worked my butt off, right? I've worked fifteen, sixteen hours a day for years, and nothing to show for it. The salary sucks, big-time," he said. "Hell, you can get laid off any day. Doesn't matter how long you've been here. Nobody gives a rat's ass. Whatever works."

Somehow, he sounded weightier on the phone. He'd gained thirty pounds in the past five years, on all those subsidized meals in the big cities. I visualized him in his office, that head full of wavy black hair shaved at the sides, the baby fat around the chin, the swollen eyelids, and that grin as he boasted about his stamina in bed. The last I heard, his levelheaded, red-haired bride was working in her severe white uniform at a VA hospital somewhere. He lived on automatic pilot, keeping himself aloft with party-boy charm backed up by the crucial ability to work eighteen hours a day while gaining another five pounds every year, his wife getting heavier along with him. I didn't trust a single word out of his mouth, but I couldn't help liking him. He could mimic anybody. He figured he could get away with anything as long as he left everybody laughing when it was over. He had appetites he couldn't control. That was hardly a crime.

Chapter 6

If I had to take one word from the dictionary with me to a desert island it would be *decency*. It was what I'd worked all these years to achieve. In college, though, I'd veered away from it eagerly toward the sort of freedom I'd tasted when my mother left me on weekends. My first year at the University of Rochester, I met Jimmy when he stood behind me in the registration line and asked me to sign him up for a class and then went outside to smoke a cigarette. He adopted me, took me barhopping. We drove to Bills games, the November snow ticking on the wipers. He fixed me up with women, rolled joints and urged me to smoke.

Saturday nights we journeyed across the river to Leroy's Birdland, for wings and hot sauce on white bread, with macaroni salad and Cokes. Smoking three joints among six of us, driving into the inner city. As the others talked about the latest Allman Brothers or the new nose tackle for the Dallas Cowboys, the grass seemed to put them in touch with the least important details of city life: little green flecks of pepper in sauce, the amusing aroma of smoldering shoe leather on the heating grate in the floor, and the way the neon lights outside buzzed like June bugs. I didn't enjoy it as much as they did. I was the dreamy one, contemplating the menu, wondering why the time seemed to pass so slowly. Jimmy majored in business and never studied, pulled all-nighters drinking Yoo-Hoo and eating chocolate-covered coffee beans, and aced the finals. I struggled but failed to better my gentleman's Cs in philosophy and literature, memorizing Wittgenstein, Carnap, Russell, Melville, Blake, and Kierkegaard.

In my junior year, I met Meg. She was the one woman I dated in college Jimmy didn't introduce me to. I met her the way I met Jimmy, by accident, in the cafeteria's food line, and ended up sitting next to her—not by accident. She was gorgeous. It took me a while to discover she was also well-adjusted, happy, intelligent, and occasionally witty. She looked solid, had the air of somebody who would keep my feet firmly planted in Rochester soil—B-flight golf leagues and tailgate parties at Rich Stadium, and Presbyterian community outreach programs on Wednesday nights—in other words, the better to stay in touch with everything I'd missed as a child.

We'd dated for only a year when I suggested a weekend in Toronto. She'd spent a week in Ohio at her father's bedside—he was recovering from a bypass. We'd been sending cards to each other, trying to be clever about how long it seemed we'd been apart: she sent me one *(to a fast mover)*, featuring a cartoon snail wearing running shoes, with his home on his back, and I sent her quotes from Lafcadio Hearn about how the Japanese named dozens of cicadas, how the insect lived underground for a decade or more and then emerged for a week to sing and die. She sent me a postcard with a Burchfield watercolor, a cicada on the branch of a tree, and a haiku, *The cicada shell, / it sang itself utterly away*, and then I sent her a glass snail I discovered at a mall. The message on both sides: *Be patient, take it slowly, and things will work out.*

When I got to the room, the drapes were parted just enough for me to see six inches of dark snow on the sill. I heard someone stir. She was waiting for me in bed, calling out softly to me, the covers pulled to her chin, her blond hair stretched over her knuckles, falling everywhere. We didn't get out of that bed until the next afternoon. All weekend, I kept stalling, thinking of the diamond I'd brought with me, afraid to offer it. I couldn't compete with her father's membership at Firestone, his Cadillac, his summer place on Lake Geneva, his seats on various boards, the Frank Lloyd Wright house outside Cincinnati on ten acres of pine and birch and sycamore and oak and mulberry. I'd played video games that taught me what having all that wealth meant: the car, the house, the boat were each like a power-up in the game, an extra life, a chunk of equity you could burn to keep you going when you failed, to protect your children from the collection agencies and repossession men. The stability, the honor, the unassailable decency of it, covered with ivy, a rock, a cornerstone, a *real* house. But how would I ever be able to equal *that?* I was beneath his daughter. He snubbed me, the one time I came to visit her parents. He told her later, if she took up with me, he'd limit her to a trust fund after his death. I figured it was only a matter of time before she told me no.

Truth was, I didn't want his wealth. With Meg, I wanted to bring up a couple kids in normal surroundings, the sort of life she'd known as a child. I didn't expect we'd become one of the prized or envied couples on the street. I didn't expect to be on everyone's A-list for dinner-party invitations or to talk late into the night about the latest Saab 900 and vacations at Hilton Head or to debate which country club we should join. It didn't bother me that I'd never be consulted for my expertise on single malts or graphite shafts. I didn't need to become a Member. All I wanted was for the two of us to move in and out of a few of those circles as a Welcome Guest and have at least a shot at raising a decent family. But I just wasn't sure if that would be enough for Meg.

On our last day in the city, we found a little Chinese gallery, with classic ink paintings on scrolls, and watercolors lining the walls, and rows and rows of bamboo brushes and ink for sale under glass. Just as Meg was walking out, I spotted the painting of a snail on a twig, and as I called her back into the shop, I saw the other, directly beside it, of a cicada on another stem, the translucent, veined wings, the painting's calligraphic black ideograms down the side and a red stamp in the corner. I put them on the credit card I'd gotten only a month earlier.

As we carried them back to the hotel, we looked at each other as if we'd been visited by something alive, intelligent, observing, leaving us this little telltale acknowledgment of our lives, these paired paintings, this odd little synchronicity. Back in the room, I pulled out my wallet and produced the ring. As I held it out to her, she penetrated it with her long, slim finger and pulled me down onto the unmade bed as we peeled away our clothes. Against all my expectations, she said yes.

Now, every time I visited Whit Sutherland's manor on Sandringham, it was clear to me how much of a guest I would always be in *his* life. When I pulled up his driveway, I wondered how much nitrogen it took to keep his acre of grass the color of jade, how cool the navy awnings kept the interior. He'd inherited the place from his father, and it was situated in the most expensive sector of my own suburb, off East Avenue, where many of the homes were still inhabited by the descendants of people who'd made their wealth during one of the many booms in Rochester's history: in flour, textiles, film, photocopies, or real estate. Driving down his winding street reminded me how much money could be amassed by a single family. It didn't seem possible to do it this way anymore, unless you won the lottery or started a software company. It was rare to see ostentation in Rochester. Usually, the only time you saw a stretch limo was on prom night or at a wedding.

It was a rare, freakishly warm midwinter day, temperature in the sixties, and everything was fragrant again, the sun warming the puddles. The weatherman was predicting snow, but it didn't seem possible with a sky this blue. When I reached for the doorbell, I realized the door was ajar. I walked into the foyer, where a marble staircase turned upward past a large, semicircular stained-glass window with a Pre-Raphaelite frieze of half-dressed women gathered under a tree. I took it all in: chandelier, flocked wallpaper, mahogany sideboard on the landing, scent of lilac rising from the carpet.

Sutherland appeared, drinks in hand. Somehow he'd already changed into a dark green golf shirt and chinos. I hesitated to take the vodka tonic he offered me, and then I slipped my fingers around it, feeling its chilly, moist surface against my palm.

"Made these on a whim. I've got single-malt too."

"I'm good," I said. "I can't stay long. I've got Alec's first basketball session to get to."

"How's he holding up?" Whit asked.

"Amazingly well. He's moving around a lot now. Not enough to play, but enough to do the shooting contest they have."

He ushered me past the living room, with its grand piano and antique loveseats. Through the dining room and the new kitchen, he led me out onto the deck he'd added in back, grabbing an open liter of Absolut on his way out. I sat in one of the two Adirondack chairs. On a little white table, he had a copy of Jimmy's brochure work, and another job jacket I didn't recognize. He picked up the copy.

"Nice job on this," he said.

"Just-in-time delivery."

"Jimmy's low on do-gas," he said.

"Huh?"

"Degree of give a shit," he said, smiling. "I heard it at Kodak this morning."

"Have to e-mail that one to Wes."

"Jimmy loves to turn everything into a nail-biter. Tell him you'll have his job next time he pulls this."

"Like I have that authority," I said.

"It's all yours if you want it."

He picked up the job jacket from the table and handed it to me.

"Two new speeches," Whit said. "Hand them off to Jimmy."

"Who opened these?"

"I did. They're from somebody higher up at Veritex," he said.

"I haven't seen the name before."

"Tish Anderson. She's new," he said. "Go to work on that drink, would you? I've got more where that came from. No need to sandbag."

I gazed down into the glass, then lifted it to my mouth and downed the entire drink in three swallows. My eyes filmed and burned as I handed him the glass of blunted ice.

"Fill 'er up."

"Killer Cahill," he said. "I like the way you take orders."

He tossed the ice over his shoulder with a deft, mechanical gesture, so that the cubes sailed over the edge of the deck and down into the flower beds. He poured two fingers of vodka into the glass, neat, and handed it back. His face said it all. Now we were getting somewhere.

"The name on that job jacket? Our new client? She and Penny are like this already," he said, crossing his fingers and holding them up in front of his face. He was grinning with more delight than I'd ever seen in his face. "The all-powerful Vince Stringer is about to get knocked down a few pegs. Or at least sideways."

"What happens to Jimmy?" I asked.

"He gets his wrist slapped. We reel him back in. Reassign him. Where he can do us some good. Writing full-time. All depends on you, though."

"Meaning what?"

"We need to pin him down on the Veritex money. Put his feet to the fire so they can straighten Vince out," he said.

"Stringer likes to be entertained," I said.

"Three thousand in one night?"

"Three?" I asked.

"Nobody can eat and drink that much. Not even Vince."

"Sounds a little extreme, even for him," I said.

"Anderson wants something on paper."

"Vince's old boss just gave him the nudge and the wink."

"I don't think his new one cares so much about the money, but his indiscretions have given her just the leverage she wants against him. She doesn't like the guy. There's also an invoice you submitted for fifteen hundred Penny's been asking about."

"Same story," I said. "I was with them on one trip. They maxed out their cards. They used mine on a couple nights."

"And what were they spending the money on?" he asked.

"Food. Drinks. Fun."

"Fun, huh," he said. "I think we need to put a finer point on it. That's where you need to go to work."

"You know what I mean," I said. "That's where the nudge and the wink came in handy."

"What I know or don't know isn't the issue."

The temperature was falling fast, and a cold wind slid down

from Lake Ontario under a front of big, bruised clouds. I watched it plow winter back over our heads, draining light from the air, turning everything gray as ash. The mercury seemed to drop a degree every minute. It was like sitting in a theater as it darkens just before the show.

"So this is management, huh?" I asked.

"No matter how bad it gets, it can't be as bad as working at Veritex. I take the Hobbesian view: corporate life is nasty, brutal, and short," Sutherland said. "Like my first marriage. Brutish. It's *brutish*, isn't it?"

"*British* for all I know. I wasn't a Hobbes guy in college."

He smiled at my remark as I watched him lean back in his chair, hanging his arm over the side, letting the neck of the bottle slip gradually through his fingertips until it settled onto the deck. He seemed completely ignorant of the temperature. It was part of the Whit Sutherland package: the immunity to all pain, including the weather.

When I got back into my car, it was snowing heavily, even though, in one part of the sky, the sun was still out. I opened my mouth to the sky and drank flakes as I closed the door. Snow: the weatherman was right, after all. Typical Rochester weather, snow and sunshine together, completely insane, with violent shifts of mood. I glanced at the digital clock on the dash. I still had more than enough time to catch Alec on his first night at the gym.

I sped through two yellow lights on the way. Halfway down Winton, across the Fairfield town line, as I was passing our street, I hit a patch of black ice. The car fishtailed, and the trees leaned in, reaching for me, and the gritty hump of old frozen snow gaped, chewing the passenger door as I slid into an icy bunker. The tires shrieked and went nowhere. Then something seemed to disengage with a clank and go loose underneath me. I stepped on the gas, the engine raced, but the car didn't shiver forward or back. Last time I'd taken it to the dealer, they'd told me the transmission ought to be rebuilt. It skipped second gear half the time. If it meant saving two thousand, I figured I could live without second gear. Now I had *no* gears.

I jogged the three blocks back to the house, called the Automobile Association and told them where to deliver the car, once they'd winched it up and pulled it out. I called a cab. As I waited, Dana appeared and disappeared into the kitchen, hardly looking at me, wearing her white buttondown shirt and little black bow tie, dressed for her shift at the supermarket. Today was her first day as cashier.

"Where have you been?" she asked.

"Where's your mother? Isn't she dropping you off?"

"No. *You* are."

"Nobody told *me*. Where is she?"

"She's meeting with Mr. Corcoran," she said, glancing at me. "She dropped Alec off. The idea was you'd bring him home if she got there too late. Can you have the cab drop me off at the store? This is so embarrassing."

"Your mother's planning to show up, right?" I asked.

"That's what she said, Daddy," she said. "See how easy it would be if I had my Neon? Think you can take me out to test-drive one this weekend?"

I smiled at the way she could lead me to whatever inescapable conclusions she wanted to hear. Some of the other parents in our suburb were buying their kids Mitsubishis and used Jeeps and BMWs with car alarms. These kids drove better cars than *we* did. Dana was still *working* toward a car. She put on her bow tie, and got her math done, and depended on us for a ride.

"Seems like your mother spends every free minute with old Mr. Corcoran, doesn't it?"

She didn't respond, but went to the cabinet, got out a large box of Honey Nut Cheerios and poured herself a bowl for dinner.

"I just think she could spend more time with the rest of us," I said.

"Pourquoi, papa?" she asked, breezing toward the refrigerator, getting out a cold bowl of guacamole and a bag of corn chips from the cabinet.

"Because of situations like tonight. I mean what are they going to accomplish until they hear something back from the Kestlers on that development?"

"Je ne sais pas, papa. Mon père," she said. She wasn't even looking at me. Apparently she'd learned to speak French as she forgot how to read English. She ate a spoonful of Cheerios, then popped a guacamole-laden chip into her mouth.

"All the major food groups," I said.

She made her nice-try-at-humor face.

"French class is going well, huh?"

"Comme ci, comme ça. Cher papa."

"Eat fast. That cab will be here any second," I said. "So, you happy these days?"

"With what?" she asked, looking at me as if I'd lost my mind.

"I don't know. Everything. Your life," I said. "I was so screwed up when I was your age. What ever happened to that girl who jumped into the canal?"

"She's fine. It wasn't like she didn't know how to swim. That was the big joke. If you're going to kill yourself, pick something you don't know how to handle. She's one of these clueless types. It's like, *That Galileo thing is, like, totally bogus. You take a mohair cardigan sweater and the receipt? You can't, like, tell me they'd hit the ground at the same time. That would, like, never happen.* She's totally bored with her life. That's all."

"You're one to talk," I said. "That's all I hear from you."

"Well, it's true! Fairfield High is so dull. The biggest crisis we've got is how they never order enough chocolate-chip brownies in the cafeteria. Or, *Oh my God, I'm going to get a D!* One kid I know got a detention and community service for bringing a bagel to homeroom for breakfast. Busted for carrying a concealed bagel. It's pathetic. Nothing ever happens at our school. But nobody kills themselves because they're bored."

She took her empty cereal bowl to the sink and rinsed it out and placed it in the dishwasher.

"There's the cab," I said. "You ready?"

"I'm so nervous."

"Hey, it's all bar codes now. You'll do fine."

After we dropped Dana off at the supermarket, the cabdriver took only eight minutes to get to the school. He didn't look as if he cared about such a small fare—he didn't even count the money I handed him. I got into the gym after everything had begun and found Meg in the stands, near the door. I joined her, sidling around several couples we knew, shaking hands and smiling on my way up. The Hot Shots competition was half finished, and players were stationed at three different baskets.

"Did I miss Alec?" I asked. "D'he shoot yet?"

"He's next, after this group."

"I had to take a cab," I said.

"What happened?"

"I slid off Winton. Triple A'll tow it home," I said. "Where were *you?*"

She didn't even look at me, but kept her eyes trained on the competition below. I stared at her, anyway, and then gave up.

"Gregg still can't get through to the Kestlers. He and I put together a new, lower bid, and we overnighted it to where they're staying on the West Coast," she said.

"Is it lower than the Canadian dealer's?" I asked.

"No. But it's close. She's trying to sell them a truckload of junk. You should see some of it. I had no idea. It's about a notch above a starving artist's sale at the Dome arena."

"And where did you have this meeting?" I asked.

"We had a drink at Hogan's Hideaway. And some wings," she said. "Took us about an hour to figure out how to put the thing together. Then we went back to the gallery, did it on the computer, and I stuck the thing into the FedEx box on the way to the gym. I hope it actually gets to them."

"Dana had Cheerios for dinner again."

"So make her a meal. You're the one who was home."

"I wasn't having a stinger and wings at Hogan's Hideaway, if that's what you mean."

I looked down onto the court as Alec came out. He looked up into the stands and saw me sitting next to his mother, waving at him. He smiled, then prepared to shoot. When the whistle blew, he tossed his first free throw, but it swirled around the rim and popped out. I felt a little ripple of dread, wondering if this would be one of those times when nothing went right for him and he fell into some kind of slump I couldn't help him overcome. It happened in Little League, midseason, sometimes. He'd start whiffing, not even nicking the ball, and the hitless weeks would start to pile up, and I wouldn't know what to tell him.

But he stayed on top of the ball for the rebound, making a couple close shots, then moving away from the basket for the higher-point shots, missing about half of them. With every shot, I could see the look of desperation mounting in his face. By the time the whistle blew, he was hanging his head. As he slouched off to the stands, I felt helpless, having to watch the whole thing from the sidelines, knowing there was nothing I could teach him.

"He can make all of those shots at home, when he isn't trying so hard," I said.

■

On the way home, Meg drove and I rode up front, letting Alec sit silently in back. No one said a word. At home, we went to our rooms, and I took off my work clothes and changed into a set of charcoal sweats and a pair of chewed-up cross-trainers. I closed the door and lay on the bed while Meg changed.

"Somebody's got to pick up Dana in half an hour," I said.

"It's your turn."

"I should go back to the office, anyway," I said.

"Aren't you ever going to get a night off?"

"We can always hope."

"What did Whit need to talk to you about?"

"They're getting all bent about the way Stringer and Jimmy are spending Veritex money when they're out of town."

"You mean at those places?" she asked.

"No doubt. Remember when I pulled away from Stringer, when they had me doing the client contact? That trip to Dallas when he spent fifteen hundred on the dancers and asked me to hide it in the invoice for the work?"

"How'd that end up, anyway? I thought they just looked the other way about that stuff at Veritex."

"They used to. Now Whit's asking for an explanation of that voucher."

"Great," she said.

"He isn't after *me*. He's just trying to get everything squared away so this new woman at Veritex can come down hard on Stringer."

"Why did it take them this long to look at what he's been doing?" she asked.

"Nobody cared until now."

It was still a turn-on to watch Meg undress, even the way she stretched her toes when she peeled her hose off her feet. I loved it when she took off everything and stretched out backward on the bed, her arms over her head, letting all the tension from her day drain through her delicate fingers, high above her head. But tonight she stepped into a pair of jeans and a sweatshirt. Maybe she didn't want to waste the show on *me*.

"Do you really think we should go through with the new house if I don't land the Kestler deal? I mean it's going to leave us next to nothing for our Future Fund."

"I ought to have a lock on a good raise, long as I land that account in New York."

"Hope so. The way things are going, who knows."

"No no no. You're supposed to say, *Yes, Rich, you are a super account executive. You are Super Suit. You are my hero, my god, and I know you will provide for us all.*"

"That's what your new clients need to say," she said.

"We're as prepared as we'll ever be. I hate to think my raise is going to be our only source of extra money, though. We never save enough. You know?"

Alec stuck his head through the door.

"Where are my headphones?" he asked.

"Downstairs. On top of the refrigerator. I borrowed them when I went running this morning," Meg said.

"Can't you get your own headphones?" he asked. He was wearing a baggy plaid flannel shirt, loose warm-up pants, and a pair of unlaced basketball shoes, and he had his Michigan cap on backward. It was his hip-hop look again, straight off MTV. In those videos the men lived like roaming dogs, unrolling their accordion packs of condoms for the camera before ducking into bedrooms with four women, grinning, a gun under the belt, a fifth of gin on the table, with a stack of dominoes. It probably looked a lot more intriguing to him than my flights to Manhattan, my regular paychecks, my lugubrious conversations with his mother about raises and promotions. It looked a lot more interesting to *me*.

"Would you help me practice some shots tomorrow, Dad?"

"After work, sure. I don't know how much help I'll be," I said. "I never played."

He sighed and nodded and left.

I went up to the attic to check my e-mail once more before I went back to the office to put in another two hours, hoping to catch up on the brochures and the video. My breath blurred the air in front of me, and I knelt at the space heater, turning it to FULL. When I downloaded my e-mail, there was a reply from Jimmy.

> TO: RCahill
> FROM: JS
> Can we get together tomorrow morning? I can do a more detailed memo on the Veritex situation, but I want to run it past you first. We need to talk. I've got a bad feeling about this situation. You and I both know how Vince spends money.

I clicked on REPLY.

> TO: JS
> FROM: RCahill
> I don't think we have any choice but to get into details. They're serious about this. I don't know what's up at Veritex, but they aren't going to leave us alone until we come up with some numbers and some specifics.

I noticed the light on my answering machine was blinking again. That red light flashed like a light in a rearview mirror. The blood surged into my neck. I stared at the machine, visualizing myself taking the cassette out and crunching it under my heel. Instead, I pressed PLAY.

The recording went on and on. Someone had called and then set the telephone down on a table or a chair. Then there were two television voices. One sounded to me like Jim Lehrer, interviewing someone. The guest was doing most of the talking: *That's right. In these years, more and more working mothers were entering the job market but aggregate incomes weren't rising. The middle quintile has enjoyed no increase in pretax income—adjusted for inflation—in the past twenty years. The richest top few percent are the only people in this country who have seen the kind of growth in income most people saw after the war and up through 1973. We're becoming a very top-heavy society.*

There was no question this information represented a threat to me. Yet, as disturbing as these facts were, this wasn't exactly the sort of threat I expected from the sort of person I assumed was its source. Nor was it exactly news: the rich got richer and the poor got poorer. I'd heard it all before. The world had been hearing it for thousands of years. Still, it was like the previous calls, its animosity intensified by the offhand, casual quality of the content. The way these phone calls refused to be what I expected bothered me as much as their persistence.

I heard someone pull into the driveway, and I went to the attic window: we weren't expecting anyone, and we almost never got surprise visits after dark. As I opened the drapes I could see the flashing light, but the light was yellow. It was my car, hanging from the back of the tow truck. I'd completely forgotten about it. I went out and watched as they lowered the wheels onto the drive; then I signed the paperwork. This time the news was exactly what

I'd expected: *Transmission's shot. Cost you two thousand to get it rebuilt. Tranny work's highly skilled.* I tipped them and got into the Saab. It was time to pick up Dana at the supermarket. I figured by eleven I'd be done for the day.

Chapter 7

Meg drove me to the airport in the morning, so I could pick up the little rental Grand Am we'd reserved for two weeks. It was one of those I've-got-nothing-to-say drives when it felt as if both of us wanted to talk, but neither of us could think of anything worth saying, even though we both probably thought there were about three hours' worth of important subjects to discuss. When I got out of the car, she waved by lifting her hand and facing her open palm at me, like some kind of salutation between chieftains, and then she took off for the gallery. It was a relief just being alone, but I felt uneasy; we found it so hard to say the most fundamental things now, as if everything in our marriage were suddenly wiggling loose from the moorings, waiting for one of us to start anchoring things down again.

I drove the Grand Am to work, and my spirits lifted as soon as I got to the on-ramp. It was no sports car, but compared to the Escort it felt unbelievably alive. I was surprised at how easily it responded to a mere tap on the accelerator. So this was what I'd been missing all these years. For years I'd been saying no to myself and yes to everybody else. I was proud of my self-restraint. But there were limits.

After I got a cup of coffee, I left a message on Jimmy's voice mail: *Come by and see me first thing. Let's get this Veritex situation pinned down once and for all.* Then I checked my e-mail.

TO: RCahill
FROM: WhitSuth

Get me whatever details you get from Jimmy as soon as you can. We're off to New York in two days. I'd like to put this thing to bed and talk seriously about your future over dinner in New York. What's the status on the Kodak brochures, the video, and the work Wes has been doing?

I called Wes, who'd been in his office for two hours already.

"Whit's on my ass. What've you got for me?" I said.

"I made a few calls to New York. We can get permission for the Late Night Clown. But the client's backing down on it. They think it would come off as if we're making fun of the beer," he said.

"Are you serious? Let me give them a call later today."

"Figures, doesn't it?" he asked.

"It's always like this. A real ad campaign, a chance to do something that really pops, and they get cold feet."

"What about the brochures? Have you looked at what Jolie wrote?"

"Yeah, I called the client and they've faxed me the words they want me to plug into the copy. Listen to this: *Your choices will be countless as the stars.* They want this in the brochure."

"Tell me you're joking," I said.

"Not only is the universe stranger than we imagine, it is stranger than we can *possibly* imagine," Wes said. "And there's a snag."

"What?" I asked.

"They did a little focus group and they're getting nervous about the tag line for the new campaign."

"Focus group? Since when does anybody do a focus group on brochures?" I asked. "How come I didn't know about this?"

"It gets better. They went down to the library and took aside the two women who handle the microfiche and asked them to read the copy. They said they didn't get it. Too many words. They wanted bullet items. Neither of these women ever actually purchased any microfiche equipment. They use it. They don't buy it. This is their idea of a focus group."

"This is after eight drafts of the copy," I said. "What the hell kind of focus group is two women at the public library?"

"They ask you to think outside the box, and as soon as you start doing that, they start screaming, *Get back in the box! Get back in the box!* Nobody's got the balls to make a decision anymore," Wes said.

"Thanks for handling all this. You've gotten more done in a day than Jolie managed to do in a week. You should be handling accounts."

"No, thanks. I was just trying to get a little more input and they dumped all this on me," he said. "Good luck."

Now I had to try to track down a digital audio recorder myself in order to transfer the video voice-overs from analog to digital.

A fine way to spend my time, considering the agency billed me out at a hundred dollars an hour. As a last resort, I figured I'd go out to a stereo shop and buy one. Just as I was reaching for the Yellow Pages, Jimmy came in.

"You got a second?" he asked.

"I hope you're here to brighten my day," I said.

"Don't put on your Ray-Bans just yet."

I grinned and motioned for him to sit down.

"I think we should draw the line here," he said, for once coming straight to the point. "I *like* Vince. I know you like him too. We can't do this to him."

"We aren't doing anything to him," I said. "And I don't like him *that* much. If it's my job or his, then I'll protect my job."

"Your promotion, you mean," he said.

"That isn't what this is about."

"You don't crucify some guy just because some woman thinks he's a pig."

"Who said she thinks he's a pig? They're just trying to straighten things out. If he's been blowing the money on dancers, then we should say so."

"I say we just stick to the story: expensive wine, big-ticket meals. Fun. No receipts. No paper trail. Up to them to prove otherwise."

"That's it, huh? That's your idea of a response?"

"It's totally political. And you're on *her* side? He hasn't done *anything.*"

"He's spent more money than they want him to. That's something," I said. "I think Vince is all right. I mean, I can see what you're—but you *know* Vince is gonna survive. They'll slap his hands and get even for whatever it is he's doing to her; then she'll move him someplace he can't piss her off. That's all."

"You don't know that," he said. "It'll just get us in deeper."

"What's deeper? I have no idea what you're—"

He stood up.

"Just stonewall them. Okay?"

"You know Whit needs to know all this. Just because you helped him spend it isn't going to get you into a lot of hot water."

"You are so out of it," he said.

"I'm not taking sides here, Jimmy."

"My lips are sealed, man," he said. "And yours should be, too. You owe me. You owe me big-time."

I avoided Whit all the rest of the day, staying out of the office, tracking down a digital audio recorder, transferring the analog tape onto the digital one while sitting in the front seat of my car in a parking garage, and then delivering the new tape to the studio. I ran errands. I tried to avoid thinking of the situation Jimmy was putting me into, and then I went directly home, without checking back at the office. If I allowed myself to think about it for more than a minute or two, I would either get angry at Jimmy or else start feeling depressed and backed into a corner.

When I got home, Alec was in the driveway, practicing his shots, and I handed off a couple passes to him for layups before heading into the kitchen. I could hear voices in the dining room, first my wife's and then Gregg's, through the swinging door. They had a tone when they were together, more casual and intimate than some married couples, as if they'd been best friends for years. There was a bottle of vodka out on the counter, and another of vermouth, and a mixer filled with ice and what was left of the martinis. I poured myself a double and leaned back against the counter, listening. Meg sounded almost lighthearted, full of energy.

"You think so?" she asked.

"We go in there tomorrow with this new bid, and we blow them away."

"It's so low," she said. "It's depressing."

I could hear the clicking of fingers on the keyboard of Gregg's notebook computer. And then the sound of ice in a glass as it hit the table.

"I'll tell you what really bums me. These guys have no idea what this Canadian woman's selling them. They don't know the difference," he said.

"You think *we* know the difference anymore?" Meg asked quietly.

"You really think the numbers are too low?"

"Ever feel like you're losing touch?"

"I still know what's good. It isn't what I would have thought was good in college," he said. "Check those numbers over one more time."

"That's *exactly* what I mean. In college, if I'd seen one of those things Keinholtz was doing back then? I would have thrown a rock through a window somewhere and gone back to my essay on Vermeer."

"There's still plenty of beautiful work. Bailey, Hodgkins, Janet Fish."

"But look at what *we* carry. I know, I know! Don't say it. I know it's good. I understand that. But I don't . . . how can I say this . . . I don't *love* it," she said. "You know what I mean? Except—"

"Well you don't have to—"

"But I love making it happen. I love the way we get in there and make it work. But that's just the business part."

"Yeah. I know," he said. "Would you just come over here and look at these numbers?"

I'd had this discussion with her before, *three* years ago. How did time pass so quickly? She'd take on artists she knew would hit it big in SoHo, like the woman who painted flat images of stick men with surrealistic *tromp l'oeil* deflated balloons for testicles, creating the illusion, worthy of Dalí, that they were stuck to the canvas with a pin, in the anatomically correct spot. She discovered a man who created fake department-store window displays with carefully reconstructed scenes of atrocities from Vietnam, Somalia, the Gulag. She built the beginnings of a career for a young Hispanic artist who did abstracts that were so alive, they seemed to shift and quiver as you looked at them, dark and splintered and ethereal—even *I* liked the stuff—and Meg thought she might actually make real money with his work in New York, which is exactly what happened but not until he was discovered dead, overdosed in the apartment of his middle-aged gay lover. This was not what she'd had in mind when she fell in love with art. None of it was anything even remotely resembling the sort of work, or the sort of people, she'd dreamed of promoting.

She knew she was making an honest living. But she felt like a stranger to herself sometimes: I could hear it in her voice from the other room.

I realized I wasn't hearing *anyone's* voice from the other room. No more conversation, no more sound of fingers on a keyboard, no more ice cubes knocking around in a cocktail glass. My heart started to pound. Alec stuck his head into the kitchen.

"That guy's back. He brought somebody with him."

As I looked out the back door, I recognized Bogardus immediately, even though his back was turned. He rubbed his lumbar muscles with the palm of one hand and held an unlit cigarette in the fingers of the other. Over his shoulder I saw someone else, with a pale gray sweatshirt hood over his head, baggy black warm-up pants, and a new pair of white Fila sneakers. He was helping Alec adjust his grip on the ball, but I couldn't see his face. His hands were deeply tanned, as if he'd just returned from a vacation in the Caymans. As I reached for the doorknob, he turned around far enough for me to catch a glimpse of his face. As I recognized him, Bogardus appeared on the other side of the storm door, opened it, placed his hand on my chest and pushed me back into the kitchen, shutting the door behind him.

"Don't! Don't! Hear me out! He has no idea you were the one at the lineup," he said.

"There is no way—"

"Hear me out. Would you shut up for two sec—I know what you're—"

"No way. No. Way," I said.

"Listen," he said.

"I'm serious."

"Rich. Hear me out," he said.

"I mean, I can't believe . . . here. Here in my own driveway," I said. "This is ridiculous. This punk out playing basketball with my son! This doesn't happen. You don't *do* this. I mean, you *promised.* You don't bring this, this *felon* to—The idea was to get him *out* of my life."

"He's teaching him. Let me finish, would you? And keep it down. Can you talk a little softer, please?" he asked.

"He's going to know, goddammit," I said, almost whispering. "He's going to know."

"He won't. Not the lineup. He knows who you are, obviously. He already knows where you live. Your phone number. You're the guy at the McDonald's. That's why he's here. To make up for what he did."

"I despise that little prick," I said. "There's no way he can make up for—"

"He's here because he injured your son. That's the deal. He gives your son some private lessons. Long as that Ignatius clinic lasts. What is it, a week?"

"Uh-uh."

"All the people I see, year after year, you know what I wait for?"

"Somebody to offer you a job in the private sector?" I asked.

"Oh, I've passed up a lot of those. I could be making twice as much heading up security for some of these companies," he said. "I could be out guarding houses at Sedgewick."

"Really? You passed that up?"

"What I wait for's to see a certain look in a guy's eyes. He blinks. He's done something wrong. He knows it. He feels what? I dunno. Ashamed? Something. Just one human being. Know what? Never happens. Everybody's got an excuse. Nobody thinks he's doing anything *wrong*. But Will. I saw that look in his eyes. Down in that interrogation room. He felt bad. Finally I saw that look. I'm not talking about just the blacks, either," he said. "And I should throw that away? Once I've gotten that look out of a kid I halfway care about?"

"What's all this going to do for him?" I asked.

"I want Will playing basketball for Ignatius by the time we're done, if I can figure out how to finance it. Get him on the bus out here to Fairfield. Make him realize there's another sort of world. This is triage, Rich. Ninety percent of what I see are walking dead. No hope. With this kid, it's different."

Bogardus was talking to himself now, using a low voice, lost in thought.

"Like his new shoes?" Bogardus asked. "I went out to Foot Locker and got him a pair. You've got to help me with him."

We were standing in the middle of the kitchen, and I gazed out at the driveway. I could hear voices in the dining room, but no one came into the kitchen to check on what was happening. The longer they stayed in the other room, the odder it seemed, especially now that they were talking so quietly I couldn't make out what they were saying to each other.

Will was crouched beside Alec, going through the arm motions of a jump shot, talking nonstop. Alec was laughing at whatever he heard as Will came halfway up, sprang his arms easily over his head and let his right hand hang limp. He was lost in the act. Then he had Alec try it. It wasn't anything I hadn't taught Alec already, but I could see the difference when he tried the shot now. He was loose in his joints, and the ball easily found its target and when it plunged through the net, it nearly swished. But this sort of thing didn't happen. Not this kid in *my* driveway.

"The kid's a punk. Someday I'll come home, and the VCR will be gone."

"Don't you see the trade-off? He pays the price for what he did, and your son gets better at basketball."

"And what do I get out of it?" I asked.

I heard the back door open, but before I could even look around, she was in the kitchen, wearing a tan vest with tight black denims and low heels. She smirked at Bogardus, who glanced sideways at me, as if he expected danger from my side of the room rather than hers. At first, all I recognized was the familiar feeling of being ambushed by her beauty. I'd forgotten how compact a woman could be around the waist and hips, what few pints of air she displaced as she moved from window to telephone to table. After two kids, Meg looked good, but certain curves didn't have the same drama, the same poignancy, as they'd had ten years earlier. The rises and hollows tended to average themselves out.

"This gone take all day?" she asked, glancing at me.

"What are *you* doing here?" I asked, smiling.

"Oh. You remember?" she asked.

"The del Sol," I said.

She moved across the kitchen and casually opened the refrigerator, leaning forward and tapping a Tupperware storage bowl with one long fingernail, trying to see through the translucent plastic into the contents. From behind, as she leaned over, the prospects were even more unnerving. I looked away, out toward the blacktop, where Will passed the ball back and forth with Alec, both of them grinning and bantering. I rested my fingertips on the smooth, cool countertop. Paulette closed the refrigerator's pale door and leaned back against it. Her straight hair hung in shining bangs, parted slightly in the middle, over her large, dark eyes. She glanced around as if she were in a foreign country with enchanting customs, Romanesque architecture, bad plumbing, bats.

"Come on, Paulette. Quit fooling around. We aren't finished here," Bogardus said. "I left you the key. Go out. Listen to your tapes."

"Why's she here?" I asked.

"Because Will can't drive," he said. "She'll be dropping him off. Paulette owes me."

"I hate my name," she said. "Know what I like? Chantilly. My mother had no imagination. Tanisha. Lavegas. Babies these days got all the good names. Shabrittany. Porsche."

"As in P-o-r-t-i-a?"

"As in nine-eleven," Bogardus said. "I think it was your father who picked your name. Your father who had a layover in Paris once and never got over it."

She ignored him. She wanted to make me wonder. But even more, she wanted to look around. She was an enthralled tourist in a world that hardly registered anymore on my retinas and eardrums: she was making me look at everything twice, to see what I'd been taking for granted all these years. It really wasn't an impressive house, but I think maybe the smell of it, the way the sunset fell on the countertops and the sound of robins in the trees outside somehow combined to make it seem to her like a little gingerbread house, without any roaring ovens in the cellar.

"Go on back outside, Paulette," Bogardus said. "We aren't finished."

"This is some *place*," she said. "I thought it would be bigger, though."

Words no man ever wants to hear. At that moment, Meg and Corcoran came through the swinging door, both of them looking as if they couldn't quite figure out how the house had suddenly gotten so crowded. He was in his typical mode: hiking boots this time, black jeans, a collarless shirt and black blazer, with the earring, hair in a little ponytail. Paulette looked Meg up and down, lifting her chin as she assessed Meg's haircut, glancing at Gregg with his notebook computer in a little purselike satchel strung over his shoulder.

"Hi, Rich," Gregg said.

"Get everything all figured out?" I asked.

"Never roll over. That's my rule," he said. "We're coming back at 'em with another, lower bid tomorrow. An offer they can't refuse."

"Hope you're right," I said.

"I think we need some introductions here," Meg said.

"Let me just get out of your hair," Gregg said, squeezing past Bogardus. "I'll give you a call right after I meet with them, Meg."

He ducked out the back door, as the rest of us watched. When I turned and looked around the kitchen, Paulette was missing.

"How are you?" Meg asked.

"Just fine, Mrs. Cahill. You must be wondering what's going on here," he said.

"You might say that."

"Where's Paulette?" I asked.

"Paulette?" Meg asked. "Would this be the young lady who just walked into our living room?"

"Yes," I said.

"I don't think I've had the pleasure of being introduced. You seem to be much better acquainted."

"Yeah, she was valedictorian of my class at Harvard. We made *Law Review* together," I said.

Bogardus smirked.

"She went into the living room?" I asked.

I gave Bogardus a questioning look. He rolled his eyes and

shrugged. I thought she'd come back after a quick peek into the other rooms, but she didn't. I found her on the couch, looking around the living room with undisguised curiosity and guarded approval. She didn't want anyone to know she could actually be interested in a place this middle-class, this *safe*, but it showed in her face.

"You mind?" I said.

"Do I look like I mind?" she asked. She blinked slowly, deliberately, pressing her perfect lips together with impatience, as if she'd mistakenly thought I might be hip enough to let her do whatever she pleased in my house. *By all means, Paulette, go on up and check out the bed. Take a shower. Help yourself to some of Meg's underwear. Here. Take my wallet, but be sure to leave it under a Pinto somewhere, so Frank can find it.* When she gazed directly into my eyes, I looked away, as if somehow *I* were the intruder. When I blushed, my body had the odd ability to shunt the color away from my face as my ears turned red and my breath caught in my throat. She tossed a copy of *Vanity Fair* back onto the coffee table, and started sifting through the contents of her little purse-like leather backpack, dumping half the contents onto the couch and then scooping back everything but a pack of Big Red gum. She unwrapped a stick and slowly folded it onto her tongue. As she walked back into the kitchen, she passed within inches of my arm, and her hand brushed lightly against mine. The first touch of a woman's skin always seemed to discharge a little jolt of something as motivating as hope, but not quite as transparent and refreshing, not quite as easy to shake.

"So the idea is to have Will show up every afternoon. Paulette here will drop him off. Is this just a one-week thing with Alec? Are there any other basketball camps he plans to join?" Bogardus asked.

"There are others later this month and next month. He's hoping to get into them, anyway."

"Then we'll tell Will he's obligated to help coach Alec for those sessions, too," Bogardus said. "Long as you see some kind of results."

Paulette ignored our conversation, chewing her gun languidly, pushing her tongue into the wad of gum, trying to form a bubble as an excuse to exhibit her oral dexterity, looking directly at me. She leaned back against the table as Bogardus explained the situation to Meg, who didn't appear to mind the idea of having Will Breedlove show up in our driveway every day to coach our son in basketball. Paulette's tongue emerged between her lips, stretching the pink gum until it broke.

"Does this sound doable?" Bogardus asked.

Meg glanced at me.

"How do you feel about it?" she asked.

I glanced at Paulette, who was pretending to attempt another bubble. She was still gazing directly at me, daring me to back down, show signs of alarm.

"Try it for a day or two. See what happens," he said.

Bogardus called Will into the kitchen. As he came through the door, her brother didn't look much bigger than Paulette. He seemed to have a sixth sense about how to move, as if the world had some kind of molecular arrangement with his body it didn't share with mine. He didn't make eye contact with me when he came into the room; his lustrous, impenetrable eyes looked filmed with resentment and anger and a set of unforgiving maxims about my world.

"You got something to say, Will?" Bogardus asked.

"Like what?" Will snapped, eyes still on the floor.

"Like what we discussed."

"Sorry," he said, hardly speaking above a whisper.

"Mr. Cahill can't hear you."

"I said, sorry."

"Can we go now?" Paulette asked. "I've got people waiting."

"What for?" Bogardus asked Will. "What're you sorry for?"

Will looked at his feet. I felt a pang of sympathy for him and held up my palm. This interrogation was more than enough. I hated putting somebody on the spot.

"That's fine. I get the idea," I said. "Really."

"You promise to come here every day to help Alec with his game, and be on time and be dressed appropriately and not use the sort of language I know you use when I'm not around and never be seen with a beeper, even one of those fake ones, or those colors I saw you wearing, unless of course you want to get your sorry little butt tossed back in the Ice Box."

"Right," he said, *still* looking at his feet.

"Right what?"

"Promise," he said. "That what you want?"

He wanted Bogardus to know he was only making a noise. He wasn't speaking a language. This wasn't the way a *man* behaved; it wasn't the sort of thing one man would ask another man to do. He refused to look at me. When he was around Alec out in the driveway, he became an older brother. Outside, with Alec, he was home. Inside, we held him against his will.

"Now, shake," Bogardus said.

When Will extended his hand to me, without leaning away from the wall, without stepping forward, I reacted without thinking. I wanted to shake his hand and be done with him, if only to show him at least I wouldn't put him through what Bogardus was putting him through. He put his hand out and gripped mine barely enough to make it count and then slipped out of my grasp as quickly as he could. As I was withdrawing my own hand, Paulette extended hers.

"I'm the driver. You be here on time, now. I don't pull up and drop off my brother to no empty house," she said, smiling, putting on a show.

Bogardus fished for a cigarette, moving toward the door.

"Yeah. One of us will be here," I said, and when I took her hand she pulled me closer. When I tried to let go, she kept pumping it, gazing directly into my eyes before she let go.

"Think I'll find another driver," Bogardus said, looking at me as the three of them went out the back door.

"No. No problem," I said.

"Maybe we'd all be better off."

"No. I can handle Paulette."

"*Can* you," he said, walking out the door, lighting his cigarette at last.

I followed them outside. Paulette disappeared around the corner and got back into the car as Bogardus lingered in the drive, watching Alec and Will.

"Your sister will come back around in a couple hours, Will," Bogardus said. "I don't want to hear you spent the afternoon amusing yourself with trick shots to impress our little friend here. I want some serious instruction."

Will nodded, without looking toward Bogardus.

"Alec? Come here," I said.

He screwed his mouth to one side and rolled his eyes as he approached. I turned my back to the others and took him under my arm, kneeling down to talk so softly I was almost whispering.

"You okay with this?" I asked.

"Okay? It's great! This guy's good," he said.

"I mean, you *know* who he is."

"Dad, you're embarrassing me."

Meg and I stayed in the kitchen, after Bogardus drove off, watching Alec and Will in the driveway taking turns with the ball until they settled down and Will started showing Alec some drills. Will had talent, dribbling in ways I'd never seen Alec even attempt, looking as if he could do jump shots with his eyes closed, backward, turning it into a hook at the peak of his jump. Air Breedlove. Alec looked as if he'd just been given permission to drive.

"So did you and Gregg get everything ironed out?" I asked.

"I would have given up by now. He just never quits," she said.

"What a guy."

"How do you know Paulette?"

"I met her on the way home from jail."

"That sounds auspicious."

"With Bogardus. He stopped at the kid's mother's house. She was there," I said.

"She's certainly full of herself."

"It got pretty quiet in the dining room a little earlier," I said.

"It got *what?*"

"They say you have to be pretty close with somebody to sit through long silences."

"It's been a long time since lulls in the conversation around here bothered you."

"Maybe I need an earring."

"I'm sure *your* clients would like that."

She wasn't getting it.

"All I know is, I'm working day and night, to the gym, back to the office, job is like quicksand, you spend two months putting something together and the client comes back and says just do bullet items—I mean, seriously, just toss out all that stuff we spent days writing and do bullet items—and then I come home and you two are in there with martinis talking about Kandinsky."

"Just shoptalk," she said.

"And the martinis?"

"Gregg declared happy hour."

"Maybe I should sleep in the attic tonight," I said. She shook her head.

■

I went up to the attic with a cheese sandwich and a mug of Ramen noodles to check my e-mail before I took Alec to basketball. When I heard Paulette pull into the drive, I went down to the kitchen, thinking she might come back in, but she didn't. I filled a glass with water at the sink three times, glancing out the window to see if she was getting out of the car, my heart racing, but she stayed inside, honking at her brother until he ambled over to the passenger door.

Upstairs, I pulled all the clothes I needed out of the closet and carried them up to the attic, then came down and got a comforter to spread on my futon, grabbed underwear and socks from my drawers and placed everything in easy reach for the following morning. The light on my answering machine was blinking. I took out the tape, tossed it into the wicker wastebasket and replaced it with a fresh one. I downloaded my e-mail and found one from Whit.

TO: RCahill
FROM: WhitSuth
Where are you??? We need to get our watches synchronized for tomorrow morning. Tish and Penny are really coming down on me for numbers from Jimmy. Let's talk in New York. Bring whatever you've got. See you at the airport.

I typed my reply.

TO: WhitSuth
FROM: RCahill
I had a long talk with Jimmy. It's complicated. Let's knock 'em dead tomorrow and then talk about where we go from here.

After I answered the rest of my e-mail, I drove Alec to the gym and sat at the top of the bleachers as the other parents filed in. When his turn came, he still missed some shots, but not as many, and the ones he made looked easier, his wrist loose as he released the ball, his rebounds more fluid. He scored well enough to move up in the ranks a couple notches, and on the way home, he couldn't stop talking about Will.

"He really helped, Dad," he said. "He showed me this thing—"

"So you want him to come back."

"Are you kidding? He's awesome. He's funny, too. I mean, you saw him, didn't you? You saw what he can do?"

"Yeah, I saw him," I said.

"He's coming back, isn't he?"

"We'll see," I said.

"All right!"

I went straight to the attic when we got home. Meg was in our bedroom, with the door closed, watching *Entertainment Tonight.* I turned on my own television, unrolled the futon and crawled under the comforter. I waited, but she didn't come up. When I finally turned off the television, I could see a clear, starry sky through the skylight and the trees outside, and a tiny blinking light creeping across the sky, a red-eye on its way to Atlanta or Philly or Chicago, up where I would be in another ten hours.

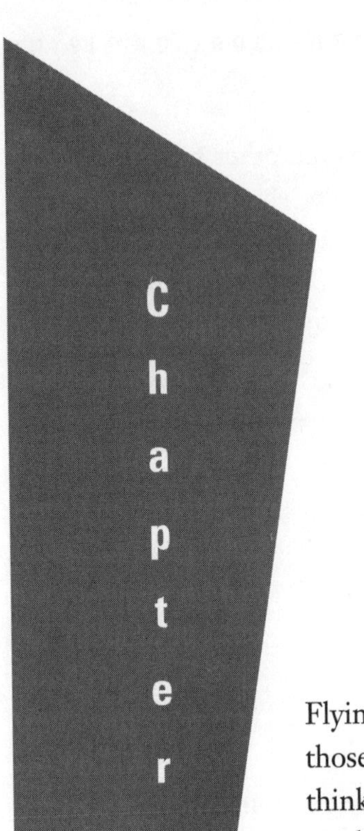

Chapter 8

Flying into La Guardia, the jet hit one of those midair vacuums and sank. As I was thinking *wind shear*, the jet tilted out of its dive. It touched down for a smooth landing, to scattered applause. I glanced at Whit, sitting beside me in the window seat, and imagined all this as an augury of welcome at our potential new client's offices: a rough time getting there, but a smooth landing, all the same.

"Only one problem now," Whit said.

"What's that?"

"Clean underwear."

In the cab, we reviewed the laptop flip charts, the folder with our proposal and samples, rehearsing what we wanted to say, all while the driver appeared to be engaged in a time trial. As we cut off other drivers headed for Manhattan, we were pushed together in the backseat, elbow to elbow, and the work samples toppled to the floor. The driver had wiry hair down to his shoulder blades, hair like plaited seaweed, half of it in dreadlocks, half hanging wild.

"Hey, where's the fire?" Sutherland shouted to the driver. Then he turned to me and, under his breath, said: "Moonlighting Salman Rushdie assassin."

Whit's sandy hair seemed brighter in the cab, his eyes darker and more opaque, gleaming coins. He was dressed in his best blue suit, black brogans, striped shirt and paisley tie.

"How about the Four Seasons for dinner tonight?" he asked.

"Why spend the money? I'd just as soon get home for dinner."

"Travel has its dividends," Whit said, leaning toward the driver. "Hey, ease up! Getting there alive is half the fun."

The driver took little notice.

"Some shit-kickers you got on there," Sutherland said, looking at my wing tips. It was the first time in two years I'd worn them. Nobody wore wing tips anymore.

"Two years old, and they still cut into my ankles," I said.

"Didn't they discover wing tips were carcinogenic? Pick up a new pair of loafers with me while we're here."

I narrowed my eyes at him: "On the card, you mean?"

He didn't answer. I wasn't sure he'd heard the question. It would have fit the picture of how people at our level lived, using the expense account to round out our experience of life. Everyone did it.

"Confucius say, one cannot work without good pair shoes."

"Racist," I said, without pressing the issue of whether Whit Sutherland, of all people, might be putting a pair of shoes on his expenses for this trip.

He leaned forward to peer at the speedometer. "You've been doing this for years, right? Repeat after me. *I've been driving cabs for years.*"

"No, mawn. First day on job," the driver said, grinning into the mirror. There was a button hanging from his license, next to his photo. The button said: PLAY IT SAFE, HAIL YELLOW.

"Rastafarian comedy. Great," Whit said, looking over at me. "Play it safe. Hail Mary."

Whenever I visit New York, I always feel I'm crashing the biggest private party in history. I know the island well enough to get around without a map. I know better than to pronounce "Houston Street" as a Texan would. Coming out of the Metropolitan Museum, I always remember to take off that little aluminum lapel button. And I know how to get from the Village Vanguard to Grand Central on foot, with ten familiar stops along the length of the island. I have my favorite little corner groceries off Lexington, and I like walking around Washington Square.

We had two hours to kill before our appointment, and Whit wanted to head straight to Paul Stuart to buy his loafers. He had me carry the flip chart, the copies of the prototype, and the bound proposal. If there was anything I envied about Whit, it was his Wasp immunity to everything degrading and laborious, darting in and out of situations and deadlines and profit plans, somehow always pausing long enough to get what he needed before moving on, never serving as anyone's porter. He always looked as if he'd known everyone for years, as if each person he met was either an old friend from college or somebody he'd run into on his *Wanderjahr* in Belgium or Morocco or Capri, or wherever he'd gone as he breezed on his trust fund through the Old World and the Orient.

After he found the loafers, he stood talking with the shoe salesman about the Knicks, timing it so that we had barely enough time to get to our appointment at the Graybar building without being late. At least he didn't hand me the shoe box to carry on the way. As we crossed Forty-second Street, he gave me another look and said: "Keep one thing in mind. We've got everything to gain and nothing to lose. We're doing this because it's a great idea. Not because we'll get it."

"They'll love this proposal," I said.

"Doesn't mean they'll buy into it."

"The power of positive thinking," I said.

"Over dinner tonight, we'll talk you through what happens next. Get you right back up on that horse."

"Is this supposed to be a pep talk?" I asked.

"You aren't hearing me. Relax. Enjoy this, no matter what happens."

"We're going to get this account," I said, as we arrived at the lobby. "We are."

We waited half an hour in the corporation's reception area. The longer we waited, the more insignificant I felt, looking at our little black portfolio of work leaning against Whit's leather-and-chrome chair. He was reading *Town and Country*, unfazed, but he glanced up at me from time to time, just checking to see how I was holding up. I distracted myself by gazing off at the huge Rothko hanging on a far wall, dominating the entire room with its hazy pink-and-yellow evocation of a distant horizon at dawn. It reminded me of Meg's conversation in the dining room, the beauty she'd once believed in, the beauty she'd once wanted to support and sell, and how few people would look twice at Rothko anymore, sitting where we were sitting, how futile the whole enterprise seemed. I wanted to get up and phone her to apologize, to tell her I loved her because of the things she loved, tell her to forget everything and dump Gregg and concentrate on getting her best people, the people who mattered to her, into galleries here in Manhattan.

Two young men emerged from a door I didn't even notice until it opened.

"Hi," the first one said, extending his hand to Whit and then to me. "I'm Terry McPherson. At last we meet."

"Hi, Terry," Whit said. "This is Rich Cahill, the fellow I've been telling you about who wants to camp out here and cater to your every whim."

"How you doing?" I asked, shaking his hand.

"This is José Santiago," he said. "He's my second-in-command. Excellent writer. Takes time off and does a piece for *Esquire* every now and then."

"*Esquire?* No kidding," I said.

"It's been a few years. Terry keeps me pretty busy. I used to do a lot of speechwriting here for the CEO, but I've gotten away from it."

We stood around the glass table for a couple beats, awkwardly waiting to be ushered into a conference room.

"Why don't we all have a seat? Can I get either of you something to drink?" McPherson asked.

"No. We're fine. But I'm a little confused," Whit said. "Do you want to do this here? It might be a little quieter if we—"

"I was hoping to have our main conference room for this, but there's been an emergency meeting convened in there, I'm sorry to report. We've got some kind of embarrassment in California and the press is doing what they usually do in these situations. In fact, I was on the receiving end of a few distinctly unpleasant looks when I said I couldn't break this appointment."

"You sure it's all right? We could reschedule," Whit said.

"No. Let's see what sort of wonderful things you've brought us. I'm not needed for another ten minutes or so," Terry said. "Have a seat."

When Whit glanced over at me, I knew we'd lost the game before the first pitch. Throughout the entire meeting, I kept chewing on my tongue, glaring at this dweeb who'd let us fly all the way here just to make us feel like total asses for even thinking we could offer these people—this writer for *Esquire*, no less—advice on how to promote a new product line being manufactured in Rochester. Whit went quickly through the proposal itself, reading from the copy—even though he had a presentation on diskette all prepared. He'd expected to be able to go into his pitch with electronic support in some kind of multimedia-equipped conference room. Whit handed a brochure prototype to Terry, who glanced through it, and then handed it to José, and they nodded appreciatively to each other and handed it back. When Whit skipped to his call to action—*We'd like to propose that you let us do a trial marketing-communications plan after a month of research with your people, at no risk*—they politely took the package of material and set it on the glass table without opening it.

"I really appreciate all this. I'd like to look this over with José and then—" Terry said. "Can I call you with any questions we have? Would that be all right?"

"But you *are* interested?" Whit asked.

"I'm always open to new ideas."

"You know where to reach me," Whit said.

They showed us to the elevator, and as I watched the two of them walk back the way they'd come, I saw them pass the table without even thinking to pick up our presentation materials which they'd left on top of the issue of *Town and Country*.

At the Algonquin, Whit revived over his single-malt, but I hardly spoke. He insisted we stop there—as if to show the occasional *Esquire* writer we knew where *real* magazine people once drank. Usually I was impressed with Whit's knowledge in areas that had nothing to do with his own survival, and I enjoyed his tendency to invest meaning in little gestures like this, but this time I just wanted to go home. We had a flight out around nine—when we could have caught an earlier flight with ease—so I was going to miss Alec's basketball session. I had to settle for a call home before we went on to the Four Seasons. We overheard enough to know the people at the next banquette were from Condé Nast, possibly talking about some new publication neither of us knew the first thing about: *If they don't get the capital, you can take that prospectus of his and cover yourself at night with it. Major interest payments before you even open up the candy store. Only question is who's going to get gored the deepest.* They were doing *real* business. I felt like a kid at Normandy Beach, toying with a couple G.I. Joe action figures and listening to veterans talk about how it felt during the landing. After I'd finished my second martini, I ducked over to a pay phone. Alec answered.

"Hey, kiddo," I said. "You ready?"

"Will showed me some awesome moves today, Dad. He might come with me to Ignatius tonight. That sheriff guy said he'd drive him home," he said. "Thanks for letting us do this. It's really great."

"Is your mom around? I thought maybe I could—"

"She hasn't gotten back from work yet. She left me a pot pie in the oven."

"So you don't know how her thing went today? With the developers?"

"You going to be home later?"

"You'll be asleep by then," I said. "Maybe I'll try calling again from the airport. Hey, good luck. Love you, Al."

"Me too."

We headed to the Four Seasons and were seated almost immediately. I'd been there once before, and I'd forgotten how spacious it felt, and how all that elbow room only accentuated how confined I felt by the rest of my life. My anger had turned to self-pity, which was now turning to fear about my raise. I ordered the prosciutto-and-melon appetizer and Whit chose snails.

Sutherland seemed unfazed, the man with the weatherproof heart.

"How can you eat those slugs?" I asked.

"A delicacy turns the stomach of the uninformed."

"So I guess our proposal was a real delicacy," I said.

"Know why these guys agreed to hear us out?"

"Get their kicks watching us squirm in their reception area?" I asked.

"Quit poking your plate of twenty-dollar cold cuts, would you? You listening? Rich? He gave us that little audience—hey? You with me here?—he figured we were horning in on their turf is all. Why farm it out to some little place upstate when they've got all the resources they need right here?"

"Then why invite us down here?"

"We invited ourselves. He just granted us the time. He probably wanted to see if we had any ideas worth stealing," he said. "You know that's always the risk in a pitch. They take your work and then show you the door."

"We didn't even show up on their radar screens," I said. "All that concern about Jimmy being late. For what?"

"Speaking of Jimmy," he said, "Tish Anderson's having a cow. She wants something definite by early next week."

"Jimmy's protecting Vince," I said.

"Why?"

"He thinks if Vince gets nailed, he's going to bleed, too."

"That isn't going to happen," Whit said. "We don't want to lose him."

"If Jimmy doesn't own up to anything on paper, what can we do?"

There was a long pause as Whit savored the last of his snails and glanced around the restaurant as if it were the only way to regain his equilibrium. The pause made me uncomfortable.

"We still set for my performance evaluation next week?" I asked.

"We are. I need serious help from somebody like you, Rich. We need to move you up. You'll love it. You belong in management."

"You know how I feel about getting chained to a desk," I said.

"Hear any irons clanking under the table?"

Chapter 9

I didn't get home until just before midnight. The whole house was dark. Meg didn't even bother to leave the stove light on in the kitchen. I felt like a prowler, sneaking into my own home. I was still wired from the espressos we'd had after dinner, and though Whit managed a catnap on the plane, I'd riffled through the flight magazine three times, letting my eyes run over most of the stories without registering a word, but without nodding off.

I tossed my little valise on the stairs and collapsed on the couch, delaying the inevitable moment when I climbed back up to the attic and crawled under the comforter. I groped around the couch, reaching down between the cushions to fish out the remote, hoping to catch

Letterman's last guest, and my fingers rubbed against a set of keys on a ring. I pulled them out and leaned over to flick on the lamp. It looked like extra keys for one of the cars and the back door. I placed it on the coffee table, and continued my search for the remote, but then I glanced back at the keys. I picked them up and held them under the lamp again. One of them bore a Honda insignia. Paulette had to have dropped the spare keys into the couch as she fished in her purse. My heart was racing, wondering if she'd left the keys there for me to find. I slipped them into my pocket and went up to the attic. I passed our bedroom door without even pausing to consider going in.

In the morning, I sat in my Tazmanian Devil silk boxer shorts and punched Jimmy's home number into the fax machine. When his answering machine kicked in, I tried the office number. He picked up after four rings.

"We need to get together and talk," I said.

"How'd the pitch go?"

"It was a bust. I'll tell you about it later. You going to be there all morning?"

"Yeah."

"I'll stop in before lunch," I said. "Whit's really pushing on this Veritex thing."

Downstairs, I poured cornflakes into a bowl and thumbed through the morning paper, waiting for someone else to get up. It was nine-thirty, and everybody was still sleeping. This wasn't a good sign. If Meg and Corcoran had pulled the deal out of the fire, she'd have been up just after dawn, making arrangements. On my third cup of coffee, I heard Meg moving around upstairs, eventually coming down slowly and trudging into the kitchen, looking completely exhausted. It was the worst time of the day for her: the first hour after getting up. Just standing in a room, she could draw all the energy out of it, as if that were the only way she could get herself started.

"So?" I asked.

"I'll give you three guesses," she said.

"You mean the amazing Gregg Corcoran didn't pull it off, after all?"

"I sat around here two hours yesterday, waiting for word. I couldn't believe, after that much time, they didn't come through for us," she said.

"Now what?"

"We pull a Brink's job. *Honey, don't ask how we're paying your tuition.*"

"Yesterday was a big setback all around. I flew all the way to New York and these two jerks made us do our pitch in the lobby before they told us thanks, but no thanks," I said.

"What did Whit say?"

"He was more concerned about Veritex. I just have to stab my best friend from college in the back and then I'll get that raise," I said. "No. Promotion. As if that's what I want."

"I have no sympathy for Jimmy. He's got himself into this mess. It isn't your fault," she said. "Did anything strike you as odd about the way this Kestler deal went?"

"Gregg strikes me as odd."

"They refused to meet with me. Didn't even want me at the meeting."

"So what? Put Gregg to work. That's what he's supposed to be doing. Negotiating."

"I'm the vendor! I'm the one who owns the business. Gregg's just the middleman. I'm sitting here at home waiting for the phone to ring. Hey, *I'm the girl.*"

"What makes you think *Gregg* wanted you there?" I asked.

"Gregg knew how I felt. But he said they insisted on dealing strictly with him."

"I think Gregg's a parasite."

"Obviously, Gregg's the only reason I got a shot at that deal."

"And look at the results," I said.

"The Kestlers aren't the only ones who want to deal with a guy. At one point or another, Gregg's managed to get his foot in the door where I couldn't. Apparently I'm the ditz who mothers her sensitive little creative types, and Gregg's the guy who can cut the price."

"*Apparently*, they don't think *that* highly of him, either."

"The bid was too high. That's all."

"All I know is, deal or no deal, we are going to get this house, no matter what happens."

I heard the del Sol pull into the drive. Will got out of the passenger side, and I stared through the back kitchen window, holding my breath, waiting to see if she would shut off the ignition or shift into reverse and pull away. She sat there for almost a minute, watching Will dribble the ball, and then turned off the car ignition. I moved away from the window as Paulette got out.

"Nice view, dear?" Meg asked.

"Why's will here so early?"

"It's Saturday. He can come whenever he wants. I'll get Alec up."

"I'm going to the office," I said.

"*Are* you?"

"I want to get this thing with Jimmy settled."

"I may be gone when you get back. Gregg's got two new developments outside Buffalo he wants to strategize."

"By all means, strategize, Meg."

I went outside.

"You sure you aren't going tomorrow?" Paulette was asking her brother. "I've got the tickets."

"I don't want to hear that guy," he said, tossing the ball to Alec.

"Go where?" I asked.

Paulette turned to face me and walked over. She wore her black jeans and a strapless, corsetlike top that cinched her waist. I could feel the set of keys in my pocket, and started to reach for them, but then held off. Would she ask? Would she wait for me to return them? Was she just giving me an excuse to see her again?

"You like the blues?" she asked.

"I love the blues."

"Young guy from Los Angeles playing Club Zero Monday night. I've got an extra ticket," she said, holding it out.

I took it, our fingers mingling for a second.

"I might be able to make the time," I said.

She lingered, looking into my eyes, smiling, and then backed away a couple steps, turned and rounded the front of the del Sol.

"You let me know," she said. "Or maybe I'll just see you there."

I found Jimmy in his office. The room was confining, with a desk and credenza and several filing cabinets. He'd covered his walls with icons of his various obsessions, a huge poster of Christy Turlington, another poster of Natalie Merchant, a framed and autographed shot of G. Gordon Liddy, several issues of a munitions magazine published for mercenaries, stacks of alternative CDs with names of groups I'd never heard and might go out of my way to avoid hearing, and an assortment of possibly a hundred other objects and photographs strewn throughout the room: a disarmed and gutted land mine he retrieved from some Army-Navy surplus shop, a half-empty bottle of Wild Turkey in his drawer (because Sinatra drank it at Capote's big party), a Beavis and Butt-head calendar, a Howard Stern poster, a distributor cap from an original Shelby Cobra, and a huge whelk shell from an island off Haiti. I closed the door behind me, and he leaned back in his chair, with an uncertain look on his face.

"That jack-off Sutherland. I can't believe he blew it in New York. That trip was a waste," he said. "Somebody needed to tell Shitforbrains this pitch of his was the biggest—"

"It was *my* idea," I said.

"Yeah, well, I mean the way he handled it."

"Jimmy Sorley. Team player," I said. "Between you and me?"

He nodded, waiting to hear me out.

"He didn't care about that pitch half as much as he cares about getting this Veritex stuff down on paper."

"I told you how I feel about it," Jimmy said.

"You aren't going to get in trouble. They want you off the Veritex account. Whit says they want to get you back into writing full-time, which I know is what you love to do. I'm the one who's going to get stuck with Veritex."

"Vince won't go for it," he said.

"Vince won't have anything to say about it. They'll move him."

"So she's taking it over?" he asked.

Jimmy pointed to the job jackets for the speeches I'd passed along to him with the new client name on the side instead of Vince's name: *Tish Anderson.*

"Tish Anderson is bad news," he said.

"Runs a tight ship."

"Vince doesn't think she's for real. They brought her in from another company, out in Los Gatos. He says she's supposed to have bigger balls than half the executive committee."

"What's going on in that place?" I asked.

"She's getting her ticket punched. While somebody like Vince works twice her hours. So what's with your name here in *my* slot?"

He pointed to the job jacket again.

"That's what I'm saying. They're pushing me into the account role on Veritex. As if I don't already have more than I can handle."

"Unfuckingbelievable."

"Jimmy. Details. Numbers. On paper."

"Won't happen on my watch," he said. "I'm not doing that to Vince."

"I can write out everything you told me. A transcript of our conversation from the other day. But they want something from you. They figure you'll just deny it if it comes from me."

"They got *that* right. How about a beer this afternoon? We can talk it over."

"There's nothing to talk over, Jimmy," I said. "My job *depends* on this. My *promotion* depends on this. It all depends on *you.* You know how that makes me feel?"

"Ought to make you feel like you owe me, big-time."

I stood up, leaning both palms flat against his desktop. Jimmy leaned back in his chair.

"I have a mortgage and two kids and two cars. I've got debts. Responsibilities. What've you got? Your apartment, your old Porsche," I said.

"I know about real life. I get news reports from Vince. He's got that house in Pittsford and his wife makes squat. And Veritex pays him half what he's worth. He's working through it, though."

"I wouldn't want to be in Vince's shoes," I said.

"Have a beer with me later. See what we can work out."

After five hours of catch-up on work, I stopped at home for a few minutes before heading to The Office for a beer with Jimmy. Alec was in the driveway, practicing his jump shots. When I saw the Range Rover standing at the end of the drive, I didn't recognize it at first. It wasn't a vehicle I expected to see on my own street, the tinted window rising too quickly for me to see who was inside. I watched, waiting for it to move on: it looked as if somebody had stopped to look at the street number beside our front door, and decided against asking directions. But it just sat there, behind the old maple tree. When I realized it had to be him, I started toward the street, moving faster and faster down the driveway, not thinking. But the Range Rover began to pull away, slowly, and then faster as I leaped past the tree and ran into the street behind it, three or four arm's lengths away from the rear bumper. Then he pulled away, and I began to slow down as he sped around the corner onto Durand Avenue and disappeared beyond the carpet store half a block away. I jogged back up the drive, panting.

As I came into the house, I picked up the phone, ready to dial Bogardus, and then put it back, and stood there, trying to decide. Everything smelled worn and stale and vaguely irritating, as if every room had the faintly repellent scent of gym socks. I wanted to turn around and walk back outside and drive to Chicago or Mexico or Nova Scotia. As I took off my coat, I saw a small white machine on the shelf below the telephone, more compact than the answering machine. The little readout looked like the one on my fax. I had no idea what it was or what it was doing there.

The phone rang. The caller ID gave the phone number and the name of the caller: Paulette Breedlove. I picked it up.

"Hello."

"Hi," she said.

"Paulette?"

"No. Princess Di," she said.

"Your friend was here."

"What friend?" she asked.

"Drives a Range Rover. I come home, he pulls up out front. I thought this was over. Now he shows up in front of my house."

"You talk to him?" she asked.

"No. He drove off."

"I think he wants to talk to you."

"What about?" I asked. "Tell him to leave me alone, would you? I'm no threat to him."

"Maybe he wants to tell *you* something."

"So you *do* see him," I said.

"How about blues night?"

"I'll try."

"Let me know if you can't. I've got other people want that ticket."

"Meg isn't real big on Club Zero. The smoke gets into her contacts and she ends up walking around half blind."

"I didn't give you a ticket for *her*, did I?" she said. "Tell Will I be right over to pick him up."

She hung up. I pulled the phone book out of the broom closet and thumbed through the Breedloves until I found her name. Only one Paulette. I recognized the street and the number. I'd driven out there for building supplies one summer. She lived near the airport, probably in one of those two-story apartment complexes I'd seen from the interstate, with cedar siding and Hot Wheels tipped over on the sidewalks and guys loitering on stoops. I wrote the street and apartment number in my Day-Timer.

I arrived at The Office early, and nursed a beer, thinking about Paulette, wondering how often she saw the Range Rover. I was watching highlights from a Skins game on ESPN. I stripped lines of sodden paper from my beer bottles and rolled them into spitballs. I liked this place. Everybody wore blue oxford shirts with the sleeves rolled up and khaki slacks or shorts in the summer. Outside, where Jimmy and I never ventured—too bright, too fluid, too much cheerful volume, where the rate of drinking seemed more superficial—they had a second bar with umbrella tables.

Jimmy didn't seem to belong here. He seemed more in his element while he bent over a shot glass at some little place out on a state highway where you'd come across an occasional cadre of armed bikers doing shots of Jack with flecks of mustard and tobacco curls in their beards. He gravitated here, I guessed, because it was right on the Erie Canal, in the suburb where he grew up and went to high school.

When Jimmy finally arrived, he took the stool beside me and ordered two beers and a couple plates of clams for us, without saying a word. He'd taken off his tie and apparently stopped at his apartment to change into a pair of jeans, though he hadn't changed his monogrammed shirt. I hated those awkward silences, and he liked to make a game of it, see how long he could sit without saying a word until I gave in. He felt untouchable. In college he looked skinny and quick, with eyes like a hawk's, bounding up three steps at a time into the library for one of his cramming sessions. Now he was slowing down, easing himself into a more comfortable spot on his barstool every few minutes, feeling his age in the seat of his pants.

He took his first swallow of beer and pried apart a clam from his little net, which the barmaid brought with the second round, along with my own plate of clams.

"What's this I hear about you and that kid who held you up at McDonald's? I mean, this is a joke, right?" he asked, glaring at me. "Wes was telling me this wild story."

"It's a deal I made," I said.

"A deal?"

"With the investigator."

"What do *you* get out of this deal?" he asked.

"Jimmy? Order some more clams and shut up, would you?" I asked.

"Are you nuts? Are you out of your mind?"

"He's just a kid."

"It's South Africa in this country, man," he said. "It's over, man. Civil rights. Affirmative action. It's over. The phone is ringing, man. Wake up. South-Central. St. Petersburg. We're next. One little nudge and things go up in flame."

"The kid's shooting hoops in my drive. Nothing's going to go up in flame except the occasional T-bone on the grill. He's helping Alec. You should see."

"Fuck him," he said. "He lost any right to help anybody when he put a gun to your head."

"He didn't have a gun to my head."

"To your ass, then," he said.

Three college women came into the bar. One of them glanced toward Sorley, managing to look away just as he caught her eye. Nodding toward them, he smiled at me.

"First time is the best, R.C. After a long time away from it. You want that feel of new skin. You remember? Or is that too far back?"

"I remember," I said.

"You've touched hundreds in your life, but it's always new," he said.

"Yeah, right. Hundreds."

"The look. The feel. The smell. The little sounds. It's always different," he said, "What's marriage? The nightmare of Friday nights. Sit home. Watch *Full House*. How do you stand it? Don't you miss that new skin?"

"I love Meg," I said. "That sort of gets in the way. But yeah, there isn't a man alive who doesn't miss it."

"That first time. Don't you want it so bad?" he asked.

"Yeah, well, then it's all downhill," I said.

"No. Then it's do it do it do it do it, and *then* it's all downhill."

"Speaking of downhill, let's talk about Veritex," I said.

"You're like a broken record, man. Anyway, Vince agrees with me. We just keep quiet."

As if we'd summoned him, Vince Stringer walked into the bar. He'd waited until Jimmy'd disarmed me with three beers and then he arrived, heading straight for us. Dark suit, white shirt, muted tie, and the burnished wings of black hair above his ears. He was even bigger than I remembered, the flesh starting to jiggle between the jaw and collarbone, the corpulent fingers wrapped around the computer. Alec would have liked this haircut, especially with that tight little bush of hair on top, all wiry and moussed back. He had one of those puffy faces, tough and yet babyish at the same time, like George Forman's, the fatty, swollen eyelids and nose and lips, with eyes that looked tucked back at the corners.

"So what is this? Boys' night out?" Vince asked, looking at Jimmy. He turned to me. "Remember that time, huh, Rich? You were a wild man."

My stomach quivered with resentment.

"I wasn't a wild man."

"Well, compared to the usual Rich Cahill," he said, getting a laugh out of Jimmy. "Been a while since I've been in this place."

"What's it been, two, three days?" Jimmy asked.

Vince laughed. "That's a long time. How are ya, Richie?"

"I've been better."

"I feel your pain," he said, doing his Bill Clinton voice. "If they're on you about that money, send them to me. I'll tell them it was a once-in-a-lifetime thing. Hey, we each spent five hundred on drinks and dances. That's the story I'm telling. Nobody'll even put up a squeak."

"That fifteen hundred isn't the issue and you know it," I said.

"You up for another night out? Fort Erie to the Queen's Highway," Vince said. "Let's rub their noses in it. Right back at ya, bitch."

Vince was grinning, wide-eyed and blinking. He was visualizing the perfect female body already, the warm downy slopes of her arms and the miraculous curve of the waist, the breasts with hardly a fold underneath. I was imagining it too, just seeing that look in his eyes.

"The women are all babes in Canada. They're young and they're thin and they're gorgeous—"

"And they're completely naked," Jimmy said without looking at us, lifting his beer to his lips.

"So you meet this woman yet?" Vince asked. "Tish the Dish?"

"Anderson? I have no idea who she is. The org chart down there changes every two days, doesn't it?" I asked.

"She's on the warpath. She's been a little cool lately, huh, Jimmy? I said the wrong thing at the Christmas party. That's what this is all about."

"Like what?"

"Like, how'd you get *your* job?" Vince said and laughed along with Jimmy. "I mean I was kidding. I was drunk. She can't take a joke. Women. They're all in over their heads."

"No way," I said. "Even you don't have the balls to say something like that. You've sucked me in too many times on stuff like this."

"I swear to God. I did. Jimmy. Back me up. Everybody was hammered. Except Tish. Big mistake."

"You don't get it, do you."

"I mean, I was just kidding her. Like what did *you* have to do to get your job? As in, you tell me what *you* had to do, I'll tell you what I had to do. It was a bonding thing, right? But she didn't take it that way. Politics. They come in and they've got to leave their prints all over everything. That's all. You could be the best, the fucking best, and they'd still cut off your balls just to have something to dangle from their rearview mirrors. The women are way worse than the men. They don't *understand*."

"Apparently she and Penny are like sisters now or something," I said. "That's the word from Whit."

"Whit's the most condescending dickhead I've ever had to deal with, from any agency, anywhere, even compared to the New York dickheads. What Whit doesn't know is that I could take all my business, tell Jimmy here to offer his services to Hickey and Reid or anywhere else in this city, and they'd hire him overnight, because he'd be bringing me with him."

"I think Penny knows that," I said.

"Sutherland. The sphincter boy."

I laughed.

"What I don't get is why you put up with them," Vince said. "You could easily make a move. We could find a place for you."

"I'd last about three weeks."

Behind his back, his ostensible manhood was a matter of some woman's paperwork, and he knew it. The world was becoming unrecognizable to him, and he couldn't bring himself to admit it. His brow looked damp. It was getting close in that place, a group of professional women behind us, crowding the bar. The noise rose, and we had to shout at each other. He looked around. There was no escape anymore.

"They're going to find out about how you've been spending the expense money, Vince. You ought to just come clean now and move on."

"Nothing to come clean about," he said. "I had the green light before she came in."

"She wants to move you out. She wants you out of her hair. That's what Whit—"

"Hey, fuck her. And fuck Whit. I've been where I am for too long to just roll over for that bitch."

"They just want the truth, Vince," I said.

Jimmy didn't say a word, didn't even look at either of us,

though I noticed at the last minute he and Vince were exchanging a private smile in the mirror behind the bar.

"So you aren't up for it?" Vince asked again. "Little trip to Canada?"

"No thanks. Not tonight."

"Big opportunity," Vince said, twitching the corner of his mouth up. "Take that rocket of Jimmy's for a little test spin, up along the lake, for a couple hours? We could have us some fun at customs. I'll get us strip-searched in no time."

"I'm in," Jimmy said.

"No thanks," I said.

"Some of my favorites are dancing tonight," Stringer said. "Hell, we could get there in forty-five minutes in that Porsche. That thing shouldn't even be street-legal. We could fold up Rich and squeeze him in back behind the seat, couldn't we, Jimmy."

"Not tonight," I said. "You're nuts, Vince. With everybody sniffing around, anybody in his right mind would be walking the straight and narrow."

"Faggot," Jimmy said, smiling at me.

It wasn't entirely a setup. He really didn't think anybody could touch him. He wanted to see me revert to the character I'd pretended to be in college, staying out all night, following the rest of them around, navigating through the old subway system with a flashlight and a six-pack. Looking at the two of them, I could predict the conversations after I was out of the picture. They had that determined look, and I was sure they'd agreed to double-team me before either of them walked through the door of this place. This was the chalk line they wanted to lure me across, even though if I went along with it, it wouldn't mean anything beyond serving as evidence that I could capitulate and become one of them again, now that I was threatening to become one of The Others at work.

"Man, you guys really don't get it, do you?" I asked. "It's over, Jimmy. This isn't college. This isn't a run to Birdland for Buffalo wings."

Stringer knew his time was up, and he headed for the door. He gave Sorley a serious look. "So long, boys. Hang in there, Rich. Keep the faith. It'll blow over. Hey, Jimmy, tomorrow."

"Tomorrow," Jimmy said, then turned to the barmaid. "One more. And the tab."

She set another two beers before us and then she grabbed his check from beside the cash register, with his company credit card clipped to it, and she rung it up. While she was gone, he pulled a wad of money out of his pocket to leave a tip. I could see only a hundred-dollar bill, wrapped around all the others. He was still doing that. All through the conversation, I kept seeing the Range Rover at the end of my driveway, the sound of the voice on the phone, the scene at the McDonald's—*Who you think you are?*

"You've changed," Jimmy said, once we were outside, standing next to the nose of his Porsche. He bent down to scrape a spot from the fender.

"Have I?"

"Know what I think?"

"What?"

"I'm toast," he said.

Chapter 10

As I pulled into our driveway, I recognized Gregg's little Talon All-Wheel Drive, the orange taillight, the spoiler, the wide tires, the kind of car I'd wanted for years—not a classic sports car, but fast enough to shove you back in your seat. I imagined him in the dining room again, commiserating, *strategizing*, as Meg put it. Maybe not in the dining room. Maybe they were strategizing in the bedroom, on the stairs, in the kitchen. How could she do this, with his car parked in view of all the neighbors? I'm gone two hours, and he moves in. The blinds were drawn in the dining room, the lights dimmed in the living room, the upstairs dark. Alec probably had a sleepover at a friend's, and Dana would be out with her posse, as she called it, on a Saturday night, riding from party to party, or hanging out at her best friend's older sister's apartment. Meg and her partner would have the entire house to themselves.

I let the car idle. I could get out and try the back door. I'd turn the key, push gently on the knob and hear it bang against the chain. Then what? Call an attorney? It was either that or resign myself to it, the cuckold, the fool, and everyone on the street would know. Hell, everyone *already* knew. I remembered listening once to a therapeutic radio call-in talk show as I drove around Boston in my rental Chevy Cavalier, the female therapist coaxing the most pathetic confessions from the caller, with his sappy little backwoods Texas drawl: *And she got me livin' in a trailer in our backyard now while she sees these other guys, and I miss her.*—You mean, Jerry, she's sleeping with other men in your own house while you live in the trailer in back?—*I don't rightly know if she's doin' that, but she steps out on me, I know she does.*—Jerry, there's nothing you can do about it, honey. You sound so sweet, you really do, but some women need to explore their sexuality this way. That's all. You have to decide what's best for you as she decides what's best for her.—*But I miss her.*—And then the male cohost couldn't restrain himself, broke into the conversation: *So, Jerry, you eating a lot of Hamburger Helper these days?* There was a long pause before Jerry answered: *No. Tuna Helper mostly.* With another man's car parked in my drive after dark, could the Tuna Helper be far away?

As I backed up and drove away, I reached over for the car phone and dialed the number in my Day-Timer. After five rings, she answered—I recognized the slight husky edge in her voice—and I hung up. She was home, on a Saturday night. I tried to imagine what she would be wearing. My heart was racing. It was a warm night, dark now except for the lights along the highway, the headlights, the winking red beacons on radio towers over Pinnacle Hill and Cobb's Hill—our "scenic" lookouts south of the city. Behind it all, the city lit up the early-spring haze.

I had the windows down, and I smelled exhaust, the brackish scent of the Erie Canal's mud as I passed alongside it, and the green odor of earth where the first needles of grass were sprouting. When I drove beneath the exit sign, I hesitated, and then I flicked the turn signal and lurched to a stop where the ramp joined the county road. I knew exactly where to turn.

I crossed the river into the heart of Birdland, this part of the city I'd grown to love when I was an undergraduate at the University of Rochester over on the other, eastern shore of the Genesee River. Leroy's Birdland was less than a mile from the main quadrangle, and was now less than ten minutes from my home in Fairfield. In those days, we were as welcome there as anyone. *Let's hit Birdland for some wings!*

It was a different deal now. Back then, a carload of white kids could drive in and out of this ward with immunity. Now people here didn't simply murder each other at intervals, they *assassinated* each other, and one woman who happened to pause at a stoplight one night was found the next day shot twice through the brain stem, minus a purse. Teenagers killed each other defending a day's profits or a new pair of shoes and then slipped the .38 back under a jersey. Now it was a place you wouldn't want to use as a shortcut to somewhere else at any hour.

I turned left and cruised along a string of little shops and bars on Genesee Park Boulevard, with Black Velvet and Camel and Colt .45 billboards overhead, ripped and peeling and badly lit. A few guys stood in a little cluster, smoking, one with triple earrings in both earlobes, another with hair sculpted into a sort of topiary exhibit. Across the river on campus, a quarter mile away, my old friend Professor Jackson Parsells taught philosophy, and now and then I gazed out the side window long enough to catch a glimpse of the Rush Rhees library rotunda all lit up, wondering what that brilliant black professor thought of his less privileged brothers this side of the Genesee. It was a jog, or a swim, from one world into the other. He probably never crossed the river for anything.

On Paulette's street, I didn't want to get out of the car until I had to. But I wasn't about to turn back, and maybe if I was bold enough, no one would notice. My ears thumped and rang. I parked on the street and saw one lone man walking unsteadily under a streetlight three blocks behind me. I imagined a knife or a gun under his coat, when all along it was probably some poor clerk in his fifties dragging home from a day behind the till at Jerome's Liquor.

I got out and started briskly along the ground-floor apartment doors, looking for her number, trying to give off a whiff of vigor and obligation. Like someone, say, with a very hot, almost late pizza. In and out, not looking for trouble or a tip. Judging by the noise coming from all these apartments, the entire tenant body had to raise its voice to be heard: *I seen you with that bitch down there one too many times, dog, I say to him, he not ready to bring hisself there, get his little punk-ass butt down to the . . . never buy any meat from that little ay-rabb shop you know the one that little guy cash you check for a fee . . . you ain't black, girl, you just a graham cracker . . . no! no! whatchyou think, you gone up and . . .* and on and on as I walked past each door toward the little number I'd written in my Day-Timer. Walking at night along the streets of my own suburb, all I usually heard was the bark of a lonely dog, the wind in the trees, and I felt grateful for the lonely monastic silence of a television's light flickering on the ceiling of an upper bedroom where someone forgot to pull the curtains. It was a street, a night, out of a haiku. In my neighborhood, you heard only your own footsteps when you walked past all the brick and stucco and siding. But here, in the city, everyone's life messed with everyone else's.

When I got to her place, I stood with my ear to the door. No voices, no television turned up, no boom box blasting the latest hit from Rappin' 4 Tay. I knocked softly.

"Come in!" she said.

I tried the knob. It was locked. I knocked again.

"Come in!"

"It's locked!" I shouted.

There was no response from inside. No sound of movement. I reached into my pocket for the keys she'd left in my living room.

Paulette was sitting on her couch, the television on, the remote in her hand. She was grinning at me. I closed the door and tossed the keys to her, but she didn't reach for them, and they fell onto the cushion beside her.

She wore a baggy sweatshirt and stretch pants: dressed the way Meg might have dressed for an evening of *Melrose Place* or *Seinfeld*. Behind and above her head, the television's glow flickered on her ceiling. The room smelled of sweet incense and another, stronger scent I recognized from college.

"Hi," I said.

"What's up?" she asked, the words swimming in her mouth a little before they came out, deflected and soft. She got up and headed for the kitchen. "You thirsty?"

I closed the door. The apartment wasn't what I'd imagined, with a plaid couch she might have picked up at The Cherry House or Portfolio, an upholstered armchair, a long coffee table, and in the back, a wide entry into the kitchenette, with all the usual brand-name appliances. The television was a big-screen model, sitting on a portable cart with a VCR and a small stereo with a CD player. The floor was strewn with jewel boxes for CDs, but not the ones I would have expected, not Dr. Dré and Snoop Doggy Dogg, Coolio, and Ice Cube, but mostly oldies and alternative: Hendrix, Aretha, James Brown, Red Hot Chili Peppers, Marvin Gaye, Nine Inch Nails. What a time span between Marvin Gaye and Nine Inch Nails. This woman knew her music. The sensation swelled quickly into longing when I looked up and saw, for the first time, on the wall above her couch, a large poster of Jimi Hendrix, mounted on foam-core behind glass.

The shot was taken by aiming the camera up at the guitarist's downcast face, so the angle's foreshortening effect made the guitar appear nine feet wide. The fingers on the Stratocaster's neck looked almost as large as the contorted face. Above his Afro wrapped in a bandana: a wide-angled panorama of clouds. The image was blurred everywhere except around the head, so the whole performance, his entire world, looked as if he'd dreamed it into existence, his body wrapped in what looked like a violet electrostatic field. Everything in the room seemed to exist against the pull of this dead star's gravity. In college, I wanted to *be* him, to have that talent, that freedom, that magnetic power.

As she opened the refrigerator, I said: "My mother wouldn't let me listen to him in high school. In college, I played *Band of Gypsies* over and over, for hours."

"I got that one."

"Really? I can never find it."

"Molson okay?" she asked, with her head in the refrigerator.

"Sure."

Strewn across the table and the floor were books and papers, textbooks, paperbacks, a zippered three-ring organizer, pencils, pens, a hairbrush, a packet of spearmint chewing gum, a half-empty beer bottle. In the center of the table, a Toshiba notebook computer, casting a faint light on the cushions. I looked at the books: *C Programming in a Unix Environment; The Anatomy of Power; Endless Love; The Computer Glossary: The Complete Illustrated Dictionary; Invisible Man; Love Online: A Practical Guide to Digital Dating; Soledad Brother; Fire in the Lake; Opportunities in*

Computer Systems Careers; Pascal: An Introduction to the Art and Science of Programming; Democracy Is in the Streets: From Port Huron to the Siege of Chicago; Class Warfare: The Attack on Working People; and *Opportunities in Computer Maintenance Careers.*

I smiled at that last one, and then it depressed me. Was Paulette actually visualizing herself as a computer maintenance engineer, digging into memory cards and motherboards and central processing units? Is this where she believed she had a future? And *Endless Love* I could understand, but where did *Soledad Brother* fit into the picture?

"You read all these?" I asked.

"Most of them," she said.

"You really into computers?"

"I'm taking night classes."

"That's what college is about now? Computers?" I asked. "They have you reading *all* these titles?"

"My friend GP gave me some of the others."

"Like this?" I asked, picking up the Noam Chomsky title.

"Yeah. I like those. This computer shit is deadly," she said and then smiled as she pointed to *Love Online.* "That one's not too bad."

I laughed.

"You don't strike me as much of a reader."

"What *do* I strike you as?" she asked. "Some bitch, you come down here after dark, give you a little thrill to look at?"

"You strike me as somebody who gets out a lot more than I do."

"No *doubt.*"

"GP's done some reading too, evidently," I said.

"Two and a half years in college. Northwestern."

"Really? In Chicago?"

"Before he realized it was mostly bullshit."

"Is he interested in this stuff? These books he gave you?"

"Used to be."

"Huh," I said, nodding.

"Always wants everything he do to mean something big. Know what I'm sayin'? Me, I just want to make some money some way don't get me killed in the process."

"Computers," I said.

She sighed.

"Yeah," she said, sounding defeated. " 'Less something else come along."

"And Bogardus made it sound like you were bad news."

"I was," she said, smiling, and then the smile faded. "Now I'm gettin' real boring."

"You're anything but boring," I said, so softly she didn't hear me.

"I hate those classes. Poli Sci ain't bad. Vietnam. The Philippines. That book about the working class. You can really get GP worked up about that shit."

I felt insanely safe in her apartment, as if it were the one place no one would be able to find me: as if laws of physics, of time and gravity and probability, ceased to obtain here. She came back into the living room holding two beers, which she set on the coffee table before she picked up the television's remote. The latest installment of *Cops* was on. They had a man at gunpoint on the ground, spread out beside his overturned car, his face nuzzling the grass next to a mag wheel, highlights shifting on the chrome as the camera panned. She flicked it off, and then knelt beside the stereo, fed a new disk into the CD, and hit the button. Immediately, it came on. The low-volume, bluesy, fifteen-minute version of *Voodoo Chile.* She handed me my beer and sat down next to me on the couch, holding out the keys I'd tossed to her.

"You keep 'em," she said and smiled.

"I don't think so."

"Wanna dance?" she asked, still holding out the keys.

I took them and slipped them back into my pocket.

"So you didn't talk to GP about me?"

"Not yet."

"What's he want from me?"

"Come on. Let's dance."

She got up, holding her beer, and maneuvered around the coffee table and started to move. When she danced, she held everything back, closing her eyes, letting her body twist so slowly I couldn't tell when she'd started to pump her hips. The motion seemed to swell up through her ankles and knees, up through her entire body, the way break-dancers push a wave from the fingernails of one extended hand and pass it through their arms and shoulders until they flick it into the air through the other fingertips. She closed her eyes and brought her wrists to her face, as if they were cuffed, hiding her eyes behind her joined wrists, her lips showing below and between the two thin gold chains riding up her arms. Her elbows traced slow circles in the air, as her hips turned. She held the can of beer, pressed between both palms. Without the can cradled between them, she would have looked like someone in prayer. Through the whole solitary dance, she held her beer aloft, above her head. It looked like an offering, as if something or someone might soon be sacrificed.

"Ever danced for money?" I asked softly, unable to catch my breath. She opened her eyes and smiled to tell me she'd heard that catch in my voice, and then she closed her eyes again.

"You know," I said.

She said nothing.

"To pay for that del Sol?" I asked.

"Not'n'ymore."

"So who pays?" I asked.

"It was a gift," she said.

As she moved, she reached up under her sweatshirt and felt behind the elastic waist of her stretch pants. She brought out a reefer, rolled tight, not as fat as the ones I'd sampled reluctantly in college. She found a pack of matches on the television and lit the hand-rolled joint, and the sweet odor drenched the room with memories of my dormitory's hazy hallways after midnight, the banging of the radiators, the black lights glowing above the lofts, the smell of toaster-oven tuna melts, the Fillmore West concert posters covering the cracked walls. All of that undergraduate liberty I tasted so dutifully until I met Meg and finally became the good father I'd dreamed of having, and then becoming.

I hadn't come in contact with this particular odor for more than a decade, and it worried me to see someone lighting up again so casually. Lines of shadow vibrated at the upper edges of the room, like quivering auras before a migraine. I could be someone else here, and that Talon could stay parked in my drive until midnight. I wouldn't give her the satisfaction of knowing I'd seen Gregg's car in the drive. I'd make her wonder who *I* was strategizing with after midnight.

"Little chronic?" she asked, as she took another hit from the joint, then extending it out toward me.

I shook my head, waving it away, so she lifted it to her lips again. I told her: "Sit down. Quit trying so hard, would you?"

She danced with her eyes closed. She looked directly in my eyes as she danced, reaching her arms above her head so the sweatshirt lifted to reveal her hips and waist and a thin line of cocoa skin above the tights.

"If you were a dancer how come you're living here?" I asked. "They make good money."

"Just spent what I made."

"On what?" I asked.

"What you see's what I got. Tuition. Stuff."

The beer was kicking in. I got up and fetched another one from the refrigerator—I was getting bold and comfortable here—and I brought it back into the living room. She was already finishing the joint and was halfway through it, gazing at it steadily, as if the thin, curling line of smoke was unfurling itself into some urgently important skywriting she couldn't quite make out. Pretty soon, at this rate, she wouldn't be able to count her own toenails.

"How many of those you go through in a night?" I asked.

"Enough."

"I think we've established you know how to dance."

"You don't like?" she asked.

"Yeah, I like," I said.

She smiled and shrugged and plopped down beside me on the couch, once again offering me the joint, grinning.

"You're no fun."

"Fine. Give it here," I said.

She wouldn't let go of it. Instead, she held it under my nose and let me drag briefly on it, with her fingertips barely touching my lips. As the smoke seared my lungs, I knew by the time I exhaled, I'd be on the wrong side of the mirror. Almost immediately, time skipped, and reversed and snagged. The entire room seemed lit with a strobe situated somewhere behind my optic nerve, and my mind registered at random a purple drawstring laundry bag, an Ajax smell, a wah-wahed e-string, the imaginary feel of velour against my arm, all of it over leaps of dead air. Nothing connected itself to anything else. *Now*, I remembered why I hated marijuana.

"How long you live in that house of yours?" Paulette asked, a dreamy look in her eyes, as if she were visualizing my home.

"Seven years. Eight years. Why?"

"It's nice," she said.

"You wouldn't want something bigger?" I asked.

"You got cute kids," she said. "You must be happy there."

"Funny how you get used to things," I said, and then got up from the couch and went over to the window.

"I ain't got used to *this*," she said, looking around the room.

As I looked out toward the street, the Range Rover pulled up alongside my car. My arms and legs were turning to rubber, supported by wire-thin, malleable bones. It was one of those moments when seconds click past like drips of honey—each minute the equivalent of an entire night—and you feel as if you've been invited to watch your own execution, instantly replaying every second in your mind again and again as it passes, little jolts of *déjà vu* and regret. I remembered, distinctly, the way he turned and studied me at McDonald's, tilting his head slightly to one side when I yelled *Who you guys think you are!* He seemed to be continuing his study.

The air around the Range Rover thickened, and the darkness itself seemed hung like drapery in the air. The night suctioned itself to my head. I watched as that strange, expensive, top-heavy sport utility turned to shadow, and I realized it was actually moving forward, away from me, away from her apartment, down the street. He was patrolling, like a deputy in a cruiser, protecting his territory. Would he know which car I'd rented? Would he recognize it on the street, two cars away from Paulette's del Sol?

"Come here," I said. "Come here! He's out there."

"What?" she asked, not moving.

"Out there on the street! The Range Rover. He'll probably come by again."

Paulette got up, but the Range Rover was gone.

"That's GP. His name's Price," she said. "Eugene Price."

"That was the guy I was talking about," I said. "That was him."

"He's not coming here. He would have called," she said. "But why not wait and find out? Tell him what it was you wanted me to tell him."

"I don't think so," I said.

"Relax. Come here."

As the song finished, and the CD player shuffled to a random track on another disk, she led me back to the couch. My legs gave out as I sat down. She reached for my beer on the coffee table and lifted it to her lips, finishing it and then pressing her lower lip with the nozzle, pulling it down, showing me the pink between her lip and her teeth. As the bottle snapped away from her mouth, she stared at me, looking more beautiful now than she'd looked in my kitchen. She scooted closer to me as she reached for the stereo remote and turned down the volume so we could talk. Her leg rested lightly against mine, and she let it stay there, without applying any pressure, without pulling away. I wondered if I would survive the night, but I wondered this with a neutral and insistent curiosity, the way you might wonder if the mail has arrived with your tax refund, without being interested enough to get up and find out how small it will be.

"Guy in that Range Rover is the one making those calls, right? Guy outside just now," I said.

"Could be," she said. "Could just be DeWitt."

"Who's DeWitt?"

"Other guy. Wears that Mercedes thing around his neck."

"Why're they calling me? Tell him I'll stay out of his way. I've got a family," I said.

"Come here," she said.

"I mean it. I don't want anything to do with that guy."

She reached around my neck with one hand, placing her other palm on my cheek, to steady her target. When her lips touched mine, they felt plush, moving steadily and gently, not pressing hard, but waiting for me to begin the pressure, pulling away and then touching again, then pulling away. Her skin felt impossibly soft and yet firm. I pushed her away and started to get up, but she yanked on my arm and I couldn't catch my balance. She pulled me onto her as she leaned back against the pillow, wedging my knee between her legs and letting my mouth travel down her cheek around her neck, pressing my teeth against her shoulder, with my hands working up and down her body, her legs, her waist, her breasts, everything moving smoothly beneath the loose fabric. Her body was so *young.* She looked and felt double-jointed wherever one bone coupled with another. She breathed harder, her eyes closed and she was pumping her hips slowly, still dancing beneath me. Then she gasped and bit my neck and giggled again, as if she were laughing in her sleep, amused by the dream.

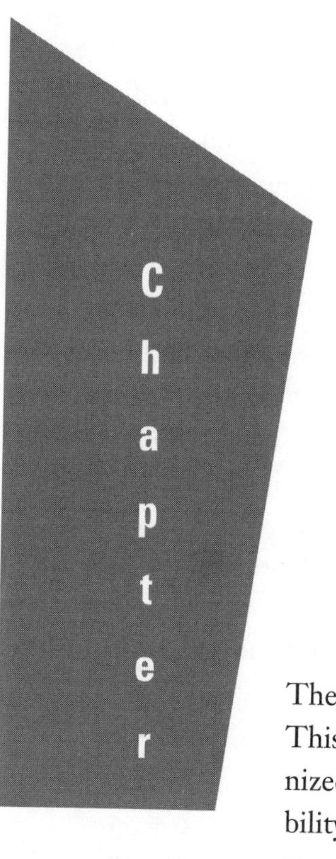

11

The world around me involved windows. This was encouraging. Outside, I recognized either dusk or dawn. One possibility made sense. The other would mean my entire world had been knocked off its axis. I tried to lift my head, but it throbbed as my heart siphoned blood through my body. If I moved even slightly, my head quaked. My scalp seemed opposed to anything resembling a vital sign. One moment I was numb. The next, I was too stricken with pain to move. I decided I didn't want to *know* where I was. I preferred to remain stretched out on the floor, with the general attitude and posture of someone recently embalmed.

As I lay facedown, my skin was chilled

from resting against the cold floor. My skull continued to torture me. I looked around, and I recognized nothing among the shadows. With a rush of relief, as I gazed up toward the gray skylight, I realized it was getting brighter outside. It was morning. I was home.

I stayed in the attic almost all day, recovering, coming down for a sandwich and a beer, avoiding Meg, speaking to no one. I wanted to call Paulette, but I kept stalling. I ached to touch her again, and every time I passed near the phone, my fingers tingled with anticipation. I kept thinking maybe she would call *me*, but it wasn't happening. Late in the afternoon, I ran into Meg on the landing between the first and second floors, and we had one of those moments when neither of us could decide which way to pass. Once we straightened it out, and she started down, she turned and looked up at me.

"Did you pull in last night and then leave?" she asked.

"Why?"

"Gregg thought he heard a car."

"Did he," I said. "I thought maybe he'd be too distracted to hear."

"Where'd you go? I missed you."

"How was *your* evening? While you were busy missing me."

"Why do you have to be like this?" she asked. "Can't we talk?"

"Don't you get enough talk from Gregg?"

"We were working on those two new developments in Buffalo," she said. "He doesn't want us to lose momentum because of the Kestlers."

"Over martinis again? Wine? You have a little fire going?"

"Where were *you?* You go to one of those places with Jimmy?"

"What's the difference?" I said. "I think maybe I should just stay out of your way from now on."

"Why are you being like this?" she asked.

"Maybe I needed somebody to *strategize* with last night. Maybe I was in the mood to *strategize*."

She took a step up, gripping the handrail and scowling at me.

"Gregg finally asked me how I felt about being left out of that meeting with the Kestlers."

"Hey, he's got an earring," I said. "He's a sensitive guy. *And* he drives a sports car. What more can you ask?"

"Let me know when you want to talk," she said.

"I'll be sure and do that."

Back in the office Monday morning, after another restless night in the attic, I checked my voice mail, but there weren't any messages from Paulette. I thought maybe she would have left word for me at work. Apparently, this woman wanted things, but didn't *need* them. It was all I could do to stay away from the phone. I looked at my list of e-mail messages. It was up to forty-two. Wes showed up in my doorway, with copy for the brochures.

"It's got all the sanitized, preapproved verbiage," he said. "It reads like a VCR instruction manual. But hey. They're the ones paying a hundred bucks an hour."

"You ever think about that?" I asked.

"What?"

"The difference between what this agency charges clients for our time and what they *pay* us. They pay us, it must come out to about thirty bucks an hour. That's a hell of a markup."

"I'm out of here in six months, tops," Wes said.

"No kidding? You been interviewing?" I asked.

"I'm going off on my own. Work out of the house. Get a new computer, an Internet hookup. Everybody who's left here in the past two years and gone into business for themselves is making at least double what they made here."

"Why does it always feel like we're trapped in a Terry Gilliam movie in this place? Get fitted for your straitjacket at the door. You know, I don't want to sit up in my attic every day at a computer. But you get more than five or six people in an office together and it's a death match."

"Won't be any less insane in business on my own," Wes said. "But at least I'll be getting paid what I'm worth."

"Sounds tempting," I said. "What ever happened on the Late Night Clown thing?"

"They chickened out. Like I said. Now it's two yuppies at the bar, talking about cars," he said. "Gotta go. I had five new job jackets in my mailbox this morning. Who the hell is opening all these new jobs?"

"Sure isn't *me*," I said. "My performance evaluation is this week. You got any of those cyanide pills left? Little pinch between the cheek and gum."

"You've had a good year. You've put in a ton of hours."

"How many people, in the past six months, have gotten no increase? No raise at all?"

"Too many," he said.

"And I shouldn't worry?" I asked. "Where's Jimmy?"

"Plotting Whit's death. Who knows."

Wes shut my door and sat down in the chair opposite my desk, under the little Milton Avery poster Meg put up for me when I moved into the space.

"This conversation isn't happening," he said. "Understand?"

"What conversation?"

"Jimmy and I were together about a month ago and he unloaded on me about Vince and this whole situation. There's more to it than wasting money on dancers."

"Like what?" I asked.

"He isn't spending the money in those places. He's just *getting* the money in those places."

"I don't follow."

"He's drawing cash off the card. You know how it works. He gives it to the bartender, who sets up a draw on the card and gives him cash."

"Right," I said. "So he can slip it into some naked woman's garter belt."

"A lot of it's been going under his *own* belt. That's what Jimmy says."

"There's always a little left over for the next trip. Expenses are like that. You always get back a little more than you spend if you work it right."

Wes sat there, looking at me, without smiling.

"We're talking thousands. He has Jimmy melt it into the invoices for the work. No receipts except the record on the credit card statement, which is just the total he draws from the card when they go into those places."

I drew in my breath. "How long's he been doing this? How much does it add up to?"

"Plenty. Over the past two years."

"I mean, he drives a Cherokee. Not a Ferrari. Where's it all going?"

"It isn't a fortune. He's taking what he needs to get by. That's what it amounts to. I can see it from Vince's perspective. They haven't given him a decent raise in three years. He's worked his ass off. You can say what you want about Vince, but he's a worker. He's a phenomenal guy in front of a group. Phenomenal. He's got more marketing savvy than all our other clients put together."

"But he's nuts to be doing this."

"I'm not defending him. I'm just telling you what Jimmy told *me*. He's just making sure he gets paid what he deserves, that's all."

"And Jimmy just hides it all in the invoices," I said. "No

wonder he doesn't want to cooperate. He's in shit as deep as Vince."

"He didn't know at first. It went on for months before he realized what Vince was doing. He kept drawing off the card, and Jimmy never realized he was keeping a lot of it. Once he found out, it was either go along with it or lose the business."

"You don't know how much I needed to know all this," I said.

"Just between you and me."

"I understand."

"You lay this on Jimmy, he's going to know I told you."

"I won't do that," I said.

"I just thought you ought to know."

Whit didn't bother to sit down or shut the door.

"Penny's going ballistic. She wants something on paper. Now."

"I'll have it for you by the end of the day," I said, stalling. "One way or another."

"We're depending on you, Rich," he said.

"I guess *so.* After a whole year of work, it's hard to see why my raise has to hang on something like this," I said.

"I didn't say that. But it would certainly help."

He left without further ceremony, my door drifting closed behind him. I recorded a message on Jimmy's answering machine at home, and on his voice mail, and I sent him an e-mail: *I need your help if you want to get through this. Where the hell are you?*

Then I checked my e-mail, with a kind of robotic faithfulness to the routines that once gave my life meaning, looking for previous e-mail from Jimmy. I wondered if Paulette had access to e-mail at school. There were five old messages from Jimmy, responding to a volley from me. I read them, half in a trance.

TO: RCAHILL

FROM: JS

You write: <Jimmy, it's getting serious. Penny wants something on paper. We really need to>

clicked on delete before I got to the end of that one ixnay on the anagerialmay ullshitbay two words for Penny uckfay off-fay

The next e-mail on the list was a shorter version of the same thing:

TO: RCAHILL

FROM: JS

You write: <Jimmy, if you don't ca>

CLICK

And then the last one:

TO: RCAHILL

FROM: JS

Let's get something straight, RCahill. The client is the guy who sets the rules, and we follow them if we want the business. When you got off the account, you could see this coming. You were just looking the other way. You were doing exactly what I've been doing. You're a part of it. And so's everyone else who looked the other way.

All right, Jimmy. You want to play rough? Let's go. Let's get this over with. I picked up the phone.

"What's up," Wes said when he answered.

"What's Jimmy's password? He gave it to you, right? When he had you intercept the e-mail he sent to Penny that time he was drunk?"

"Why?" he asked.

"I need it."

"What're you looking for?" he asked.

"Anything."

"I wondered if you'd think of this," he said.

"Butthead."

For a brief moment, I closed my eyes and thought the next sound I heard would be the click of Wes hanging up on me. But then I realized he wasn't referring to *me*. I shifted the phone to my right ear.

"That's his password. *Butthead*'s his password."

"Thanks," I said.

I wandered down to Jimmy's office and closed his door, once I was inside. I rooted through stacks of paper on his desk and in his drawers. There were unpaid bills, record club mailings, J. Crew catalogs, skin magazines, along with endless drafts of various brochures, sell-sheets, advertorials, and speeches, with about twenty job jackets strewn on the floor.

Finally I turned to the computer. I typed in Jimmy's name and then the password when the system prompted for it. I scrolled down, looking for VStringer. After about fifteen e-mails to other people, I found it. I double-clicked and waited for it to come up, shutting my eyes, hoping. When I opened my eyes, there it was, as long an e-mail as I'd ever seen from Jimmy.

TO: VSTRINGER

FROM: JS

Vince, you've got to rally. There's no paper trail. You think Cahill has been keeping track of any of this? He doesn't have a clue. He's as clueless as he was in college. He never would have guessed what you were doing if you hadn't pissed off that woman. When you set up a draw on the card at the bar, nobody can pin down how you spent the money. They may say you have no selfcontrol, but there's no law against spending it at those places. There's no record. Just stay cool.

TO: JS
FROM: VSTRINGER
You haven't kept any records? None?

TO: VSTRINGER
FROM: JS
I mean there's obviously a record of every cash advance on the card. On the statements. It wouldn't be hard to estimate how much you've taken by adding up all our charges at those places. But the thing is, nobody has any proof. We just say you spent everything we drew off the card right there.

TO: VSTRINGER
FROM: JS
Is there any way we can lose those card statements?

TO: VSTRINGER
FROM: JS
What's the point? The card company would just replace them. You can't ask American Express to destroy the record, right? Just lie low.

I leaned back in Jimmy's chair and closed my eyes. It was all here. Everything I needed, everything Whit and Penny wanted to know. I copied all the e-mail onto a diskette, and then I went straight to the accounting office and asked for the American Express statements for Jimmy's card from the past two years, which I copied. I put everything into a manila envelope and placed it in the back of my file cabinet. I called Wes.

"You seen Jimmy yet?" I asked.

"He's right here. You want to talk with him?"

"Send him down to my office."

It took him ten minutes. He waited long enough to let me know I couldn't simply fetch him with a phone call to Wes. He had his tie loosened and he hadn't shaved. He slumped in the chair, clearly recovering from the wrong ratio of Jack Daniel's to Amstel Light.

"You been thinking about the situation?" I asked.

"I just told Wes I'm not putting anything on paper."

"I'm not as clueless as you think I am, Jimmy," I said.

"Nobody said you're clueless."

I wanted to throw my lamp at him.

"Whit's setting me up. Whit's going to say I should have been keeping an eye on the expenses. He's going to say you had me fooled. He's going to say I couldn't come down on you because you're my friend. And you know what?"

He stared at me.

"He's going to be right," I said.

"Fuck Whit."

"It's my job on the line. What if I don't get a raise this year because of all this?" I asked.

"That won't happen. I'm not going to rat on Vince."

"Vince doesn't give a shit what happens to you."

"And you do?"

"Yeah, I care," I said.

"Doesn't show. If you cared, you wouldn't be calling me in here," he said. "You owe me, man. You still owe me. I saved your ass in college. I went to jail for you, man."

When the deer hit the windshield, we were halfway to Rich Stadium at two a.m., where Jimmy, drunk, wanted me to pass him a football in the dark, after breaking into the stadium. Only seniors in college, and I was sure we were going to die. The car smashed head-on into a pole, and the deer slid down the hood and into the pole as my face pounded against the wheel and I passed out. I was drunker than Jimmy.

When I opened my eyes, Jimmy was shoving me into the passenger seat. He knew my traffic record. He knew I'd be in jail if I was arrested for DWI, and he knew how I would fare, because he'd been there already in high school, seen those losers when he went for his hearings, the guys they bring into the courtroom in cuffs on a DWI, accountants and insurance agents—normal people who screw up when they get into a car—hosed down, in fatigues, cuffed like killers. He knew I could never fake my way through walking a line or reciting the alphabet backward, and he knew how many other drivers saw the wreck, how fast the troopers would get there. And he felt responsible: it was his idea to go to Buffalo, despite my protests; he talked me into it, and—one of the few times in his life—decided to take responsibility. The flashing lights were behind us already, and they pried open the doors and led Jimmy to the cruiser after the paramedics took a look at him. I saw him walk the line and fail, and as they got the stretcher for me, they led Jimmy into the back of the cruiser, where he sat, his eyes closed, probably sleeping, indifferent. And in the months to come, he didn't rub it in, even after a night in jail, and then going for the hearing and the plea and getting his fine and sentence and sitting through a whole series of classes on drinking and driving and faking his way through AA meetings until the sentence was served, and he was back at it again. And in all the years afterward, not a word about what he'd done for me, never once asking for a favor in return.

"It isn't that big a debt, Jimmy," I said. "That was years ago. That was DWI. This is a felony, man."

"It'll blow over if you just let it."

"I'm going to stall Whit one more day. That's as heroic as it gets. Tomorrow I want you to go in there with me and together we'll have something on paper. Nobody's going to get prosecuted for this. No way. Just own up to it and get on with things."

"You don't know that," he said. "Never in a million years."

"You've got a day to reconsider. Then I go in there without you."

He grinned.

"Like there's anything you could show them."

After he'd left my office, I opened up my e-mail and sent off a brief message to Whit: *I'll have what you want tomorrow. I want to give Jimmy one more day. I'm hoping he'll decide to cooperate. Tell Penny and Tish not to worry. I guarantee I'll have what they need.*

I left early, and no one was home when I got there. There was a note on the kitchen table: *Gregg and I are in Buffalo today. Right back up on the horse!* An image flashed in my mind, the wrong image, and I ignored it. *Can you handle a run to Burger King? Alec's got two more nights of basketball. I know how hard you're working, but I'm going to be late. Could you take him? Let's not fight.*

Maybe it was possible. Maybe *anything* was possible. Maybe it was strictly business between them. Maybe Will would get into Ignatius and play basketball and Paulette would get a computer job with General Motors or Paychex. Maybe I would get the raise we needed to start building that nest egg. Maybe I could find a way of building a normal middle-class family four days a week and live the rest of the week on a mountaintop somewhere, finding the right balance between engagement and contemplation, and life would finally be meaningful and important, and every gesture, every word, would count for something, and *happiness* itself would brood over our lives. All of which was about as likely as my waking up and finding my little children at my knee again, offering me their Crayola drawings from school, asking to hear me read *Goodnight, Moon* to them one more time before bed.

I went out through the back door and did what I might have done any other year of my life at this point in the season. I walked around our tiny backyard, trying to be the person I'd always believed I was, even though something else gaped inside me when I touched Paulette, and it was devouring me. I hunkered down to see how high the daylilies were getting, poking the soil as if it might need a little extra compost for the roses Meg wanted me to plant. Then I got a folding aluminum chair out of the garage and the white wrought-iron umbrella table, and I set everything up on the brick patio, imagining where the impatiens would go in May (with the little imploding pods Alec loved to pop, spraying seeds everywhere), where I'd put the begonias in June, and how many ferns I'd transplant near the house from along the fence in back. It was still a beautiful day, the sun out and the smell of crab-apple trees blooming three lots down from ours. Yet this little yard offered me no refuge. I would have to go back so many years, back past so many decisions, to an earlier fork, to make everything right again.

As I cranked the umbrella open, the kitchen phone rang.

"Dad?"

"Alec?"

"What are *you* doing home?" he asked.

"I came home early for once. I needed a break."

"Can you pick me up? I missed the bus," he said. "I was shooting baskets and I forgot what time it was."

In the car, on the way home, Alec looked preoccupied.

"Where's Mom?" he asked.

"In Buffalo. On business."

"Is she with *him?*" he asked.

"Yeah. They're making some calls on developers there."

It wasn't *me.* He could see it, too. It was like a disease nobody wanted to talk about, but everybody feared. I was the fool, I was the one making all the mistakes, and everyone knew it. Even Alec.

"I'll be there at basketball tonight, Alec," I said.

"You wouldn't believe what Will's showing me," he said.

"Hey, Al," I said.

"Yeah."

"You know I love you," I said.

"That was so *random,*" he said, as cool as ever, but smiling.

After I got back home with Alec, the del Sol pulled into our driveway as Alec was tossing the ball toward the noisy little, backboard I'd jigsawed from pressed particleboard and then painted with enamel. Paulette parked the car halfway into the drive and got out even before Will did. She wore her stretch pants again and a tank top over a torn T-shirt, no bra, and it was hard to quit gazing at the way those pants clung to her legs all the way up to her waist, where they ducked under the wheat-colored top over her small, defiant breasts. Just enough, and never too much, anywhere, everything in harmony with everything else. So much energy and life packed into such a tiny space. Her shoulders were completely exposed, her nipples just showing under the fabric in the cool breeze. It seemed a little early in the year to be dressed this way.

When Will got out, he was wearing his hat backward, the Nike swoosh behind his head, with an old sweatshirt, the sleeves completely torn off and a pair of long basketball shorts that reached down past his knees. He scowled at her as she crossed his path to get to me. I glanced over toward Alec to see if he was watching, but he was intent on the ball, which Will stole from him with a grin; then the two of them were into their usual one-on-one game.

Now that his arms were exposed, I noticed a mark on Will's arm, up near the shoulder. It was about the size of a quarter, and from where I stood, it looked like a pitchfork enclosed in a circle. I could see it clearly, embossed and pale, as if the lighter flesh extruded itself through the darker surface, the scar raised up. It was a brand, like something out of Auschwitz or the Deep South during slavery. I'd seen them on blacks who assembled on Main Street when it was cordoned off every year for a marathon of three-on-three basketball games, the Main Event, which Alec always dreamed of entering. It looked like a tattoo, only one degree deeper into the flesh. My stomach went cold.

"What *is* that?" I asked Paulette.

"What?"

"On Will's arm," I said.

"Can I come in?"

"Sure," I said, without moving toward the door.

She gave me a little sideways nod, full of sudden annoyance, which was supposed to get me to follow her inside the house, but I stood my ground, watching the game. She paused, looked irritated, and then went inside, banging the screen door behind her. I counted off the seconds to a full half-minute; then I went inside, too. She wasn't in the kitchen, but I could smell her perfume in the air. It was Trésor, which Meg kept hinting she wanted, coming home with it on her wrists after a quick trip to Kaufmann's for new pillowcases. On our budget, a bottle of it would have been considered a luxury, and she didn't want to feel guilty buying it for herself, but I'd never bothered to get it for her, for Christmas or her birthday or Mother's Day. And now here was Paulette in our house, wearing that scent.

Once again, I followed Paulette into the living room, and this time she sat upright on the couch, with her hands knit together over her knees, her elbows planted on her legs. She was staring at the floor. In this pose, her tank top rode up to expose about three inches of firm, flat stomach. I sat on the end of the couch, facing the front door. She'd taken off her sandals and placed them side by side on the carpet, and she was digging her toes nervously into the pile. She'd painted her toenails bright red.

"Why'd you leave so soon?" she asked, frowning. I realized she must have been waiting for me to call her.

"I couldn't go through with it."

"Was it me?"

"You don't know how much I wanted to stay. I've been trying not to call you for two days now."

"Why? What are you afraid of?" she asked.

"Afraid of? Put yourself in my position. What would *you* be afraid of?"

"You like me, don't you?" she asked.

I moved across the room and sat beside her on the couch, facing toward her, with about a foot of clearance between our legs, just far enough away.

"I've got a life here. I've got a family. You understand?"

"Why can't you just let things happen?"

"Because people depend on me."

"Come to the concert tonight," she said. "Just for the music. I know you'll love it."

"I've got Alec's basketball."

"Main act don't start until ten."

"But the whole idea is to stay away from you."

"You feel the way you feel, a man got to *do* something about it. Otherwise it won't leave you alone. How many women, you see them walk by, how many make you feel the way I do?"

"It's been a long time."

I got up and stood on the other side of the room. It was too hard sitting a foot away from her on the couch. I took a deep breath.

"That thing on Will's arm. That from this guy Price?"

"Uh-huh. Like a Folk Nation sign, out of Chicago? Show's you got quoted. Will got it right after the McDonald thing. From Price. That's what that was all about."

"Is it burned in or what?" I asked.

"That one is. Sometimes it's razors," she said, but in a remote voice, thinking about other things.

"It's crazy," I said.

"Way you get in with Price. You get quoted," she said.

"So you're in with him?"

"Not yet. Once you in, you in for life," she said, with the look of a troubled woman who wasn't about to give me the details. I heard a car pull into the drive.

"Meg's home," I said.

"Be there tonight," she said.

I imagined Dana in Paulette's position, without me, without this house, without this suburb, without this family, without a father. Paulette's wrists and ankles and waist were so tapered. Her body's narrowest passages went straight to my heart. The world was a blunt object, ready to break her.

The back door opened, and I could hear the rustling of paper bags as Meg walked into the kitchen and put groceries on the counter. Quickly Paulette slipped her sandals back on and stood up to leave.

"I'll have Will call you when he's done," I said.

"Don't need to. I'll pick him up on time," she said. I walked her to the back door as Meg went upstairs to change, without saying a word to either of us, as if we weren't even in the room.

As I opened the back door, she whispered: "Be there tonight."

■

Meg moved silently around the bedroom without looking at me, standing at the window and poking her finger into the Levelor blinds, prying them open.

"She gone?" she asked.

"Where were *you?*"

"In Buffalo. Didn't you see my note?"

"So you were included in the meeting this time?" I asked.

"One of them was a woman. The other seemed to like me better than he liked Gregg. I think Gregg's earring put him off."

"So I guess it wasn't the crisis you thought it was, not getting invited to the Kestler meeting," I said.

"I didn't say it was a crisis. I said it made me angry."

She stared out at the street, which I imagined covered with little whirling shadows tossed there by clusters of pale green leaves on the maples. I saw hints of spring in the brighter angles of light, the steeper slant of shadows, and I heard it in the *sweet sweet sweet* of the cardinals. It was the only songbird in our neighborhood. I kept listening for the mockingbirds I heard as a child in our backyard, but they never came around now, as scarce as warblers, the endless repertoire of sounds they could make, little guttural trills, sweet riffs high up on the scale, noises like human conversation: all of that improvisational freedom and power in one little bird's voice, that sense of possibility and variety and surprise, the way life itself was supposed to feel.

"That was Trésor, wasn't it?" she asked.

"What?" I asked.

"When I walked in, I thought maybe you'd bought it for me. I could just imagine Dana spraying it on her wrist to see if she liked it better than the CK we got her. And I thought, *Oh great. Dana had to spoil it for me.* But no. Paulette had to spoil it for me. What was she doing here?"

"She was dropping off her brother," I said. "Who's stopping you from buying a bottle of perfume?"

"I don't buy myself anything," she said. "You know how much your raise is going to be yet?"

"No," I said. "Listen, Meg. We've worked for this new house for years. I don't want us to back out now. That lot isn't going to stay vacant. It's one of the last lots left around here where you can build. We've earned that house. We deserve it." I wanted it, and I wanted her to know I wanted it, and her, more than anything, even as I felt myself pulling away from all of it.

"Since when do people get what they deserve?" she asked. "So what was Paulette doing in our house?"

"I told you," I said.

"She didn't need to come inside to drop off her brother."

"She likes this place," I said. "I think she's curious about us."

"Tell her she can move in when we move out. Until then, I don't want to see her in my house."

"What's *your* problem?" I asked. "You can dish it out, but you can't take it?"

"I'm not dishing it out," she said.

"I'll say you're not."

"Oh, like you're really deprived. Since when have I said no?"

"It isn't a matter of saying no," I said. "It's obvious you aren't interested."

She reached into her jewelry box, plucked a small metal object—it looked like a pendant from where I stood—and tossed it at me. I recognized it when it was halfway across the room and caught it just in front of my face. She'd thrown it hard enough to cut me. It was the ring of extra keys from Paulette.

"I found them in your pants," she said.

"I haven't done anything," I said.

"Not yet, huh?" she said.

"And what about *you?*"

"I don't have a set of Gregg's keys," she said.

I could smell the Trésor again. It took that long for the scent to ride the heat drafts up from downstairs. The sun cut directly through the blinds, casting distinct bars of light and shade on the wall above her dresser, filling the room with a peach-colored glow. In that light, Meg's skin suddenly looked acutely desirable. Anger brought color into her cheeks, made her lips seem fuller. I wanted to bring everything to a standstill, get everybody back on track, and do my best to remember what the word *decency* meant. Meg stood there with a whole new posture, her neck upright, her shoulders back, her eyes level with the window's latch. I wanted time to stop with exactly this angle of sunlight and the faint sound of wind in the maples and ginkgos along the street, the creak of tricycle wheels and the smack of the basketball out back, the laughter, the shuffle of sneakers on the blacktop, the whole cool pressure of a spring afternoon on my taut, dry skin.

Without another word, I turned and walked out and went up to the attic. I stretched out on the floor, looking at my print of William Blake from college. In that posture, I wondered how, exactly, it would feel to be rescued by some Superior Being or at least someone in a higher tax bracket. I'd even settle for Ed McMahon with a check for several million at my front door or else a sub-sub-factotum at the MacArthur Foundation who spotted the seeds of genius in a Veritex sell sheet I once rewrote in a pinch, when all our copywriters called in sick. Someone—anyone—who could carry me to my refuge, crank up the sling, tighten the truss, poke the IV into my wrist and slide the remote into my fist. *Lean back into the drip, friend. I'll take care of things from here.* Someone who could pare my schedule down to a life-support system, or a robe and a bowl and a timetable of sweeping duties, or an icy cave somewhere with a Sherpa and a loincloth, a life of air, earth, water, and fire, without a pocket calendar, without a telephone. I listened to Meg move around in the bedroom and then go down to the first floor. I heard the doors slamming, the Saab revving. Soon the house was silent.

■

In the gym, Meg sat with some of the other mothers, talking and laughing as if she didn't have a doubt about her life at home, as if she didn't know I was there, on the other side of the bleachers. What did she expect me to do? Call an attorney? Call off the new mortgage? Retract our offer on the lot and lose our deposit?

As I headed out of the Ignatius parking lot, I glanced back, but no one else was coming out yet. I was on my own now. I headed downtown and parked in a garage about a block away from Club Zero. I'd been there before, to hear The Story one week and The Ramones on another when they were on one of their revival tours. It was a dungeon, with pinball machines and a pool table in one room, a glass case of souvenir T-shirts, and a big room with wooden posts bearing signs that warned: NO SLAMMING.

I stood at the bar, watching the door, but Paulette didn't arrive until the first band was finished, and the main act—a young black singer from Los Angeles, with a set of acoustic guitars and no band—came out to get the soundboard technicians working on the right mix. I was disappointed: no bass, no drums, no lead guitar, just a man and six strings and a bottleneck slide and a pick. I wanted to feel the music in my ribs. This was going to be *old* blues, Delta blues, like scratchy plastic recordings from the thirties, Robert Johnson in San Antonio and Dallas. She was wearing her usual uniform: a tight black top and jeans. On her way toward me, she stopped to talk with a little group sitting in white plastic chairs the owners had placed across the floor in rows. I sipped my beer and waited, but she was in no hurry, so I turned my back and tried to occupy the old bartender in a conversation about the Red Wings, but it wasn't going anywhere.

Finally, the singer came out—tall, black, classy, and quiet, dressed in a white oxford shirt and dark slacks, with a vest, very friendly and humble with the crowd—and started on his first number. Paulette was still talking with one of the women, and I was getting annoyed. But the music immediately charmed the room, all eyes on the stage except a few drunken clusters of people in back, and when he sang the first few lines, his voice was like warm firelight. People hooted from the back of the room, the drunks first, once they paused long enough to realize he was playing, like a congregation shouting in a church, and he went straight into his second number.

I ordered another beer and felt a hand touch my waist.

"Hey," she said, the scent of Trésor following her.

"Who were those guys?" I asked, trying to catch my breath, not wanting her to know how weak she made me.

"People from school," she said. "Isn't he great?"

"Excellent. I wish he had a band. It would be fun to watch people dance."

"This guy's as good as it gets. Wanna go upstairs?" she asked.

"What's upstairs?"

"See the balcony?"

I looked up and saw, for the first time, the railings around the little balcony above us. It faced the stage where the ceiling went up a floor, like a mezzanine around an atrium.

"You can get up there?" I asked.

"I know the owner," she said and took my hand, lacing our fingers together. "He probably doesn't want us up there. But he'll never know. Come on."

We went out past the rest rooms, through the billiard room, and through a door I didn't know was there until she opened it. The stairs were lit by a single bulb at the bottom, and we stumbled a couple times, Paulette falling against my arm, her face brushing against mine. She pulled back and smiled as she looked into my eyes, and then started up the stairs again ahead of me. It was an empty space, a wooden floor surrounded by round metal railings, and it looked more like a place to store sound equipment than an upper-deck seat for the show. We sat cross-legged behind the railing, so the bartender wouldn't notice us and send up a bouncer.

He began the fifth number; it was a slow one with long pauses and painful licks that he strung out, bending the strings on notes between chord shifts.

"Now *this* is it," she said.

"I like the slow ones best."

"Me, too," she said, getting up. "Come here."

"Where?"

"Back in the corner here. Nobody'll see."

We backed into the shadows and she hung her arms around my neck and pressed herself gently against me and started to sway, slow and easy, bending, pulling me down, her leg between mine, then coming back up, her hips moving in circles, then pulling away. She danced without touching me, her eyes closed, like the dance she'd done in her apartment. She turned to face away from me and slowly backed into me, her ass rubbing against my pants, reached back, placing her hands in my back pockets and pulling just hard enough to feel me growing stiff behind the denim. Then she let go and danced alone again, her eyes still shut tight.

Slowly, she inched closer again, and looked up into my eyes with her hands locked behind my neck, her wrists gently resting on my shoulders. I leaned down to kiss her, but she dodged my lips and then locked eyes with me, drawing me back into the dance, the music, our bodies not touching except for her hands on my arms and my fingertips riding her waist, her hips. I slipped my fingers down and around and felt the perfect curve. The smell of Trésor clouded everything. I hooked my fingers into her belt loops and drew her closer, but she pushed away.

"What?" I asked.

"Just dance," she said.

She didn't want to be distracted from the singer's voice, its pain. I had to wait. The music came first. I let her go and she danced alone, in front of me, as I leaned back into the corner.

"I don't want to lose you," I said.

She wasn't listening. Maybe I'd spoken too softly.

"You think I'm in love with you?" I asked.

She didn't seem to hear me. She shook her head from side to side, in rhythm to the music. She opened her eyes and looked at me without smiling, then closed her eyes until the song was done. She moved toward me in the shadows and put her arms around me again, and pulled my face down to hers, holding back for one, two, three seconds, letting our lips touch and then pulling away to look at me, then bringing her lips up to mine, and we kissed gently until she pulled away.

"Let's go," she said.

In her apartment, she didn't bother to turn on the light. She pushed me back against the wall and ran her tongue around my lips, circling the gap, retreating when I pushed my own tongue toward hers. She ran her mouth along the jawline and then down into the little pocket of space at the base of my throat, where my collar parted. I ran my fingers over her waist and her ribs and her arms, my fingertips gently touching her shoulders, then hovering in the air around them.

She pulled my shirt over my head, the fabric tugging at my ears, pulling my chin up, and she clamped her teeth onto my neck again with the shirt still wrapped around my head, holding my wrists together with one hand above my head. I was blind and helpless, and she used that, held me there, pressing the length of her body against mine, her breasts soft and warm and firm under the black cotton fabric rubbing against me, her leg pushing my legs apart, pushing upward. I pulled my wrists free from her tight grip above my head, letting her draw the rest of the shirt over me and toss it aside. I grabbed the back of her top and yanked it up, peeling it off as she pulled away from me, keeping her distance, teasing me, smiling, lowering her lips to my chest, running her tongue down the length of my stomach, tasting my skin, releasing my belt, nudging the zipper. I reached down and stepped out of my pants as she slipped out of hers, and then I took her hair into my fist and gently drew her upward and we stood there in the dark, a foot apart, her fingers mingling with mine, between us, our eyes adjusting to the twilight, the light shining in from outside, falling like frost on the couch, the creamy wall, the table, the carpet.

She let go of my fingers as she slowly brought her lips up to mine and kissed me, gently pushing her open palms against my shoulders, holding me off, making sure nothing touched except our lips, and then she pulled away and slipped her fingers into my hair and held my head between her hands as she started to sway and turn, the music still echoing in her head, the room silent and gray in that light borrowed from the street. As she danced, I knelt in front of her, my face moving slowly past the twin crescents of shadow under her breasts, she holding me off, letting me smell the perfume and the other scent, pushing my head down until my knees touched the floor, my face level with the little wedge of black lace stretched around her hips, the little shard of dark fabric curving down and looping under and around her legs. She pulled hard and pressed my face into that spiced thicket of lace, and I tugged at the hem as she stepped free of the fabric.

"Come on," she said, smiling.

She led me into the bedroom and moved quickly off to the bathroom and shut the door. I lay back, listening to the muted sound of people in the next apartment, the faint sound of bickering over the television laughter. I studied the dark shapes on the walls, posters, a mirror, a set of tragedy and comedy masks in porcelain, gleaming in the light through the window. It was a small room, and the cool air settled on my chest. I heard the toilet swirl and then she moved softly around in the bathroom, and when she opened the door the light flashed across the room, until she reached back and flicked the switch. In that moment, with all the harsh immediacy of a strobe, I saw her body, perfect even in that unforgiving light, the slope of shadow diving downward from beneath her breasts, down to the gradient of her waist, curving out toward her hips and legs, long and sleek, tapering to her tiny ankles, her entire body so weightless I could seize her, lift her into the air, and lower her onto me. I knew I would never last the first time, hoping she'd be patient enough with me.

She came to the side of the bed and placed a small square foil wrapper on the nightstand.

"I hate those things."

"This time you won't," she said. "But first things first."

She straddled my legs, and I couldn't restrain myself, reaching out to hold her breasts at last, but she deflected my hands with her wrists, a little jujitsu delay, and she knelt to her task, letting her hair dangle and stroke me, swinging her head back and forth, bringing me to the edge. When I moaned in warning, she stopped, ran her hands up my legs, dragging her limp fingers upward, the nails running along my glistening skin, until she nested her fingertips under me, at precisely the right spot, and I let my legs fall apart. She brought her mouth down onto that same little quarter of skin where everything came alive and veered out of control—the trigger of the gun. She flicked it twice with her tongue. Paused. Covered it with her lips, and, inside her mouth, she plucked me, faster and faster. It lifted me off the bed, the heat and shock wave spreading out to my fingertips and head and then back again, outward and inward, like bathwaves in a tub.

As my shuddering began to subside, she took a hot washcloth

she'd brought from the bathroom and cleaned up, and then a towel, and then she lay beside me.

"Boy, were *you* in a hurry," she said.

Making love with her was like riding a whirlpool, revolving slowly around the edges, circling into tighter and tighter orbits until I dropped straight down. I began by gently rolling her onto her stomach, straddling *her*, running my tongue along her shoulders and down her back, feeling the rhythm of her vertebrae, the skin stretched over the ladder of bone. She moaned softly and her breath caught whenever I took tiny pinches of skin between my teeth.

I pulled her shoulder and rolled her over. I ran my fingertips slowly over the length of her body, down along the insides of her legs to her ankles, and on the way back up, I followed my fingers with my tongue, her skin smooth as an apple. Then I was at her breast, her nipple a firm pellet, rolling my tongue over it and then pulling away until she grabbed my hair and forced me back. I reached down and parted the folds, and I moved my fingertip lightly, in circles, until I could hear what I was doing in the way she breathed. I'd reached that point where everything starts to happen on its own.

She reached over to the nightstand and took the foil in her teeth, tearing off the wrapper, then she rolled me onto my back, bringing her mouth down hard on mine, teething my lower lips, kissing my eyes—sending a sobering shock of sad tenderness through me, because it was something Meg did when we were first married—and I could feel the condom start to unroll around me under her fingers. Then she lowered her head and slipped her lips around the tip, taking the condom oh-so-gently between her teeth and she cautiously pushed against the white ring, unrolling it before the advance of those teeth, taking me deeper and deeper into her mouth, her tongue starting to work again, until she knew I was ready, and she pulled away unrolling the rest with her fingers.

She lowered herself onto me slowly at first, guiding me in, and she rode slowly astride my hips, moving forward and back, then in circles, never easing the pressure, until I knew I could go all night like this, but she started to move faster, and I reached up to stroke her breasts, and she leaned forward, coming down to give me her nipple again, her hips working harder, getting herself into just the right position.

"Slow down," I said. "Make it last."

"We don't stop with this one," she said, biting her lower lips, wincing with the severity of it, and then with a gasp and a cry that started deep in her throat as she bit hard into my lips, trying to stifle another scream, pumping hard and then beginning to ease up, panting, kissing me on the chin, the cheek, biting my ear, then running her tongue along my forehead, licking away the salt.

She toppled sideways, and pulled me with her, so that I didn't fall out. And she pushed up against my chest until I lifted myself a few inches away from her and she began to go to work again, pumping against me—just like Meg—and I slowly began to time my thrusts to her steady tempo, moving faster and then easing up as she got closer. When she opened her eyes and looked hard into my own eyes I knew she was ready again, and I pulled away, completely pulled out.

"No, no!" she said. "I'm almost there."

I lowered my lips to her breast and teased her with my tongue, just slightly touching. She had her hands behind me, one cheek in each fist and she pulled me toward her, arching her back and opening her legs. I thrust hard, missing the first time and sliding back past the mark, but she quickly grabbed me and slid me inside, and she came immediately this time with a long, rumbling moan, and at that sound, I came, letting our bodies slap together, but as I came, my arms began to shake and I lost all control of the muscles. It was like a seizure. I collapsed on top of her, her sobs in my ear, until we rolled apart and lay on our backs, staring up at the ceiling. When I looked over toward her, she was weeping. When I reached for her, she pushed my hand away and rolled onto her side.

"What? What is it?" I asked. "You all right?"

"Just give me a minute."

As I lay there, the gray afterwash of guilt rose up, and soon I felt tears in my own eyes. It was as if some rude god became whole between us, and then withdrew, moved on. We'd been used and discarded. Leaves rattled on the walk outside. My sadness deepened when Paulette turned to me and rested her arm over my stomach, pressing her face into my arm. I reached for the towel, kissed Paulette once on the forehead, and headed for the bathroom. For a moment, on my way, as the blood drained suddenly downward into my arms and legs, I lost all sense of direction, of where we were, of the time, the date, of where I'd been earlier in the day, of who I might be and where I might be going. One brief soothing, disconcerting episode of oblivion.

Then it all came back to me. I leaned against the wall and breathed. When I recovered, I knew I would feel a long way from home.

Chapter 12

When I woke up in my attic, I stared at the beacon of winking red light by my desk. I crawled and hoisted myself into a standing position and wobbled over to the shelf where my answering machine blinked. I stabbed the PLAY button with my finger.

A long silence, and then the voice, this time without any of the cocksure, mocking intonations. Dead serious now, urgently getting the information across: *We need to talk. You the nigger, except you don't know it yet. See, you the nigger, and I'm the man. Other people get rich off niggers like you. Cuz. I got free of all that. Which is why you wanna be me. You and me, we gone have a little talk. You wanna know who I think I am? Think it's about time I show you. About time I show you who you are, too.* And then a little sound of jostling and a click and the line went dead.

I picked up the phone and hit star-six-six and hung up. Within seconds, the phone was ringing, but in an unfamiliar pattern, with less volume and less time between rings. I picked it up and the ringing began at the other end of the line. The phone company computers were connecting me to the last number to call my upstairs line. After six rings, someone picked up.

"Yeah?" they said.

"Who's this?" I asked.

"Who you want?" they asked.

"Who've I got?" I asked.

"Thunderbird. We aren't open."

"Sorry," I said, and hung up.

The blood drummed and throbbed in my head. I heard Meg's footsteps. She was wearing her quilted robe with a pattern of tea roses. She didn't come all the way up to the attic, but stayed on the landing where one flight of stairs made its U-turn into the next. I could smell the cigarette smoke in my hair from Club Zero.

"Bogardus is here," she said. "Something's happened."

"What?"

"Where've you been?" she asked.

"My head is killing me," I said. "Why's Bogardus here now?"

"Come on down. He'll show you. Somebody left something on our back door last night," she said, walking beside me down the stairs. "Alec found it when he left for the bus."

In the kitchen, nothing was disturbed. As I crossed the room, I saw Bogardus outside, holding the storm window from the screen door in his hands, lifting the Plexiglas up to his nose. What looked like a small square of paper was stuck to the glass. He was looking close, touching only the edges of the window. It was an envelope taped to the glass. He motioned to a pair of gloves at his feet.

"Put them on," he said.

"What is that?" I asked, as I stepped outside and picked up the gloves. It was warmer than I imagined it would be, like a day in May. Bogardus could probably read the entire history of my previous day by paying attention to the rotation of odors as he moved around me. He didn't flinch, though, or turn away.

"You tell me," he said, holding the window up to my face. "Check out what's inside for me."

I pulled the envelope from the window and looked inside. It contained a key and a sheet of paper. I recognized the key: it was the extra one we kept hidden in the garage. Slowly I removed the sheet of paper from inside and unfolded it. It was handwritten on a sheet of paper, in a fluent and scrupulous cursive. *Check it out. These the people turn homeys like you into a nigger. Murdoch, Gates, Milken. Ain't no way to lock them out of your lives. Ain't no way to lock me out, either.*

"I used this key the other day. Locked myself out of the car and had to fish it out," I said. "He must have been parked on the street or something."

"Maybe he had somebody else watching."

"You said you were going to do something about this guy," I said, handing the picture back to Bogardus, keeping the note. "Who *is* he?"

"I'll need that note," he said, reaching for it.

I read through it one more time, and then handed it to him.

"Can we go inside?"

I stared at him as he took out a cigarette, lit it, and took three deep drags. As he was getting ready to drop it, I grabbed it and dragged on it myself, then dropped it to the blacktop and let him smash it with his toe. I realized I had nothing on my feet. Then he put the note into the pocket of his corduroy jacket. I hadn't seen one of those sport coats in years, complete with suede elbow patches. It looked like part of the wardrobe from *All the President's Men*, something honorable and Ivy League and completely out of place in the contemporary world.

"We've got a trap on your line. Your wife tell you?"

"I did that star-six-six thing. Got through to a place called The Thunderbird. Sounded like a bar," I said.

"Bar. Pool hall. Strip joint. Men's room serves as a pharmacy," Bogardus said. "Up near Ridge Road. Price used to hang out there years ago. Nobody sees him anymore. He's gotten too far up. If he was really at that McDonald's, it was the strangest thing he's ever done. Totally out of character."

We went into the kitchen. Meg was upstairs, getting dressed.

"I mean, I've got Will here in my driveway every day," I said. "What are you doing on your end of the deal?"

"It's tough. Price has got people on his payroll. I'm sure of it. Otherwise, we could have had him long ago. Guy's a real fucking prize. Thinks he can get away with anything. I'm sure you know he's got a thing for Paulette."

"A thing."

"Yeah," he said.

"What kind of thing?"

"What kind of thing? You had a thing for her after thirty seconds."

"Is she why he's still around?" I asked.

"He's got too much pride to tie her up and toss her in the trunk."

"I can't believe you got me into this."

"You look wrecked," he said.

"I was out."

"Out where?" he asked. "I swear to God, if you went to see her last night—"

"Don't lecture *me*," I said. "You can't even nail this guy."

"The other thing is, that guy in the hospital? Guy they knocked down when they were leaving McDonald's? You saw the paper, didn't you?"

"No." I couldn't remember when I'd last read a newspaper.

"He died," Bogardus said. "Homicide thinks they've got themselves a collar. I don't think Price has any pull in homicide. Maybe he thinks you saw him knock the guy down."

"You've got to do something, Bogardus."

"You aren't helping."

"I mean, have somebody trace these phone calls or—"

"I told you we have a trap on the line. I explained to your wife how to activate the trace, unless it's a car phone. Look, I've got to get downtown. You going to be all right?"

"Oh, yeah. I'm just great," I said. "Hey, stay in touch. Send me a postcard sometime."

After he'd left, and I was ready to walk out the door for work, Meg came down. She stood in the kitchen, filling a glass from a little stream of water under the egg-shaped filter attached to the tap, waiting for an explanation.

"So?"

"This is the guy in the Range Rover that day," I said. "I was right. That was him."

"You can't just come onto somebody's property like this. What's Bogardus going to do about it?"

"I'm not sure he can do *anything*. Looks like this guy does whatever he damn well pleases."

She sighed and looked down and then up.

"This is all because of her, isn't it?" she asked. "He wants her to stay away from you."

"This is because of the thing at McDonald's. That's all."

"She's obviously attracted to you," she said. "And she's with him, isn't she?"

"I don't know who's with who anymore. Do you?"

"I used to think I was with you," she said.

I sighed and looked out the window.

"I feel like shit," I said.

"You look it, too," she said. "You sure you're okay?"

"I'll survive."

"What are you thinking?" she asked.

"I'm thinking I've got to do something about this guy. I'm thinking about the house. The job. Jimmy. You. Me. You want the whole list?"

"Where were you?" she asked softly.

"Don't worry about it."

Outside, it was warm enough for shorts and a T-shirt. In my cramped little office, I wasn't even curious enough to look at the seventeen things I'd listed in my Day-Timer's To Do column. Nothing in the office seemed quite real to me. My life felt like a golf game where every swing is a surprise: the ball spins right, cuts left, skids across the ground, soars past the green into the water, and you don't have a clue what you're doing wrong, because it's always something different, with every swing its own little unique sin against good form.

Memories of the previous night started to surface, the blues licks at Club Zero, the way Paulette's body moved against me as we stood, unseen, on the balcony, my hands touching her naked waist, and then in her apartment, the perfect texture of her skin, the smells, the sounds she made. And then the betrayal in what we'd done, the fear that every minute I remained there I was in danger, an interloper in Eugene Price's preserve.

Whit peeked into the room. He was wearing his glasses again, and his hair was perfect: the sandy coif, the distinct hairline, the impeccable layering on top. The man with the classic 1963 Austin-Healey wintering in the garage on cinder blocks. It was so long since I'd gotten it cut, the hair curled on my neck.

"Where's Jimmy?" he asked.

"No idea, as usual."

"What happened to *you?*"

"Don't ask," I said.

"Out with Jimmy? You know you're an enabler for him."

I snapped my head up and said: "Who's *your* enabler, Whit? I've seen you put it away pretty good."

"You *are* in bad shape," he said, smiling, though I could almost see him filing away my remark for future reference.

"I am."

"So is Jimmy with us or against us?" Whit asked.

"I have to talk with him one more time this morning."

"Tish thinks we're covering for Vince."

"I still don't see why this is all *our* job."

"Because Jimmy's the one who's been helping him do it," Whit said. "Because—"

"Jimmy only did what the client wanted. No problem, long as nobody above Stringer made a stink about it. Now this woman comes in."

"She's the client. We're doing what she wants," he said. "What have you got for me?"

I glared at him.

"What's my raise going to be next week?" I asked. I knew it was a mistake, but I couldn't stop myself.

"In two days, we'll let you know what—"

"I need to know now," I said.

"I don't think Penny would want me to—"

"How much?" I asked.

He moved to the window and turned his head in circles, loosening the bones in his neck.

"Two thousand. Two and a half. Ballpark. Assuming you come through for us on this."

"Are you serious?"

"Many people in this agency have gone two years without a raise," he said.

"Two?"

He nodded.

"Two thousand?" I said, standing up, leaning forward. I lowered my voice for emphasis. "That's two thousand dollars a *year*, right."

He looked at me without expression, until he couldn't look anymore.

"You know everybody's getting slimed. You aren't the only one."

"She's got that place in the islands. You've got the company car. And I know you make six figures. The rest of us settle for no raise or two thousand?"

"I got hired when times weren't quite as lean," he said. "That's all."

"Times aren't ever going to be lean for *you*, Whit."

"Don't get greedy, Rich," he said. "Hang tough, man, and we can—"

"It's greedy to want to put your kids through college?"

All the years seemed to roll themselves forward in my mind, all the hours, all the work I did for them, knowing they charged our clients three times what they paid me for each hour I worked, knowing they didn't have *that* much overhead. I earned a wage. They made a profit.

"I'm done hanging tough. This is bullshit."

After he disappeared around the corner down the hall, I was

still standing. It would have been easy, comparatively painless, to slam a hole into the drywall behind my chair. It *had* to be cheap drywall.

I reached behind my filing cabinet, took out the envelope with the hard copy of the e-mail in it, went downstairs and made a Xerox of it, and slipped it into Whit's mailbox. He wouldn't find it for an hour or two, long enough for me to get out of the office. When I arrived back upstairs, the phone rang.

"Hi," she said.

Something in the way her voice came over the wire carried the memory of her lips, the way her shoulders arched when I pressed my palms into the small of her back; it all rose up as she spoke, along with a swarm of little irrational side memories flashing from years ago, the way I'd felt with Meg when I met her, unable to stay out of bed, back when every kiss, every whisper triggered these flashes that connected me to bigger things. I couldn't remember the last time I'd felt this way with Meg.

"You get home all right?" she asked.

I closed my eyes.

"Yeah. Fine," I said. "Your friend Price. He left something on our back door last night. Do you think he knows, I mean, about—"

"Us?" she asked.

"Yeah. Us. Which was a mistake, Paulette."

"I knew you'd say that," she said.

"I want to see this guy."

"Let's talk first. Can you meet me this afternoon? At Cobb's Hill?"

"You'll have him there?" I asked.

"I think you ought to consider—"

"Then do it. I'll be there."

She told me when to meet her, and, when she hung up, I tapped the phone's plunger and finally went through my voicemail messages. One of the earliest ones, from the previous evening, was from Alec. He'd learned to call in and leave a message when his mother and I were both still at work and away from our phones. This time, I could hear the timid concern in his voice. *Will wants to go with me to Ignatius. My coach says it would be all right. I thought you'd want to know. They're going to let Will play on one of the teams next year, I think. See you tonight, Dad. This is the big one.*

I felt a thousand miles away from that voice. The fragile, unprotected sound of his words trapped in that machine seemed like a little taste of everything he'd face as an adult, the impersonality and silence of all this machinery and all these strangers. I wanted to go home and put my arms around him.

I continued through my voice mail and came up against another of the Phone Calls. There was silence for about half a minute, with bar sounds in the background, and finally he said: *Time you and I had a talk, Cuz. Don't call me, though. I keep trying. I'm sure you pick it up one a these times. You and me, we got some business to conduct. But I can wait.*

"Yeah, well, *I* can't," I said.

I dropped the phone into the cradle. I knew what I needed to do next. Once you get beyond a certain place, the fear drops away. Because once you move past that place, you don't care *what* happens.

Chapter 13

I walked along a side street, not far from City Hall, with my face down. Crossing at the light, I passed the parking lot on the corner, the OTB parlor, a bar, a Thai restaurant, a tobacco shop, and then I glanced casually through the front door into the interior dusk of the place I wanted. In the window, a large, handwritten bill advertised the sale price for a Model 60 Lady Smith snub-nosed pistol. I walked past a shoe-repair shop, a café, and another bar, looking over my shoulder to check how many people were out walking, trying to gauge how far away they would be if I turned, went back, and entered the shop. Would any of them recognize me?

Seeing other couples out for a noon walk, junior managers from Kodak headquarters, U.S. District Court bailiffs from the federal building, securities brokers from the Four Corners tower—the whole scene made me feel like someone emerging from a manhole. They were all there, on this early-spring day, running blameless errands, sunlight on their hair, lunch in their crumpled bags, snapshots of children in their wallets. Life *could* be good.

I turned and walked south along the same stretch of sidewalk. When I arrived at the entrance to the shop, I ducked through the door. It was a tiny place, where most customers arrived knowing exactly what they wanted. The only thing hanging on one wall was a poster with a cutaway drawing of a Beretta 92F, a sixteen-shot semiautomatic pistol. I didn't want to touch anything. The room seemed coated with some kind of residue, like the gray, oily soot from a grease fire.

I was captivated by the glass display counters. They reminded me of an expensive jewelry shop, all the product under locked glass, everything spread out on strips of dirty green velvet, handguns, and nothing but handguns, with the exception of two semiautomatic pistols converted into machine guns.

As I was looking at an unusually large weapon, with a carved grip in dark hardwood, the clerk emerged from behind a mirrored wall in the back. He entered the room without a word, a man of mixed race with a freckled-looking face. He was wearing a greenish-yellow silk shirt open at the collar, with black slacks. He had a trout's complexion and looked as if he swam regularly beneath the reach of sunlight and was now coming up for air. He stared at me, waiting, blinking occasionally. One eye looked at me and the other wandered. Then they seemed to switch roles, with the good one wandering. I wondered which was watching. Which eye did he aim with?

"I don't know exactly what I want," I said.

"Gun, right?"

I didn't know if he meant to sound like a wiseass. Maybe he

sold other instruments, other substances, in back, and this was some kind of essential, qualifying question.

"Yeah, a gun."

"Then you in the right place."

"Don't know which one."

"That happens," the clerk said, without moving away from the back wall.

I moved to the counter at his left, without touching it.

"I mean, what's the difference between the one and the other?"

"Well," the guy said, his left eye wobbling. "Size of the gun."

He wasn't making this any easier. He moved behind the counter and stood across the display case from me, looking down at the row of guns, one silver, one blue, another silver, another blue. He folded his arms and waited for my next question without moving, squinting and frowning.

"What's the size of that one?" I asked.

He said nothing, looking out the window. Maybe he needed to know my tax bracket, what kind of car I drove, what dental and disability plans I had, before he could bother to answer such blatantly stupid questions. Maybe he figured I was thinking out loud and the best thing to do was not to interrupt my train of thought.

"I mean, if we wanted to have one around the house, to protect the house, my wife was wondering, what would you say would be a good thing to get? As an example."

He looked at the display case and pointed to the one on the left.

"That little Colt, that's a police gun. Fit real nice under her pillow," he said.

"What's the difference between the silver and the blue?" I asked.

"All I know is, either one gone calm some homeboy's nerves real quick."

"What size is that one?" I asked, before I realized *size* wasn't the word I wanted. *Caliber* might have revealed I'd held a gun in my hands before. Nothing I'd said so far would have led him to think such a thing. He knew I had no idea what I was doing. I wanted *him* to do the talking, but he wasn't going to oblige. I didn't want to handle any of the guns. I certainly didn't want to *use* them. I wanted to *own* one. By purchasing a gun—without firing it—I hoped to go on with my life, the way someone goes to a doctor to hear him rule out cancer, without doing a biopsy, because even though his voice doesn't rid you of the pain or the potential tumor, you feel better having at least passed on the burden of anxiety to someone else. I could let the weapon worry for me. I wanted to load it and put it in my glove compartment and never touch it again.

Contrary to the impression I made on this clerk, I knew how to aim and shoot a gun. I'd gone to a gun club with a friend in middle school, when his father bought him a .22 rifle to give him some practice handling a firearm before he took him deer hunting in Pennsylvania. The two of us lay on the floor and aimed at little faded cardboard targets clipped to wires. I hid my targets, with their cluster of holes, in the living-room bookshelf, inside an edition of Shakespeare my mother quit reading in favor of T. S. Eliot and Flannery O'Connor and Dostoevsky. Sometimes I'd take out those targets and press my pinkie through the holes with little florets of torn cardboard sticking out the back.

"Got a permit?" he asked.

"No."

"No permit, no gun."

"How do I get one?" I asked.

"County clerk's office. Take six months."

"Six months?"

"That's right," he said.

"That's where you get a fishing license, right?" I asked.

"Couldn't tell ya, brother."

He'd probably done less than his fair share of fly casting on the Salmon River, probably wondering why a white guy from the suburbs would come window-shopping in this place. I saw doubt in his eyes, a slight edge of paranoia, as if maybe he thought I was a rookie undercover ATF agent putting him to the test.

"Got to fill out the forms. Shame, isn't it?" he asked. "Write your congressman, man."

"But six months? I need one of these now."

"I hear you, bro'. Nobody care about that, do they? Man out a luck he need a gat in a hurry."

I'd never get a gun in time to make a difference. I wasn't sure whether I felt frustrated or relieved.

"You have a permit, you can come in and carry one of these out the door?" I asked.

"Y'all don't have no sheet," he said.

"No felonies. Not yet, anyway."

"You young," he said, smiling. "Plenty a time for that, right?"

I chuckled nervously. I wanted to get out of this place, but instead I moved farther down the counter. It was unnaturally quiet, no music, only the muffled sound of a bus as it passed. Lifeless. There was no way to comprehend what was happening behind those dilated pupils, those little peepholes into his cranium.

"What about this one?" I asked, coming back to the big handgun with the carved wooden grip. He squatted and looked at the upside-down numbers on the end of the box: .357.

"That'll knock him right on his bootay," the clerk said.

"Clint Eastwood caliber."

"You got *that* right. Gat like that get you plenty respect."

We'd reached the end of the display counter and there was nowhere to go but out the door, unless I could come up with something else to say. In a gun shop, over the lunch hour, once you reached the end of the display counter, and especially if you lived in the suburbs and dressed the way I was dressed on this fine spring afternoon. As a last resort, I'd come prepared to suggest something illegal.

"No way to get around that six-month thing?" I asked. "Nobody can speed it up? Like I said, I've never been arrested."

"There's ways. Ways you get you ass busted," he said.

"Like what?"

He looked out at a city bus blowing exhaust as it waited for the light. Apparently he was lost in thought. I reached into my pocket and took out a sheet of paper folded twice into a square. I could see the denomination of the hundred-dollar bill through the thin paper. I placed my offering on the countertop.

"My permit's in there. I forgot," I said, feeling like a total ass. "Take a look, see if everything's in order."

The clerk gave me a long, level look of suspicion, caution, and avarice. Then, without even looking down to watch his own hand, he fingered the edge of the paper, wedging it open and lifting it enough to glance down for only a second, long enough to see the amount of my bribe. Then he let it sit. He motioned for me to follow him down to the other end of the counter—with the money right out in the open where I'd left it—and he scribbled something quickly onto an old Lotto stub and handed it to me.

"This guy help you out," he said.

He headed back toward the money, but it was still sitting on the counter when I walked out. As I went through the door, he called out to me: "When he ask, tell him Terrell."

"Thanks," I said.

It was a single-story motel in Gates, not far from the exit ramp. I always wondered who stayed in these cheap hourly rooms, aside from hookers and people fooling around on their spouses. The place was designed so you could discreetly pull up to your own door and park your car within ten heartbeats of the room itself, secluded enough from traffic to duck inside without being seen. I let my engine idle, parked near the edge of the blacktop, a hundred feet from the room number on the ticket.

It was depressing: the broken shutter on one of the bungalows, the crumpled blinds in the office window, the pickup truck with the NRA bumper sticker and the Copenhagen Tractor Pull Championship Finals logo and a University of Margaritaville decal. If there was anywhere in the world I didn't belong, it was here. I belonged in Paulette's apartment more than I belonged here.

As I sat in the car, I imagined what might happen if I went through with this. I'd knock. A man would ask, through the closed door, who'd sent me. I'd say Terrell. The door would open, and the motel-room merchant would be a small, grizzled man with a face like a dried chamois. The odor of something odd in that room, dry dog food or French fries, would be hard to identify and hard to take. He might be sporting a large Chinese dragon tattoo that ended discreetly several inches above his wrist.

On the bed would be a large leather case, and when he opened it, all the samples would be wired in place, or maybe held by leather restraints. He'd remove one after the other of the weapons, hand them to me and ask how they felt. He wouldn't overdo the patter about range and muzzle velocity. I would pick a midcaliber revolver and ask how much it cost. Then I would reach into my envelope of hundreds and fifties and select the amount, rounding it up to the nearest fifty. On my way out, I'd ask for a box of shells, and that would be it. Unless we had a little heart-to-heart closing conversation about the Dutch tulip mania or the indomitable Dow Jones industrial average or Hegel's theory of dialectic materialism. Nothing to it. *Jesus Christ, Rich. You've got to be kidding.*

I shut off the engine, reached around to press down all the locks, and, resting my fingertips on the door latch, glanced back at the onrushing traffic. As I reached to turn off the radio, the announcer said: *For VCR repairs that won't take a bite out of your bank account, come to Burgess Electronics.* The word *Burgess* nagged me. It was the street where Wes lived in the city. How could I have forgotten about Wes? After a street fight a block away from his house at three a.m., and two weeks after a pair of killings five blocks away, he bought a home security system, a can of Mace, a rape whistle, two deadbolt locks, a maladjusted Doberman, and a pistol.

I drove for several miles looking for a phone booth before I finally glanced down and remembered I had the car phone now. It was one of those rare moments when I remembered to use it before the need had passed. Wes was still at work when I reached him.

"Still have that gun?" I asked.

"Why?"

"Ever used it?"

"Few times on the dog," he said.

"Ah, the limp."

"No. That's when I ran over him with the car," he said. "Now *that* was an accident."

"So you said."

"What's up?" he asked.

"Can I borrow it?"

"The gun?"

"No, the *dog*."

"Long as you promise not to use it on Sorley," he said.

"What's he up to now?"

"What else? Spy versus Spy all over again. He called me from this cellular phone he's got in the 911 now. Told me to go into his e-mail account and unsend something he shot off to Penny this morning. I checked. She hadn't read it yet."

"Wha'd it say?" I asked.

"You don't want to know."

"What?" I asked.

"He was trying to load this whole thing off onto you."

I sighed loudly into the phone and shook my head. "He's got to stop drinking."

"A gun, huh?"

"I'll get it right back to you," I said. "You mind?"

"Like, right now?"

"Well, I mean, what're you doing? Can you get away?"

"You serious?" he asked.

"For a little while, you know?" I said. "Somebody tried to break in last night. Would make Meg feel better. I mean, until I can get a permit."

"This about that McDonald's thing?"

"Meg's spooked."

"Tell you the truth, I'm not sure I remember where I put the damn thing," he said.

"Until we can get an alarm system installed," I said.

"I'm, like, in the middle of a sentence here," he said.

"Won't take long. You don't live far from the office, do you?"

"Make it quick," he said.

"One other thing."

"Yeah?" he asked.

"You got any shells?"

■

We didn't talk about the gun as he searched the junk drawers in his kitchen and then up in his bedroom, and finally behind the headboard of his queen-size bed. It was hanging in a holster behind his wife's pillow. He talked about other things. He told me how, the night before, he'd realized the comedian Bill Maher looked like he'd been separated at birth from Buddy Hackett and, then, how some guy on the Comedy Channel went to Hanoi and got a group of women in some public square to exercise along with a Jane Fonda videotape: he had the television and VCR all set up on a park bench. When Fonda told her attentive Vietnamese students to turn to the right, the comedian said, "*I'll* say she turned to the right." Wes was using all of this conversation, as usual, to distract us from what we were doing. He looked a little rattled. I think my urgency bothered him more than actually loaning me the gun.

It looked like the snub-nosed models I remembered from *The Untouchables* and other film versions of Prohibition high jinks. He handed it to me to see if I liked the feel of it. I raised it up to my nose, but there wasn't even a trace of gunpowder smell, and it wasn't pearl-handled. The dark-grained wooden grip fit perfectly in my palm.

"Good solid six-shooter," I said, holding the gun at a safe distance from my face.

"Five," he said.

"Five?"

Then I glanced at the side of the gun and saw the name engraved into the gray metal: Lady Smith.

"Are you kidding me?" I asked.

"Model 60. Got it on sale."

"It must *always* be on sale," I said.

"Huh?"

"Never mind," I said.

"Hey, I don't care what it's called. It's still a .38 caliber. I was in the same fix. Kim's the one who wanted it," he said. "Where I got it, they said a lot of guys carry this one. It's lightweight and it leaves as big a hole as any other .38. That little Swiss Army knife I've got? It's a woman's model. I like it better. It doesn't have the toothpick. Who needs the toothpick?"

"Does this come with a toothpick?" I asked.

"Little nail polish brush in the stock."

"What's this thingie?" I asked. It was a little cap, a hood, barely big enough to fit over the gun's hammer. It looked like a thimble you'd slip over the mouth of an especially territorial Bedford Stuyvesant cockroach.

"That's to keep the gun from snagging on your bra strap," he said, grinning.

I glared at him.

"Seriously. You're supposed to wear the thing close to your body. It'll always be under your clothes, even though it's illegal to carry it that way. You don't see too many people wearing these out on their hip. Here's the holster. Fits right under your arm."

"That's illegal, right?" I said.

"Illegal?" he said. "Not having a license is worse than concealing the thing."

"It isn't loaded, is it?"

"I think *so*," he said, taking the gun, checking and then tilting the gun until three shells fell into his palm. He didn't have kids.

He took hold of my arm.

"You sure you want this?" he asked.

"I'll give it back," I said. "Just give me a couple days."

"That isn't what I mean."

"I know what you mean. Yeah, I want it."

Chapter 14

Paulette brought a dog with her, a big friendly blond lab, and she let it climb in back when she got into the passenger seat. She hardly spoke as she pointed for me to pull around to the other end of the reservoir. We locked the Grand Am, and she led me and the dog into the woods. She said it was Price's dog, and he'd left it with her. I'd brought the gun with me, slipped behind my belt, under a baggy golf shirt with a Players Championship logo, and we descended into Washington's Grove, a little wooded park with hiking trails and hills and hollows and spots where kids built campfires in the summer and drank forty-ounce beers. I'd jogged through those trails, back when I was jogging, thinking Boo Radley thoughts, watching the leaves fall. Every trail circled around on itself so that you could never really get lost.

Then the dog got loose, and Paulette chased him down the path, yelling for me to follow. The dog was as good as deaf, and fast. As I ran, I tripped over an exposed root and went facefirst into the underbrush. My forehead was bleeding as I climbed back to my feet and tried to catch up, practically choking by the time I went down the other side, trying not to slide off into the leaves on the downslope, finally spotting Paulette through the foliage. The trail opened up to a cul-de-sac on the far side, where she'd caught up with the dog and had his leash back in hand. She was getting into a Dodge Intrepid—an unmistakable rental—parked in the cul-de-sac. As I emerged from the woods, she backed the car up and opened the passenger door.

She took side streets to East Avenue, driving toward the city, pulling in behind an apartment complex on East Avenue, not far from where Whit Sutherland lived. Around back, she parked beside the Range Rover. She rolled her window down an inch and left the dog in the car.

"We be back, honey," she said. "Now you just lie down and behave."

The Rover looked as messy as Jimmy Sorley's apartment. The unmistakable sign of a man who answered only to himself, a man who didn't have to clean up. I saw magazines and newspapers strewn around in the rear. As we pulled back out onto East Avenue, I checked out the little piles of periodicals: *Money*, *Forbes*, *Business Week*, and "The Pink Sheet Bulletin." There were *Wall Street Journals*, with big empty blocks of space where someone had clipped stories from the front pages.

At my feet, on the floor, I found a scrapbook with cheap square pages. Inside were taped magazine and newspaper articles. I skimmed through the headlines: *dow breaks four thousand*, *yen declines against dollar*, *interest rates hit all-time low*, *income distribu-*

tion favors top 5 percent, first-time starter homes harder to buy even for two-income families, and *profits rise dramatically as corporations cut more jobs.*

"Is this Price's car?"

"Yeah, it's GP's."

"Where we going?" I asked.

"Somewhere we can talk," she said.

"Price will be there?"

"Relax," she said.

Paulette drove north toward Ontario Beach. We found a secluded road into the park, winding uphill to a sheltered group of picnic tables. Paulette kept checking the mirror, watching as other cars passed. Several drove back and forth on the road, one of them about five times. The drivers kept looking over at us, as if we'd stumbled into some kind of situation where this particular spot would soon be urgently needed for something I wouldn't want to know about. It was possible Bogardus or someone else was having both of us followed, too, but I didn't think they'd be so obvious about it. At one point, a low-rider pulled up and idled a couple car lengths in front of the Range Rover.

"This place has changed," I said. "I used to take the kids on walks around the pond."

"Let's go out on the beach. It's warm enough," she said.

"Is he going to be there? I want to talk to this guy, Paulette."

"Be patient. *We* need to talk."

The driver of the low-rider smoked a cigarette with his booming stereo turned up as we maneuvered around him and drove deeper into the woods and then out, crossing the highway, and parked at the beach. Lake Ontario was gorgeous in the morning light, a freighter far off near the horizon, the sunlight flashing on the chop. As we got near the water, Paulette took my hand, intertwining her fingers with mine. It felt perfectly natural. I could have spent days doing this, the sound of the gulls above us, the scent of the water, the seaweedy breeze. We walked maybe a quarter of a mile, past an area under construction, a big bunker of soil and sand, bulldozed into what looked like a levee, surrounded by orange tape, like the kind used to quarantine a crime scene.

Along the beach, she paused a moment to watch a mother with two toddlers walking along the water; the mother—dark hair, jeans, red sweater—looked lost in thought, but never seemed to let the children get more than ten or fifteen feet away. I didn't realize Paulette had stopped to watch the little threesome, and I had to walk back to where she stood. When I got close to her, she looked toward me, smiling, and then we continued on.

We found a secluded little patch of sand surrounded by willows and tall grass. As we talked, something about Paulette's face, the sound of her voice, the way she walked—it all worked on my nerves like a painkiller.

"Is he waiting for us down here?"

"He's leaving town soon," she said.

"And?"

"What I mean is, you don't have to see him," she said.

"Then why's he keep calling me?"

"Because he wants to meet *you.*"

"What am I? His class *project?*" I asked.

"You want to see him, I'll take you there, right now. But I want you to think about it. You can just wait it out. That's all I'm gone say."

"I won't feel right if I don't get this thing square with him. He'll never leave me alone if we don't get this straightened out. I'm sure of it."

"Maybe. Maybe not," she said.

She looked out across the water.

"I like you," she said. "You never do what I expect you to do. You look like a good father. Got a decent job."

"People getting laid off left and right everywhere. You take whatever they give you because you've got that pink slip hanging over your head."

"Everybody got something hang over them," she said.

"You feel that way too?"

"Till I meet GP. Only man I know got a plan."

"You don't seem the type. To be with him," I said. "You in love with him?"

She looked out at the water and smiled, glancing at me and then toward the water again.

"He's smart. Smarter'n *you* from the look of it," she said, smiling, putting me on.

"That doesn't exactly distinguish him. A lot of people fit that description."

"See. That's what I mean. I like when you say things like that. Don't nobody I know say things like that. With you, it's a whole different thing, way you say things."

She leaned over and pulled my head down as she kissed me, and I drew away, but then relaxed and let it happen, until we were stretched out on the sand and I could feel the length of her body alongside mine, our legs intertwined. It was happening all over again. This wasn't the place. I tried to hold back, but every contour and surface seemed to give and move beneath my hands and arms and legs. I kissed her harder and ran my hand under the sweater, her breasts firm under the blouse, her chest rising and falling as she breathed harder. What was it? Why did she respond to me this way? I hadn't felt this way for years, the liftoff and flight, the intoxication of it, everything about her—the color of her eyes, the sound of her little groans—made me hard and fierce, grabbing her wrists and holding them tight in one hand, high above her head, so that her back arched. The gulls screeched overhead. Then I pulled away and rolled onto my back, listening to her breathe. I felt the gun behind my belt, under my shirt. I wondered if *she'd* felt it.

"You sure you want to meet GP?" she asked.

The only thing I wanted was to *do* something to lessen the pressure, to act, to *confront* my life.

"I just wanted you to think about it before you go see him. GP can be persuasive. Once you go to see him, something in you gone change."

"Let's go. I've got my son's basketball game I want to get to. I just want this guy out of my life."

She drove us downtown, and parked in the South Avenue ramp, a short walk to the back entrance into the Hyatt. I still had the handgun behind my belt, under the tail of my untucked golf shirt. It was digging a permanent imprint into my stomach.

"Nicest place in town," I said. "Figures."

"Only the best for GP."

We got out of the car and then rode the elevator up to the hotel's garage entrance, got off, walked down the posh hallway, and then directly into another open elevator door off the lobby. Within minutes, we were walking through the door of a corner suite in the most expensive hotel in the city.

"Is he supposed to meet us here?" I asked.

"That's right."

Inside, it seemed more like an apartment than a hotel room. A minibar and a Stickley couch, and a bedroom off to the side, three telephones, and two televisions. Paulette immediately turned on the one in the sitting room, clicking until she got MTV. I looked at my watch, marking time until Alec's Hot Shots competition.

It was twilight outside, the days still short, people everywhere locking up their doors and windows for the evening, ready for whatever shows they usually watched on this particular week-night, *Frasier* or *Home Improvement* or some "def comedy jam" on HBO.

"I be right back," Paulette said.

As she went into the bedroom, I sat on the couch, watching a Smashing Pumpkins video. I heard movement again and turned to see if Paulette had changed already. Two men emerged from the bedroom and walked slowly around the armchair, the tall, bony one taking a seat on the edge of the coffee table, not even looking at me, and the larger one, the one I remembered from the Range Rover, sitting across from me in the armchair. It was Eugene Price. I remembered the shape of his shoulders as he came into the McDonald's, the way he walked with one shoulder slightly lower than the other. *Who you guys think you are?* He must have thought I was out of my mind.

"What up, Cuz?" he asked.

I extended my hand, and held it in the air, but he refused to shake it. I let it drop. He wore a silk shirt with a tab collar under a crisp black blazer, a sort of clerical look, with sharkskin trousers and black brogans. He was wearing the Oakley sunglasses again: thermonuclear protection.

Price was large, with a regulation NFL neck, almost wider than his skull. I imagined sliding a pair of calipers down the sides of his head until it nudged up against those neck muscles. He'd had his hair shaved so close around the sides that you could see that nose tackle's crease of skin high up on the skull, the flesh bunching up into a fold, all that neck muscle with nowhere else to go but up. Finally, I got a close look at the other one, tall and gaunt, with one of those grunge knit ski caps with flaps and ties hanging down each side. His neck looked considerably skinnier than Price's, with his head bobbing around when he got excited. He looked to me the way I imagined a crack baby would look if it got rationed enough vitamins and mood stabilizers to make it to adulthood. He was painfully thin, with a long, ragged jacket over a black Georgetown University sweatshirt and a pair of big, ballooning warm-up pants. You could see little, significant hatch marks shaved into the stubble above the ears, the White Sox logo peeking out from under the cap. And through his sweatshirt, from underneath, the bas-relief of the Mercedes hood ornament.

"DeWitt. Turn it down," Price said.

Instead, DeWitt got up, unlocked the minibar and took out two miniature bottles of brandy and a Heineken. Downing the cognac in three swallows, he plopped himself into an armchair and clicked open the beer can, suddenly bewildered by the Smashing Pumpkins video. "What *is* this bullshit?" he mumbled.

"Paulette?" Price called. "Get out here."

He waited a few seconds, and then said to me, "You got to excuse me." He got up and disappeared into the bathroom as Paulette finally emerged, dressed in sweats now and sneakers. She no longer seemed aware of me, biting her nails, sitting on the couch, her eyes on the television, though nothing appeared to register. The lines of her face were still as beautiful as ever, but she looked more lifelike than alive. Price came back into the living room, the sound of the toilet refilling behind him. I wanted to make a trip in there myself. As he came in, Price flicked a light switch inside the door, flooding the room with lamplight, making his second entrance with no less authority than he would have enjoyed on a suddenly illuminated proscenium.

This time, he was carrying a fat red candle and a Bic cigarette lighter, and a small greasy brown lunch bag, rolled up at the top. He placed all three objects on the table beside me, glanced at me, and then took a seat on the couch beside Paulette, saying nothing. He was heavier than I remembered though not quite as tall. He could stand there and look like a big chunk of something blocking a road somewhere, blasted out of a rock face to make way for a tunnel. I opened the bag: a cold hamburger and congealed fries. I thanked him but told him I wasn't hungry. On the music video the singer screamed, *Despite all my rage, I'm still just a rat in a cage.*

"I could use the bathroom, if you guys wouldn't mind," I said.

Price didn't react to this. Didn't say yes or no. He just kept studying me. The question was, should I get up or stay put? What would Letitia Baldridge suggest? Or Emily Post? All those authorities on proper social behavior I'd studied secretly in college. I could imagine Ann Landers in the morning paper: "An advertising executive, one R. Cahill, from Rochester, N.Y., asks: *How, exactly, in a potentially life-threatening urban standoff, should a gentleman from the suburbs such as myself indicate his need to visit the bathroom?* Well, in situations such as these, one must be cautious, Mr. Cahill. I think maybe the best policy would be to wait as long as you possibly can and then pray to Jesus to save your sorry white ass, you poor stupid son of a bitch. Who the hell do you think you are, getting involved with these people? You also ask: *At what point, once a person is snugly situated in the bathroom, might he appropriately pull out his best friend's .38 pistol and emerge with the intention of winning new friends and influencing key people in the living room?* Forget the gun. Do not, I repeat, do not deliberate on any of this. It will only make you feel helpless and small and infinitely more entomological than you already feel, considering everything else your life is putting you through at the moment. By all means, stick with your strengths. In other words, keep smiling.

"He won't do what you want, GP," Paulette said. "He just wants you to leave him alone."

"You want me to be quiet? Is that what this is all about? No problem," I said.

"It ain't what I *want*, Cuz. It's what you can *get*," Price said. "How much you worth? Net worth?"

I hesitated. I'd never thought about it, never added up all the separate assets. But then rattled off the numbers, and, as I did, realized it didn't amount to much: mutual funds, 401(k), equity in the house, checking account. A pathetic sum.

"Right. You get it in tens, you ain't got enough to wipe you ass from now to the day you die. You got investments? You got, what, some CDs? Got an IRA? Got that retirement all planned out already?"

"I'm not driving a Range Rover, if that's what you mean."

"You *could* be, Cuz," he said.

"What I'd really like is to go to the bathroom," I said.

"Let him go, GP," Paulette said. "Go on, Rich."

It was the first time I heard her utter my name. Even in bed with me, she'd never called out my name. Her voice had changed since they came into the room. I wondered if she'd ever thought I might be some kind of serious alternative to Price. This didn't appear to be the case.

"Shut up," Price said.

I winced.

"Don't talk to me like I'm somebody's bitch. I ain't nobody's bitch. Ain't even a G yet."

"Yeah, well, you gone be. Either you in or you out. You in, and we head outta here. You out, and you never see me again," he said, and then turned to DeWitt. "Go get it."

DeWitt moved across the room and into the bedroom. While keeping his eye on me, Price leaned forward and picked up the candle and the lighter; he lit the fresh white wick and tilted the candle sideways, letting enough wax melt to make the flame brighten, the wax dripping directly onto the carpet at his feet. There was something thrilling about it, watching him ruin that carpet without a second thought, not worried about the consequences of anything he did. I'd never once felt that way about anything, especially a length of carpet like that. I looked from the candle to his face, back and forth, and I saw something in that face I'd never seen before, a look of what seemed absolute fearlessness, as if he just didn't care the way other people cared, as if he'd achieved the sort of liberation I imagined my mother sought in her retreats upstate, but through completely different means.

As DeWitt came back into the room with a long, bent wire clothes hanger in his hand, he looked over his shoulder at their bickering and smiled, as if this were one experience in life he'd been fortunate enough to miss. I tried to meet his gaze as it came back around on its way to the television, but his face went rigid as he saw me smiling with him. He stood beside the couch, waiting for word from Price.

"And I still haven't made up my mind," Paulette said.

"Yeah, well, I made up you mind, 'cause I got no time for this. Most bitches on they own be decided by now. Talk about, dinner this and dinner that. You always like this. I's aside the car half an hour waitin' on you, last time we ever went anywhere. Y'all slow me down," Price said. He was beginning to sound like a husband, and it all seemed at least categorically familiar. Price glanced over at DeWitt and then turned back to Paulette, "Now's my turn to slow *you* down. Go sit in that chair by the desk. Pull that chair over here, DeWitt."

She got up slowly and moved toward the high-backed desk chair. "I decide my ownself what I gone do."

"Sit down," he told her, without getting up from the couch. "Sit in it like this. You arms on the back."

DeWitt had come over to the coffee table, extending the metal hanger's bent tip into the flame. From where I stood I could see the little circular tip, tiny pieces of smaller wire welded together to form a sphere with four spokes in the middle, twisted into the shape of a pitchfork enclosed in a circle. Paulette refused to watch, keeping her arms crossed in front of her, facing toward Price. She tugged the fabric to reveal more of her shoulder, and she held the blouse down, staring at the carpet with a grim look in her eyes. When I glanced over at DeWitt, I saw the tip of the brand glowing orange as he brought it over to where she sat. I dug my fingernails into my palms. I knew I'd need to visit the bathroom in the next three minutes, or they would see a grown man wet himself, which, as far as I knew, may have been one of their objectives for the evening.

"How can you do this?" I asked.

Price got up deliberately and stood over me, without taking off his sunglasses.

He moved away, sat on the couch again and nodded toward DeWitt. "Get busy."

DeWitt thrust the brand back into the flame, and it turned orange almost immediately. He moved quickly over to Paulette, and she hunched over the chair backward, holding one hand over her eyes and gripping her forearm tight with the other hand, as if to hold it steady. DeWitt quickly lowered the brand onto the pale brown skin of her back, above where her bra strap would've been if she'd been wearing one, which she never did, and she flinched, jerking forward, so the brand fell away from her skin. The orange glow was completely gone. There was no way to tell from looking at it how hot it was. Slowly the room filled with a repellent scent, like burning hair.

I turned away and held my breath, but I couldn't wait it out. The odor hung in the room. DeWitt pressed the brand back onto the mark he'd already made and held it one, two, three seconds before he pulled it away, and this time Paulette gave out a little lovemaking kind of cry as she sat perfectly still, biting her lower lip. Then DeWitt pulled the brand away from her back and took two steps away from the table, holding the wire in both hands, waiting for her to straighten up.

"You all right?" Price asked quietly.

Paulette sat up and opened her eyes and nodded as she pulled her blouse up. She was smiling. Before she covered it, the burn was already raised, swollen and paler than the skin around it. Just looking at it turned my stomach. But underneath the horror, there was something else. A small, insistent thrill. She belonged. She was a member. She'd moved through to the other side. Making love made her cry. This made her smile. She had the power of that group within her now.

"Can I use the bathroom?" I asked.

"Come over here," Price said, taking out his gun again and laying it on the cushion beside him, without having to hold it, just making his point. Or maybe simply to show he was disarmed. "Have a seat."

Everything seemed to happen in some kind of dreamscape, one of those worlds or streets or staircase-ridden houses you infiltrate repeatedly in sleep, year after year, as familiar and real as anything you've known while awake. I thought of Dana when she was a preschooler, squealing with delight when she heard me open the back door and come home from a long day at work. I thought of Alec, looking up into the scuffed gymnasium grandstands to see me watch him play. I thought of Meg, in Toronto, the paintings, the ring, the *yes*. Is this what she'd said yes to?

"One little trip over there. That's all I need," I said. "Then you have my full attention."

"I got you full attention," Price said.

"Two minutes in there. That's all I need."

"You don't have any idea what you need. I know things you ain't never dream of. I live or die it's all the same to me. Once you know it ain't no different alive or dead, then you got the edge. 'Cause then you got no fear. You don't know what *life* is until you not afraid to die."

He stood and walked away from the coffee table and came back, as if he had to cross the room to collect his next few thoughts and bring them back to me.

"See, *you* the nigger. But you don't understand that."

"Nigger this and nigger that. I don't get it. How can you people talk that way?" I asked.

" 'You people'?" he asked.

"That's right."

"You one of us *people*, Cuz. I see that the minute you say, *Who you think you are?* You, down there on the floor, ready to spit in my face. You more a nigger than anybody in this room. You a nigger to the woman run that company. To the man run the IRS and the police and General Motors and the television network. Know what? I got a piece a them. Which means I got a piece a you. This country, you got no choice, 'cause they make sure you a nigger, no matter who you are, what color skin you got."

Price looked at DeWitt, who had the twisted wire back in the candleflame, heating it. Finally, he looked up at Price, who'd grown silent in thought. All of us looked toward Price, waiting for him to go on.

"Saw my own baby brother beat up, killed on my front lawn. Detroit. Fourteen years was all he got. Out one night cops spot him walkin' home, think he be the homey kill some bitch three blocks over, 'cause he black. Bring him back home in they squad car. Put him in a coma right there on the grass, my mama watch the whole thing and I got to watch her watch it."

He paused and then continued.

"Once I got past the urge to burn the city, I decide to do what I'm doing now. Lot a ways to get even."

"Word, GP," DeWitt said, a grin leaking onto his face. He leered at me as if he expected Price's words to inject some long-overdue and righteous pain into my white soul. I was thinking mostly about my daddy.

"As if what you're doing is political," I said.

"It is. But I ain't out there burnin' down City Hall, now am I?"

"Looks to me like you've gone Republican. It's all just money to you, isn't it?"

"What I learn is, you got to set up you *own* rules. What I do, I spend eight years, build up my business, and I manage not to fade but three people in those eight years. And that's only because they like to fade me first. But now I'm just this nigger got to run and hide, just like always, like all those eight years just disappear. Don't have to tell *you* how that feels."

DeWitt moved closer to me but Price raised a hand and waved him away, turning back to face me.

"I know it's time to get out six months ago, but Polette, she want to stay. Then Polette talk about, I got to watch Will because DeWitt tell Will this the way he get quoted, stick up that McDonald's. Understand? And I say fine, cause DeWitt, he gone take over for me here, let me move on to other things."

"You did it to look out for Will 'cause I ask you to," Paulette said.

"Wha'd I just say, huh?" he snapped at her, then turned back to me. "Then that old man die. So we got to leave town sooner than we thought. One last little pickup tonight is all."

"Pickup?" I asked.

"I tell you all about it. First, we got to get *you* quoted."

"I'd just as soon—"

"Know what you don't know yet?" he asked.

"What?"

"I die tomorrow, I still be more alive than you *ever* know," he said. "Let's get busy."

He pulled his sunglasses up so I could see his eyes. Intelligent eyes. The eyes of somebody who could imagine himself in someone else's seat and picture it, feel it. He *did* feel things, after all. I recognized him now. He *was* the man I saw in the BMW reading the business page, when I went into the McDonald's. The one who came through the door at the end and cleaned up and leaned down to whisper in my ear: *What did you say?*

"Where you want it?"

"I don't *want* anything," I said.

"Yeah, well, we see about *that.* Show me you shoulder, then," he said without taking his eyes off my face, intent on seeing every expression that darted though my eyes. He couldn't miss my hands trembling. I was so numb by now, I couldn't *feel* them trembling, but if I looked down I could see it. When I glanced at the table, it looked as if my fingers were jumping. I grabbed my left shirtsleeve and shoved it up to expose my arm all the way to the shoulder.

As the brand dug into my flesh, like a cluster of hornets, I felt my pants grow warm and wet, and then with all the effort I could manage I made it stop, but not before I felt it soak across the top of my legs. From the corner of my eye, I saw DeWitt grinning at me.

The walls seemed to turn a filthy avocado and then lighten up, darken, lighten up, and the boomerang patterns in the rug spun outward and returned, disappearing into the kaleidoscopic flashing around the edges of my vision. I wondered if I would stay conscious, and realized I was gasping for breath, and I clamped my teeth together and held my breath, struggling to hold back the dizziness and nausea. I didn't know how Paulette stayed composed. And then everything seemed to ease a bit, and Price watched my face, having nudged the sunglasses up on his nose again, hiding his eyes.

"We all done. Bathroom's back there. Look like you already got a head start," Price said. DeWitt grinned again.

I locked the bathroom door and did my business, which seemed to require several minutes, and then I leaned back against the wall, sliding down until I was sitting on the floor, with fresh towels hanging over one shoulder. I felt for the gun: it was still there. I could hardly keep from pulling it out. On my way down to the floor, I looked at myself in the mirror, hair stuck to a crust of blood on my forehead, dirt smudged on my cheeks, the swelling around my eye from my fall in the woods, my shirttail half out and half in.

As I turned the knob, the door smacked my forehead, knocking me back, and my head banged against the tile floor and rested against the toilet. DeWitt grabbed my ankles and dragged me out of the bathroom, and then yanked me up by my shirt, ripping the fabric, his own gun in his hand now, the muzzle resting against the bone behind my left ear. I let it happen, coiling up into myself, but I was waiting, ready to uncoil, feeling the surge of energy already through my heart and muscles, the countdown to what I knew I was going to do. The gun was still under my shirt, pressing into my skin. As I got up from the floor, I pulled it out, aiming the stubby barrel directly at Price's mouth. All mirth leaked from his face, but he didn't look worried. Angry, impatient, frustrated, maybe, like a man's expression when he gets bumped off a flight, but not worried exactly, not concerned, not fearful. Then amused at the way my hands were shaking.

"I'm going to leave. And I'm not ever going to hear from any of you again. Understand? No more. This is as far as it goes."

"Hey, DeWitt," Price said, starting to smile. "That little gun you always want. For you purse."

DeWitt cackled again.

"Maybe he let you try it out."

"Didn't you hear me? I'm talking to *you*," I said, pushing the muzzle within an inch of his cheek.

"Back off, Cuz," he said, his face turning cold and hard. "I mean it. Back off."

I pulled the gun away from his face, but kept it trained on him. He relaxed and the good humor returned. He pointed toward his own gun, resting on the couch.

"You need a *real* gun. Go on. Have mine," he said. "DeWitt. Give him his advance."

"Now?" DeWitt asked. "Sure you don't want me to just shoot him?"

"I don't want to say it twice," he said.

"Sheeit, GP. You gone soft, let some crazy-ass white bitch get away with somethin' like this," DeWitt said, starting to reach into his jacket.

I shouted at him: "Stop! Paulette, take it out slowly. Let me see it."

She stepped over to DeWitt, who spread his arms wide, and reached inside his jacket and removed the wrapped package about the size and half the thickness of a brick. It looked like a perfectly cut chunk of tofu wrapped in butcher's paper. She placed it on the table beside me and stood back.

"It's an advance," Price said. "Go on. Take a look. It's all yours."

I picked up the package and pulled it open. It was a stack of fifties. From the thickness of it, it must have been five thousand dollars.

"Go back to you car now," Price said. "You say you got to get to that basketball game. You take that money. After the game, you bring it back or you keep it. You keep it, you got to do little job for me. And I pay you the rest. Another five. And that's only the start."

The nature of the whole situation had changed so radically, so abruptly—my understanding of what Price wanted from me undergoing such an about-face—I had to fight not to feel overwhelmingly grateful to him for everything he'd just done to me.

He wanted to pay me for my cooperation. Apparently, this is how he hired people. I lowered the gun and sat down.

"You think I really need a few thousand dollars this badly?"

"How much *do* you need?" he asked.

How much did I need? It seemed no one had ever asked me this. It was startling to hear him ask it that way, not as a taunt, not with any sarcasm, but in a voice I'd never heard from my employer: a genuine curiosity about what I required to live the way I wanted to live, to get what I felt was coming to me. How much did I need? I needed enough to start building a future: a good home, an education for my children, money for my retirement, a car less than three years old. I didn't want luxuries. I needed my share, not just what the people who had power over me could afford to give me and still keep me productive. I needed more than he would ever give me.

"Right now? What do I need? I could use about twenty thousand dollars," I said. "So I appreciate the offer, but I think we're done talking, aren't we? I want to go now. Keep your money."

"DeWitt," Price said. "Add another five to it."

"Five?" DeWitt said. "GP! Are you—"

"You heard me. Go on," Price said, as DeWitt slunk from the room, giving me a look of stifled outrage, and returning from the bedroom with a larger stack of bills, setting it on the envelope. Price looked over at me. "That makes ten. Another ten if you go through with it. This here's the ten you take. That's just thinkin'-about-it money."

"Ten thousand?" I asked. "Are you serious?"

"I could use somebody like you tonight, Cuz," he said.

"What if all I want is to get you out of my life?"

"You take that money, then go to see you boy," he said, looking at his watch. "Then call me. I pick you up, you do the job, I give you another ten. That makes twenty."

"Twenty thousand?" I asked. "You kidding? You can hire people to *kill* somebody for less than that."

I looked at him, wondering.

"Nothing like that, Cuz. Just one night's easy work."

"One night? And then you're done with me and I'm done with you?"

"That be up to you," he said.

Twenty thousand. Seven or eight for each college fund. Five to add to our 401(k). Or a nest egg to get me started in business for myself, join Wes if he left the agency and do it on our own.

"What is it you want me to do?"

"Be down with you homeys. That's all."

"Let's go," I said. "The basketball's already half over by now."

At Cobb's Hill, Price handed me a matchbook with a phone number marked on the inside of the lid. I reached over and put both the gun and the stack of money in the glove box. I tried to focus on getting to Alec's game. I was sure I'd missed his turn at shooting. He was high in the standings now, and he'd be one of the Hot Shots starters.

I kept translating that ten thousand into the things it would bring me. I felt the heat of it, the way you can feel an act of revenge warming itself up, some angry recompense for all the things done to you. You feel it in your muscles, the anticipation, the constriction in your stomach.

I was trembling, and my arm felt as if someone had taken a scalpel to it. On the way to the gym, my life hollowed out. Nothing hung together. In front of me, green numbers circled a wagging red needle. What were they for? Memories and sensations pricked me at random. Streetlights hung their heads. I remembered my mother wore square-toed shoes and stretched out flat on her stomach in church to pray. I remembered at

Christmas she had me bite into a garlic clove dipped in honey. Opposites fused into one flavor. She wouldn't recognize me now. She wouldn't want to.

I couldn't remember my own mother's face. I hardly recognized my eyes in the mirror. My tongue was numb. At the horizon, the sky ripped itself from the earth. I sat inside a strange car, a ghost inside a stranger's body, or a memory of myself inside a stranger's ghost. I couldn't touch what *real* meant anymore. I couldn't *feel* anything. *Let me stay together. Let me get through this, please, for Alec's sake. For Dana's sake. I'm not like this. This isn't me. It'll be me again tomorrow.*

At the school, I parked in the cul-de-sac. I knew I needed to go inside and impersonate the individual I'd worked my whole life to become. There was no hiding tonight, no escape, from the people who would see me here. *Whenever a gentleman attends any social occasion with dried blood on his brow, his hair oily with fear, and his shirt ripped from fleeing through the woods with an urban criminal's accomplice, it's best to stay near the back of the crowd, especially if other family members will be present.*

I removed my golf shirt, leaving only my gray University of Rochester T-shirt, soaked under the armpits. At least it wasn't torn. I checked my watch. There was still time left. I got out of the car. I put one foot in front of the other, back and forth, left and right, up the steps, through the door—learning how to walk again—down the empty hall. In the dark trophy case, I could see my bruised reflection.

I headed slowly into that packed, painfully lit-up gym. It was all I could do to wedge myself into the throng of parents standing inside the door. All those people waiting, watching. I imagined Alec scanning their ranks again and again, waiting and hoping to see my face. Slowly, I pushed my way past one person and then another, getting first annoyed and then startled looks, trying to get far enough forward for Alec to see me as he moved onto the court. My eye was swollen half-shut, and many of the parents, some of whom I recognized, looked at me with confusion and disapproval.

Alec was coming out of the stands. He rubbed his hands on Will's head—Will sat on the bottom bench—for good luck. Will smiled and grabbed Alec from behind and flipped him over his shoulder, so that Alec landed perfectly on his feet on the shining floor, and he jogged up to the free-throw line and took the basketball from the coach, waiting for the starting whistle.

I moved from behind several taller men and a small boy with a T-shirt that said NO BLOOD, NO FOUL, until finally I stood in front, where Alec could see me before he started shooting. I was as scared of seeing the look on his face as I was eager to make eye contact with him. I raised my hand into the air, like a rear-row student wanting to get picked, and I waved, again and again, as Alec took one last, quick look around the gym before the whistle. For one brief moment, I caught his attention, and he smiled with recognition, just as the whistle blew.

When Alec tossed the ball for his first shot, I could tell, before it left his hands, it would swish through the net without touching the rim. He moved to the outer lines and tossed the ball again. Again, net. *Yes!* And then again. *Yes!* Then one-point layups, again and again, then from farther away, bounce and spin and in. *Yes!* And then back outside the three-point line, using his entire body to get the ball into the air, arcing it high and through the basket, no rim. A few kids in the back of the bleachers were standing up to watch. Soon, the noise of conversation ceased.

"Yo, Alec!" Will said. It was so quiet, he said it in what was almost a normal voice, full of admiration, and it carried throughout the gym.

Again and again, score, score, a narrow miss, score, then a miss, then around the rim and in, another miss, another score. When the buzzer sounded, they announced the count: thirty-five points. It was enough for him to hold on to fourth place. He was beaming. He'd pulled it off. I could see he was flushed, breathing hard, elated. I ached to feel his arms around me and to tell him how proud I was. For the first time in my life, looking at Alec, I understood what the word *thrilled* meant. You could see it all through his body. I felt it myself. He didn't need a trophy. He'd prevailed. He'd gotten around the obstacles and scored.

He didn't look my way as he sprinted back to the bleachers. He walked swiftly over to Will, who gave him a high-five as he stood up and messed Alec's hair. I looked up into the stands and saw Meg, just as she noticed me. She put her hand to her mouth and started to get up, then paused and slowly lowered herself back onto the bench. I glanced around and realized a few people were staring at me, at my lump of an eye, and I glanced away, looking toward my feet as I moved slowly out of the gym.

When I'd made it past the trophy case, out in the dark hall, I heard Alec call out behind me, "Dad! Did you see?" I turned around in the darkness and saw him coming through the doorway, facing into the shadows, sprinting up to me. He looked bigger than I remembered. He jumped up and clamped his legs around my waist, though he was almost too heavy for this anymore.

"Did you see my moves?" he asked.

"You were awesome."

"I don't get a trophy for fourth," he said.

"Who needs a trophy?"

"What happened to your eye?" he asked.

"I slipped and fell."

He pulled back, trying to see me clearly in the dark. "You all right?"

"As all right as I can be, I guess."

"You coming home?" he asked.

"For a minute. Then I've got to go out again," I said. "You

remember where you were last year? You were in, like, twentieth place or something. You were amazing out there, Alec. Even with your leg."

"It's because of Will," he said, pulling back. "You should've seen him. They're going to get him into Ignatius next semester. They want him. He can take a bus. They've got it figured out. He called his mom and told her. He might not have the money for the three years, though.

Over Alec's shoulder, I saw Will appear in the doorway, watching and waiting for Alec to return. I put Alec back on his feet, and looked back up at Will. I could tell he was checking out my eye. I wondered how much he knew, how much he suspected.

"You did a great job with Al," I said, raising my voice.

Will shifted from one foot to the other, without looking at me, nodding to Alec: "He's got the arm for it."

"Coming here next fall?" I asked.

"Hope so," he said.

Alec put his arms around me, and hugged me around the waist and then let go and looked up at my face, as if his world were starting to make sense again. I wanted to sling him over my shoulder, the way I did when he was five or six. I wanted to carry him out to the car, and come to his room and sit beside his bed as he slept, keeping watch, making sure I was there when he woke.

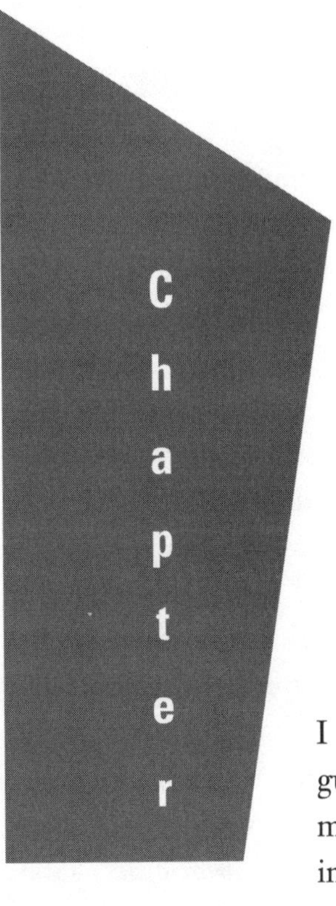

Chapter 15

I got home before anyone else. I left the gun and the money in the glove compartment. The phone was ringing when I got inside. I let it ring until the answering machine in the kitchen kicked in. It was Whit.

"Rich? You there? Pick up. We met with Jimmy and went over the e-mails he sent to Stringer. You came through for us, buddy. It was everything we needed. He told us the whole story. Tish met with Stringer at Veritex half an hour later, and he's agreed to move to another position. Jimmy agreed to go back to writing full-time, and we'll be passing along the Veritex account to you shortly. We're setting up a schedule for both of them to pay back the money. Call me when you get in. We can talk about that raise. Maybe we can see clear to go as high as three. Talk to you later."

The call only made me more determined to go ahead with Price. I took the matchbook out of my pocket, picked up the phone and dialed the number.

"I'm at home."

"I pick you up in fifteen minutes," he said.

I wrote a note for Meg: *I'll be back. I've got one more thing to do. I love you.* I meant those last three words. I kept glancing out the dining-room window, hoping Price would arrive before Meg got home. I recognized his Range Rover as it pulled around the corner. I went outside, reaching into my car to get the pistol, putting it behind my belt and under my shirt, and then climbed into the backseat of the Rover, with Paulette. DeWitt was sitting in the passenger seat, up front. As I got in, I glanced over at Paulette, but she was looking out the window, ignoring me. To sit down, I needed to clear off a news clipping he'd left on my seat. He'd cut it from the Op-Ed page of the *Times* or the *Journal*. The letter, submitted by an associate professor of economics at Harvard, ran the length of the page:

> The economy, by most measures, including Gross Domestic Product, is booming. Profits are up. The Dow keeps going through the roof. Yet look around you. You finding any of those profits in *your* pocket? Why are so many of us on the verge of insolvency? The credit card lenders smell blood. Their telemarketers call nightly at the dinner hour to every home that carries a balance. You in debt? Why not get deeper? That's the message. Over the past twenty years, during the greatest bull market in our history, the average income for male workers has dropped from around $34,000 to $30,000, and though the entry of women into the workforce obscured that reality, their own wages started dropping six

> years ago. And hundreds of thousands of workers get laid off every year, finding only lower-paying jobs or no jobs at all. These are college-educated workers. This is all during a time when the richest segment of our society has gotten even more obscenely rich, and more visibly so, which only makes it more painfully obvious how stagnant everyone else's income has become. The average middle-class family needs to spend half its income on housing, health care, and utilities. Hard work isn't enough anymore. As another writer put it in this newspaper not long ago, these are uncharted waters for American Democracy. The American Dream has priced itself out of reach, and it's only going to get worse.

"So what am I doing?" I asked.

"I like that uncharted-water part," Price said as he pulled out onto the interstate. "Little uncharted water what we head into tonight, Cuz. How that arm feel?"

"Hurts."

"That's good. You learn from that kind of pain," he said.

"Still do a lot of reading?" I asked, holding up the newspaper clip.

"I got a book full of those."

"So you're an owner now, huh? You up there in that top percentile?"

"Got me an acquisition to make after tonight. Consolidate my holdings."

"Out shopping for a satellite network?" I asked, smiling.

"No."

"So we can cross a leveraged buyout off the list?"

"I got me a radio station I want to start. Right here."

I stared at the back of his head, then saw his eyes, lit up by oncoming headlights, catch mine in the mirror.

"Got four already, other cities. No overhead, all profit. Little homey preachers come in, talk to the brothers and sisters for free, and those advertisers, they line up. Donations come in by the bag, and the station get a cut of that. Only overhead you got's the equipment. No salaries. Black-owned stations. Black preachers do it just for the exposure. Detroit. St. Louis. Got big margins on them stations. Legit."

"You *own* them?" I asked.

"Majority share. I'm pretty much the silent one, know what I'm sayin'? Company owns four stations. Only got but one competitor in Pittsburgh. After tonight, I get out of town, have DeWitt here start me up a station right here in town. They little money machines. Little gospel stations, all they do is talk. Preachers come on and talk they asses off all day and all night. Don't ask for a penny."

I glanced over at Paulette and she raised her eyebrows, still without looking at me. "I told you GP got a plan."

I frowned, looking back and forth between Paulette and GP. Neither of them was smiling. This was no prank.

"So fine, ain't she?" Price said. "We be out a this town three hours from now, baby."

"We better be. No more a this after tonight, GP."

"You got *that* right," he said.

I could see luggage piled in the rear, a few boxes, probably filled with Paulette's things. The dog was sleeping, squeezed beside the pile of luggage. It wouldn't have surprised me if they left behind everything but their clothing and their cash. I kept looking over at Price, wondering why, all my life, I'd wanted to find the median of all demographic measures and use it like the needle of a compass. A man like Price just seized what he wanted and followed it to whatever extreme. He was his own chief executive officer.

"Where's DeWitt fit into all this?" I asked.

"He want to quote Will, have Will work for him once I gone.

I say no, but Will insist. Even Paulette couldn't stop him. DeWitt get a nice piece of what we do tonight and then he be here to run things at the station I plan to start up. I be off in Chicago. Ain't that right, DeWitt?"

DeWitt stared out his side window, looking almost forlorn, as if he wasn't sure he wanted to be running a radio station. On the other hand, I couldn't imagine DeWitt slipping the right people the right amount of money to keep himself out of jail. Price pulled off the highway at one of the last exits before the Thruway, keeping it under fifty-five, checking his mirror and generally driving in a way my wife would have admired, using his seat belt, no music on the radio, no distractions, no risks. He pulled off into a park and stopped in one of the rest areas.

"DeWitt's customer, guy named Blanchard, built a house in Great Heron. You know it?"

"They had Home-a-Rama on this street last year. We took a tour. Those places are way out of our league. Meg likes to look, though."

"Polette and me, we almost decide Blanchard gone sign that house over to us," he said. "Just as a what-if."

"To you?"

"Me and Polette. Blanchard find out he's getting transferred to Florida two months from now. Got to put that house on the market before he even live in it," he said. "Idea was, what if me and Polette move in once he leave."

"Here? In Great Heron? You were going to move in *here?*"

"Not anymore," Paulette said. "But that would be sweet."

"Whole neighborhood slit they wrists they see who live down the street," Price said, grinning.

"Like to see that!" DeWitt said.

"But pretty soon they see I got a chain of little gospel stations. I'm not so bad. They get used to it. People get used to anything. I get a whole new life, don't got to watch my ass every time I walk down a street," he said, looking over at me, as if to see if I bought it. "That *would* be something, wouldn't it?"

I imagined what it must feel like, being Price. I could feel the glee of moving into that house, walking next door to introduce himself. It was bizarre enough to be exactly what someone like Price might dream of pulling off: the pinnacle of his accomplishments, revenge and success and justice all in one. It would have been a one-man affirmative-action campaign waged as guerrilla warfare. Charlie himself tunneling into your basement. I grinned at the vengeance of merely buying a house there.

"Nice to know you *could* do it. Why go through with it, once you know you *could* pull it off, right?" he said. "Today my supplier from downstate make the drop in that home. Little delivery straight from Thailand, hear the man talk about it. Nobody stepped on it yet."

He told me this supplier sent a white man and woman to look at the empty house in Great Heron Heights earlier in the day. They left a package in the basement. He wanted me to go into the house and bring out the backpack they'd dropped in a storage room in the cellar. If he sent DeWitt, the neighbors might see him and dial 911. If the neighbors spotted *me*, I could say the realtor gave me a key. They would drop me off at the gate, and then pick me up here. I would need to come through the woods, following a trail leading back to this spot, turning left at every fork in the path.

"You got to be quick," he said. "The longer you spend in there, the more things go wrong."

"That shouldn't be a problem," I said.

"I wait twenty minutes. Then you on you own. I can't be sitting around out here."

"I understand," I said. "When do I get the rest of my money?"

He grinned and glanced back at DeWitt.

"He learn fast," Price said, then looked back at me. "When you get back. But you don't get it until you deliver."

He handed me a pair of black gloves.

"Put those on. Don't take them off until you get back in this car," he said, and then handed me a key. "This will open the storage closet in the basement."

I slipped on the gloves and took the key. The gloves were new, and a size too small—Isotoners that fit skin-tight with little strips of leather along the fingers. He handed me a keycard for the gate into the development and a key to the house itself, along with a piece of paper with the code for the security alarm written on it. I lowered my head and breathed deeply. I opened the door and walked.

As I approached the house on foot, I had to stop and check the street number he'd given me. This stucco-and-stone palace couldn't possibly be the home he'd considered buying for Paulette. How could they need that much room? It had to be six thousand square feet, big bay windows projecting beneath copper flashing carved out from above in big scallops, with gray slate tile for a roof, three tall fireplace chimneys, with stone mortared into the walls as a base for the muddy marzipan of stucco rising to the eaves. The yard could have hosted an NFL playoff game.

Next door, a massive party surged in and out of the house. Cars lined the entire street, where huge Colonials, other faux-Tudors, and castle-like structures with turrets all seemed to hover and rise in ranks up plush velvet slopes, the backyards giving onto the woods, all that privacy and opulence poised at the edge of the trees. There were Mercedeses and Audis and Saabs and Jaguars lining the street, even a white Corniche tucked protectively into the turnaround drive. I spotted people through the bright windows, their voices rippling from the backyard, shrieking with laughter and shouting punch lines over the music. The entire house was like a membrane throbbing with the beat from what had to be huge speakers, maybe even a live wall of guitar amps stacked in the basement. These people were young and rich, maybe younger than I was. I'd seen people like them driving early to their offices, clean-shaven and fragrant and oblivious, their music cranked up, their heads bobbing like dashboard Jesuses, or with cell phones to their ears. I knew even my most brilliant moves in life weren't going to result in anything that looked like this house.

I passed it by and came to the silent house next door. I followed the flagstones up to the entrance. I felt as if we were all on Long Island with little lights winking over the Sound. Though I had some difficulty imagining Price in that sort of setting, clothed in seersucker and silk, posed beside a croquet wicket, gazing up at the stars, at the dock lights on the water, it wasn't much of a stretch to envision him consorting with people who fixed national sporting events as an amusement.

At the door, my hands shook so badly, I fumbled the key. I had to open both locks to get in, which I finally managed, stumbling across the threshold, groping for the light so I could find the alarm keypad, the red button winking, daring me to punch the code in less than thirty seconds. I was counting down the seconds, unfolding Price's little sheet of paper with the security combination Blanchard had passed along to him. The first time I punched the code, I slipped and mixed up the numbers: four, five, six, two, one. I looked back at the sheet of paper. I had ten seconds left to get it right. Carefully, I pressed each button. One. At. A. Time. Five. Four. Six. Two. One. The red light turned green, with about three seconds to spare. I leaned my head against the wall until I remembered to breathe.

I walked past a bank of windows in the living room that gave me a clear view of the party next door. I paused, because I thought I recognized Vince Stringer. He was standing beside a blond woman, clearly not his wife, in a tight black shirred minidress. He was holding some kind of hors d'oeuvre to his mouth. Then I spotted Penny McKee, in an uncharacteristic erotic red. And then Jimmy Sorley, in a sweater and jeans. And Wes? Maybe. Jennifer Dewinter. With each pop of recognition, another fuse burst in my nerves, firing through my fingertips into the expectant air around me. How could they have been invited, and I'd known nothing of that party? I would never have enough to make my way into that sort of place, certainly not when I was getting only three thousand more a year. I rubbed my eyelids and shook my head. My wounded arm ached.

When I opened my eyes again and squinted, looking carefully, I realized I didn't know any of them. It wasn't Penny in red. It wasn't Jimmy. No matter how familiar they looked, they were all strangers. I leaned back against the wall and slowly slid down until I sat on the floor, my knees pulled up against my chest.

Then the doorbell rang. I remembered: like an idiot, I'd left the foyer light on when I turned off the alarm. It rang again, two chimes, apparently to signify the front door. Quickly I peered through a front window. It was somebody from the party next door, with a drink in his hand. There were two others with him, standing back, waiting to come in.

My heart wouldn't slow down. I headed for the back of the house, looking for the way down to the basement. The doorbell rang again—this time only one chime—and my heart fired a volley the way it did when the phone woke me up from a deep sleep. Now they were trying the back door. If only I'd gone straight to the cellar, gotten my package, and left, none of this would be happening. I crept along the wall to where the corridor met the kitchen, turned and found myself in a little nook that contained the door to the basement. I opened the door and stepped carefully down the stairs into the dark cellar.

The back doorbell rang again. I groped around the corner at the base of the stairs, feeling my way forward, able to pick out only the largest and most indeterminate shapes by way of the dim light that filtered in through the sliding door facing the woods. I got the key out of my pocket. Next door, every floodlight burned, all of it aimed back across the rolling expanse of turf into the dark stand of oak and sycamore and maple, where I would be sprinting to safety soon, if everything went as planned.

I paused and pulled the gun from my belt. I aimed it toward the ceiling, though I knew there was no possible reason to produce a gun in this empty house. The darkness, thick and almost silky with the scent of fresh waterproofing paint on the cinder block, clung to my skin and parted to let me through. I could *feel* the darkness, the viscosity of it, more real and palpable than light, the thrilling touch of it on my skin. Every cell in my body came alive, alert, ready to receive. Creeping blindly through the cellar gave me goose bumps. I heard every sound magnified, the ticking of the furnace, a resonant and steady ping in the water pipes—all the little crackling noises a house makes—and finally the voices moving around outside the house, the neighbors peering through the windows.

I found the closet doorknob with one hand, inserted the key into the lock and turned. The door swung open. The doorbell went off again upstairs, this time twice. I squatted and reached through the dark, imagining some crouching dog opening its mouth. My eyes were adjusting, and, in horror, I saw a figure approaching the basement door. Apparently they'd split up. I moved inside the closet and felt the pressure of something large and soft on my shoulders, imagining raccoons hanging from the rafters or unsecured strips of insulation. It was the backpack, hanging on the wall. I lifted it, feeling the buckles and straps, the snug weight of it on my back. I glanced at the glowing numbers on my watch. I had eight minutes to get back to the car.

I heard the door slide open.

"Hey, iss open!" the intruder said softly, slurring it.

The others weren't with him.

Inside the closet, holding my breath, I held the gun, clicking the safety off.

"Man! Floor paint down already," he spoke to himself, now inside the house. He was clearly drunk, talking to himself without listening. I could hear the ice in his drink. "The size of that water heater! But no drywall? Thought there was supposed to be drywall. Look at the size of that water heater!"

I heard him moving around, his shoes sliding on the concrete floor.

"Look at these cabinets," he said. "Man. Why not come down here and just snowblow your money into that furnace."

I heard him move toward the closet, opening and shutting the built-in storage cabinets. With every step he was trying another set of doors. He was so close, it was hard to tell whether or not he'd arrived at my door.

"Would you look at this?" he said. "What's this asshole need with all this. *Hey Skip! Skip! You got to see this!* Where the hell is he?"

Finally, he reached the closet door. My heart throbbed. I could hear the rattle of the latch. I squeezed the gun with both hands, spreading my feet apart, one foot forward and one back, bracing myself. I wasn't thinking. I'd reduced myself to muscle tissue, nerves, a pair of eyes, a pair of ears. His lazy, self-indulgent voice infuriated me. I glanced at my watch. Five minutes left. The seconds were slipping by, making it less and less likely Price would be waiting for me on the other side of the woods. By the time he decided to leave, I'd be finding my way through the woods to an empty parking lot. The moron: instead of looking around himself in wonder and thanking his dumb blind luck for giving him a rank in life he clearly didn't deserve, he had to come over to his neighbor's new house to check out the water heater, just to see if he needed to replace his own with a bigger one. If I owned this house I could have shot him and no jury would convict: he was a burglar in his own neighborhood. I wanted to kick the door open, fire a round into each of his knees and tell him to crawl home and thank God he wasn't me. All I wanted was to get out of this obscene suburb alive. But no, he just couldn't resist. I imagined his gaping lips sucking on the cubes he brought to his face before spitting them back into the cocktail—I could hear him do it again and again as he came closer—and I wanted to shove the gun into his face and say *How could you possibly need anything more in your life than you've already got, you rich, spoiled son of a bitch? All I want right now is the life I had before I went into the wrong place on the wrong day for a burger and fries.*

He grasped the handle of the door—in less than a second he would have it open and the muzzle of my gun would be in his mouth, and things would tumble into sudden ruin as he looked into my eyes for one moment too long. I found myself praying, saying the simple words my mother taught me to say, not asking for anything, just saying the name: *Jesus Christ, Jesus Christ, Jesus Christ.* Open a door and all the underpinnings of my universe would give a little seismic shrug and everything I knew and trusted, everything I'd built for myself, would collapse—but then he let go of the knob and shuffled away.

"There they are. Hey. *Hey!* What the . . . where they going? I'm down here! *Hey!*" he shouted and started for the sliding glass door.

They were still too far away. If they heard him, it was all over. I'd never get out of the house. I kicked the door open, took three steps to the right, lunging at him as he moved unsteadily toward the door, pressing the gun against his neck with one hand and grabbing his sweater with my other fist, pulling him back, poking the gun into his ear. He dropped the cocktail glass, and the Bic lighter he'd been using to see. The glass shattered, splattering our legs, and the lighter skidded across the floor. It was too dark now to see anything except silhouettes, but he started to look around anyway, and I shoved his head back with the gun, before he could get me into his peripheral vision, and I kept shoving until he was looking straight ahead, freezing in midstride.

"Come over here, by the furnace," I said softly, almost whispering. "I just want to get out of here."

"And what if I don't," he said, refusing to move.

I shoved the gun into his ear.

"Shut up," I said. "Now move."

"Fuck you. I'm not going anywhere. Just get your ass out of here and leave me alone," he said.

I didn't know what to say. I was a little impressed. Maybe he knew it was a Lady Smith. Was he so drunk he didn't understand what was happening?

"I told you to shut up," I said, getting angrier and louder. "I want you to get inside the storage closet over there."

I hated everything about him, his self-assured, drunken voice, the smell of secondhand smoke in his jacket, the way he crossed his arms and shifted his weight as he stood in the dark. I glanced at my watch. I had three minutes left. Then something about the weight of the load on my back changed. It ceased being a burden, a goad. It became mine, my accomplishment, my little half hour of lucrative work, my leverage. There was no way Price would leave without it, not after having gone this far. His little deadline was just the sort of thing Whit Sutherland would have put on my path. I had the package. Price could leave. I didn't care. I would find my own way home. A relaxed feeling of power surged through me and got stronger, giving everything I did a sense of greater weight and significance and influence. Everything depended on me, and I was absolutely convinced I could pull it off, and the only obstacle I faced was this drunken asshole who'd stumbled across my path.

"Move, jerk," I said.

"I'm not moving. I'm staying right here. Go on and leave."

"I'm in no rush. What I want is for you to get inside that room."

"You aren't locking me into any closet, buddy," he said. "You guys think you can do anything. Car full of you niggers came through here last week, tossed seven or eight of those empty forty-ounce bottles onto the Kaisers' lawn. This is where it stops, homeboy."

Did I sound black? But then, what did black sound like? Professor Jackson Parsells didn't sound black on the phone. Price and Paulette had their street talk, but that was different, that was a style.

"I'm not—" I said, and stopped.

"You're not what?"

"Go on. Move."

"I'll let you go, but I'm not getting into that closet. I'm not moving an inch," he said. "I don't even like elevators, man. I'm not going in there. You put me in there and I'll go fucking nuts. Just leave me out here and go."

I pulled the gun around to the back of his neck and pressed the muzzle into his skin and pushed harder and harder, but it was like pushing into the trunk of a tree. He was big. No matter how I pushed, he wouldn't budge. I wanted to shoot him in the back of the head. I felt for the trigger, holding the muzzle against the back of his neck.

"I want you in that closet," I said.

"No way."

It was past my deadline with Price. But I didn't care. I wanted to hurt this guy for what he was doing to me. I slid the gun off his neck and held it about three inches from his right ear, and I fired two rounds into the wall. He dropped to his knees, crying out with the pain, holding both hands to his right ear, doubled over. The explosion probably burst his eardrum. I kicked him as hard as I could, and he yelled again.

"Now move!" I shouted.

He crawled toward the storage closet, on his knees, and watching him, hearing him weep despite himself, was one of the strangest, most disturbing pleasures of my life.

"Get in. Keep your head down, you jerk," I said. "That's it."

"Don't hurt me," he said. "My wallet's in my back pocket."

"Shut up. I don't want—" I started to say and then paused. "Which pocket?"

"The right one. My right."

I reached carefully into his hip pocket, trying not to touch him while I pressed his wallet between two gloved fingers. It wasn't easy. There was something so nakedly pitiful about pulling this man's wallet out of his pocket the way I was trying to do it, as I kept the gun's barrel up against his neck, not pressing too hard now.

He crawled through the doorway and I shut the door behind him, but I didn't lock it. I backed up slowly, until I was close enough to the door to pull his New York State driver's license from the wallet and look at his face in the photo, using the light from the party, filtering faintly through the window. It struck me how much he looked like me. Bigger, heavier, but same brown hair, same cut, same kind of sweater I'd be wearing if I could afford it. Even his voice reminded me of mine, that same wary cast in the eyes, same kind of jowls I got when the lens looked up at me from below my chin, same trace of amusement in the mouth rather than a full smile.

"Carter Henderson," I said. "Nice to meet you, Carter. Not a word of this to anybody."

I tossed the wallet through the air, and it slid across the floor. I backed out through the sliding door and shut it. The door was hidden behind a row of cedars. I peered through them over toward the neighboring house. Most of the revelers on the deck had gone inside, the air suddenly cold with little flakes of snow blowing south off the lake.

I ran halfway to the woods, watching my shadow lengthen in front of me, the farther I got from the floodlights next door. I could hardly catch my breath. It wouldn't take Carter Henderson long to realize he wasn't locked in that closet. Then I heard shouts from the neighboring deck, but I kept running, choking on the cold air. I glanced back over my shoulder as I got closer to the trees, and one of the drinkers was pointing toward me. I plunged into the woods, bearing left as Price told me. I ran and stumbled and fell, and got up running through the brush again, the big sumac seed pods swatting me softly in the face, the moon filtering through the bare trees, the air smelling of clotted leaves and pine needles, bearing left whenever I could see a fork in the trail, panting and running and still running without coming to an opening. The more I slowed, the harder my heart pounded.

I saw a faint light through the trees and headed toward it. As I emerged from the leafless bushes, pine needles crackling underfoot, I realized these were the floodlights from the party, as well as three other bobbing lights to the side, getting larger, three men moving toward the woods to start searching. I'd circled back. I closed my eyes. *Don't let this happen.* I slowly moved back into the darkness, away from the approaching flashlights, and then when I was far enough down the path, I started running. I crouched low, looking to the left, trying to spot the fork in the trail I'd missed. I ran faster, and each time I looked back, the lights were dimmer. I took one more turn to the left, and came across a gully I remembered, the one I'd tumbled down on my first circuit through the woods, what felt like days ago. I came up the other side and at the top of the rise encountered another sharp turn to the left, with a branch fallen across the turn, hiding the trail beyond it. The moon was out, full now, and I could see the trail clearly.

I leaped over the branch, and as I did, I got my second wind. Something else took over, my breathing eased, and my whole body shifted into a higher gear, as I ran through that compliant darkness. Nothing else in my life felt this way. Then I shuddered, stumbling to a halt, looking down at my hand, where I'd snagged torn vines, trailing from my thumb: I still had the gun drawn. Moonlight splashed across the stock. I stopped, put the safety on and slipped the gun back behind my belt. I started running again through the dark. I fell three or four times on the downslopes, sprinting through the woods. It was wide and worn, and there weren't any forks. I didn't slow down, though. I ran faster and faster, the bag bouncing on my shoulders, my feet slipping on the icy patches, the lower limbs and the unseen briars scratching my face and slapping me as I bounded through them.

Finally, as I started to panic, completely turned around—north? south? where'd the moon go?—I came to a dim gray clearing where a few picnic tables and an old stone barbecue blocked my way. I stopped and looked around. I spotted the parking lights a quarter mile away in the lot surrounded by a low log fence. It was the Range Rover. Still there. It sat on an expanse of bone-white pavement, pale, coated with dried salt. It was like running into an old, faithful friend, true to his word, watching out for you when you least expected it. The moon led me across the field, and as I closed on that shiny sport utility, snow started to fall again. I slowed to a stop.

"Hey."

I spun around, the gun drawn, squinting into the dark shrubbery and brush.

"It's me," she said, moving out to where I could see her face. "Come here. He told me to come out and listen for you."

"Come on," I said. "They're following me. We've got to get away."

"Come here," she said.

I put the gun behind my belt and moved closer to her, until I was right beside her, under an overhanging branch of sumac with vines tangled and twisted through the leaves. She took my hand and pulled me into her arms, wrapping herself around me, even hooking a leg around my leg. She looked up into my face and kissed me, a long, soft kiss, gentle and full of feeling. Then she rested her face against my shoulder.

"I may not see you again after tonight," she said.

"You don't have to go with him," I said.

"And do what?"

"Stay in town. Get a job. Maybe I could help."

"I'm with GP," she said. "I'm going."

"It's going to hurt, not seeing you now," I said.

"Last night never happened, you know what's good for you." She squeezed tighter.

"You aren't all that tough, Paulette," I said.

"Nobody's all that tough. Not even GP. Just got to make everybody else believe it."

"I think GP's about as tough as they get," I said.

She looked up and kissed me again, then pulled away and led me out of the shadows. I approached the car, but all the windows were up and I could see nothing through the dark tint. My legs shook. I reached for the door. It was unlocked, and I let Paulette climb in first. *After a major drug run, a gentleman is advised to let his gansta bitch get into the car first.* As I got into the Range Rover, the lights on the dash gave a blue cast to Price's face as he turned around to watch me get in, waiting for me to hand him the back-pack. DeWitt looked bored. The dog was still asleep. Nothing had changed, except me.

"You got it?"

"I got it."

"Check it out, DeWitt. Got to get you ass out of here," Price said. "How'd it go?"

He said it as if he were telling me where to pick up my weekly paycheck. I handed the backpack over the seat to DeWitt.

"Just get out of here," I said.

"Easy, wasn't it?"

"Actually it was the hardest thing I've ever had to do," I said.

He grinned.

"Always good to rise to a new challenge in your career," he said.

At that moment, hearing the routine sound of Price's words, I understood how he looked at the world. Nothing surprised him or shocked him or frightened him anymore.

"It's in there," DeWitt said.

"Then give the man his money," Price said.

Paulette was staring out the window. The moneymaking part of life seemed to hold no interest for her. She sat there and watched everything happen for her benefit. Price glanced back at me as we started to move.

"Better'n sex, huh," he said.

After a pause, as my heart started to return to normal, I grinned back at him.

"I knew you'd dig it."

He burst into a big laugh. My heart started pounding again.

"I could have lost everything back there," I said.

"Makes being alive feel like a whole new thing," he said as DeWitt handed me another envelope. "Take a look."

I took the envelope, prying it open with one finger. It was packed with hundred-dollar bills, though not as crisp as the others he'd given me earlier. Out on the interstate, we were all silent for several miles.

"Like I say, Cuz. You got the nuts for this. You and I, we make a good team."

"I'm going to put this money to good use," I said. "This isn't for me."

"Whatever does it for you. More where that came from."

"No. This is it. That was the deal," I said, starting to calm down, to reflect on what I'd done, the acrid aftertaste. "I'm doing this because I owe it to my family."

"Don't get self-righteous with *me*, Cuz. I don't force that junk in nobody's vein. I don't blow it up some slob's nose. They do that."

"This money's all I want. I've earned it," I said. "But this is where it ends."

"Here," he said, and handed me another matchbook. "That's a number you can reach me at in Chicago. Not me. But somebody can find me. Case you change your mind."

"Can we move this thing along?" Paulette asked from the backseat.

"Chill, babe."

"I'd've kept my mouth shut without all this."

"Now I *know* you keep you mouth shut. Now you one of us," he said. "And now you know who I think I am. Since you asked. Now you know who *you* are too. Back there, in that house, you *were* me, Cuz."

It struck me maybe this was all Price wanted. He wanted both of us to know that he could get *me* to do what he needed someone to do. Like a salesman asking for your pen, even though he has one hidden in his own pocket, just to see if you'll do what he asks you to do, for the pleasure of it, the practice, the power.

I looked at Paulette until she looked back at me. She'd recovered her usual air of indifference and boredom.

"Your brother's going to be a little disappointed you left," I said.

"Will gone be fine. And so am I."

When we got to the on-ramp, Price pulled to the side of the highway.

"We never see each other again. No phone calls," I said. "That's the deal."

He didn't answer as he came to a stop, but he pulled his gun from the holster around his ankle and pressed the barrel into my cheek. He had such long arms, he didn't even have to lean in my direction. I wasn't frightened. I conceded simply because there was nothing to resist anymore.

"The deal is," he said, "you just as deep in this as any of us. Now we all in this together. That's the deal. Enjoy your life, Cuz. You never hear from me again, consider it *your* bad luck. I'm just who you need."

He lowered the gun as I picked up the envelope full of money and weighed it in my hand. He returned the gun to the holster as I turned to glance at Paulette. Just as my eyes met hers, a light blinded me, and with a grinding sound, the Polaroid in DeWitt's hands poked out a blank. I watched my face emerge on the white square, the little demonic red pupils in my eyes, the mouth gaping with paparazzi-worthy candor. In the picture, Price faced me, both of us framed in white.

"Just to remember you by," Price said. "So long, Cuz. Give me a call you wanna talk business."

I got out. Snow swirled like dust on the dry pavement. As I shut the door, Paulette rolled down her window and motioned me to come closer. As I stood beside the open window, she stuck her head out, tugged my head down and kissed me on the cheek.

"Tell my mama I be fine," she said. "You make sure Will go to that school. Tell him he can have my car. He knows where to find the keys."

"You sure you want to do this?" I asked.

"You been working out?" she asked. "You look like you work out."

"Yeah. I'm all out of breath."

"That's just from the kiss," she said, smiling.

She pulled back into the Range Rover, and they drove off, heading west. It took me half an hour to make my way back to the office parking lot, and I drove home in silence, still feeling the quiver in my fingers and feet, the delicious edge it gave to everything, as if I'd never before seen snowflakes dust my eyelashes or heard tires rip through slushy pools on pavement. It was a strange new planet, yet I wasn't all that far from home.

Chapter 16

I stood for a while out in the street, the sudden wind stinging my cheeks. The stormfront kept moving in from the west, erasing the stars. Such a little house. So many good years in those awkward rooms. Each leaded window was packed with diamond-shaped wedges of orange light, glowing from within, like eyes in a pumpkin. I just kept standing there in the street, freezing my ass, making a target of myself. Little cyclones of snow spun from the gaps where the wind whistled between stucco corners and downspouts. A house down the street kept burning Christmas lights. Wink, wink, wink every year, from the solstice to Easter. Green. Red. Gold. And as I watched, they went off, all at once. Bedtime, not Easter yet. I realized how late I was getting home from work. Same old story.

I climbed into the car, unlocked the glove compartment, and took out the first envelope of cash, then slipped all the cash into one envelope. At the back door, I turned the knob slowly and came into the kitchen, glancing at my reflection in the dark window. I was hunched over with a sullen, surprised look in my eyes, an old man in that kitchen light, an intruder in his own home. I could hear Meg getting up in the dining room. She stood in the doorway.

"What did they *do* to you?" she asked, moving closer to me, reaching up like a caveman's woman to pull something from my hair, a leaf or a stick or—who knew?—a clump of dried blood. What must I have looked like to passing drivers on Durand?

"I'm okay," I said, moving over to the heating vent in the floor and standing over it.

She put her arms around me, almost exactly the way Paulette held me in the woods. I was sure she could smell the Trésor again, but she didn't let go. She leaned her head into my shoulder and talked, without looking up.

"Can you tell me about it?"

"Let me warm up here," I said.

"Whatever it is you're doing, is it over?" she asked.

"It better be," I said.

I saw a note on the table: *Whit called.*

"What's that about?"

"He said he wanted to talk."

She looked up at me and then put her head on my shoulder, as if we were doing a slow dance.

"Let's go in the living room," she said.

"Anything left to drink? I can smell it."

"Just a little of this gin left."

I saw the glass in her hand now.

"Straight up? You turning into a lush on me?"

"Why does gin smell like evergreens?" she asked.

"God, it's cold outside. Is this winter ever going to end?" I asked.

"You want one?"

"Whatever."

She moved to the counter and filled a rocks glass with the rest of the gin.

"Where the kids?" I asked.

"Dana took off with the Saab. She's past her curfew. God only knows where she went. Alec's upstairs. He was very worried. The way you look—what in the world did they do to you?"

I handed her the envelope Price gave me.

"Go on. Open it."

She slowly pried it open and slipped the stack of bills out onto the coffee table next to the glass decanter of shells from a trip to a friend's house on Captiva one year, the whelks and worm shells and one bleached pure-white Scotch bonnet. Meg riffled through the money like a loan shark, using nothing but her fingertips to count.

"My God," she said. "How much is this?"

"Twenty."

Her face went pale.

"Nobody got hurt. Nothing like that. It's over. That's what counts."

I studied her eyes. This was going to be tough. This was what I'd dreaded as I stood on that manhole cover in the middle of our snowy street, waiting for a pair of headlights to scare me into my own front yard.

"Go on," she said.

"He had me pick something up for him. That's all."

"What was it?"

"I don't know. I didn't look," I said.

"And he paid you this much?"

"He asked me how much I wanted. Can you believe it?"

"Not really. No," she said.

"You remember Great Heron Heights? The Home-a-Rama? One of those houses. He had the key. I went inside, picked up a package, and brought it out to him. That's all."

She sighed and tossed the money onto the coffee table.

"I did it for us," I said.

"For the money."

"I told him I wanted him gone. I do this for him, and he's out of my life. Our lives. This much money for something like that? Imagine how much he makes."

"We can't keep this money," she said.

"Yes we can."

"It's going to just hang over us. We could take it to Bogardus. Tell him what happened. Turn it in."

"He'd arrest me in a minute," I said. "He'd use me."

She looked at the money again, thinking about it.

"You know how fast we'd go through that money? That's what your life, your career, amounts to? You're willing to risk everything for *that?*"

"You know what? I almost feel *good* about it," I said. "I *did* something. I took a chance. I did a job and got paid."

Meg looked at her hands.

"After what I've been through the past week—New York. Whit. Jimmy. Vince Stringer. The whole mess. Look, bottom line, it's done and now we live with it. That's all. Now we go on to better things."

She was looking at my forehead again.

"Are you sure you don't need stitches?"

"Wait'll you see what they did to my arm."

"What?"

"Let me just get in the shower."

She lowered her head and closed her eyes and then leaned back against a cushion and rested her head on it, with her eyes still closed.

"This is our future fund."

"Some future that's going to give us," she said.

I followed her upstairs, and as she went into the bedroom, I went quietly into Dana's room. I sat on her bed. Her walls were covered with the vodka advertisements she'd been tearing from magazines and collecting for the past year—ABSOLUT MANHATTAN, ABSOLUT DOW SIMPSON, ABSOLUT MONTE CARLO, ABSOLUT ROSEBUD—along with all her posters, of Alanis Morisette, Dave Matthews, and a huge black-and-white poster of sad-eyed Kurt Cobain, with the dates of his birth and death. Little strings of foil stars, purple, silver, and teal, ran up every joint in the walls, and a large winged pink plush pig hung by an elastic tether from the ceiling.

I looked through her desk drawers, and her dresser, and the little lacquered box with tiny drawers where she kept her jewelry. Beside it, folded three times, I found a clip about an Audrey Hepburn festival at Flicks, a little discount theater not far from Cobb's Hill. I'd taken her to see *Clueless* there, just the two of us, and she'd spent the following three weeks doing Alicia Silverstone imitations. They were showing the Hepburn movies now, on the anniversary of her visit to the Eastman House, and the films were to run until midnight.

When I wandered into the theater, it was almost too dark to see anyone. Once my eyes adjusted, I realized there were only a few people left, watching *Roman Holiday*. They'd saved her first film for last. I wandered up and down the aisles, trying to make out the few faces, until I saw Dana, sitting on the far left, up next to the wall, her knees practically in her face, her feet wedged into the gaps between the seats in front of her. On the screen, a young Audrey Hepburn was sitting in bed, talking sadly about the sweetness and decency of young men as her secretary rattled off her schedule for the coming day as a princess visiting Rome. I knew the moment. It came just before the princess broke down into a fit of frustrated weeping about how imprisoned she felt in her life, before she goes out onto the balcony and gazes down at a humble dancing party she can see through the forest, imagining what it would be like to be invited to a simple dance, imagining what it would be like to be one of *them*, to belong.

I sidled along the row, crossed another aisle, and slowly approached Dana, who looked up at me warily, wide-eyed, and then recognized me, and looked back at the screen. I sat beside her, watching the movie silently. The doctor arrived to tell the princess what she needed: " 'Best thing I know is to do exactly as you wish for a while.' "

"How'd you find me?" she asked.

"It's past your curfew."

From somewhere behind us: "Shhhh!"

We watched the movie as the princess escaped and wandered through Rome and eventually fell asleep on a low brick wall, where she says: *What the world needs is a return to sweetness and decency in the soul of its young men.*

"Let's go," I said.

"The movie just started."

"You really want to stay?"

We maneuvered to the side exit and went out into the cold air, the sky filled with stars now, the brief storm gone, a breeze in the big oaks and maples in the yards behind the theater, with young leaves sprouting. I was parked in the grocery's lot across the street, under a streetlamp, next to where she'd parked the Saab.

"Anything you want to talk about?" I asked.

"I just wanted to get away from it."

"From what?" I asked.

"Everything. What's going on."

"What is it you think is going on?"

"I don't want to know, all right?" she said. "Can we just go home now?"

"It would be nice to think she was right, wouldn't it?" I said.

"Who?"

"The princess. About what the world needs."

"Doesn't seem like too much to ask," Dana said.

"It's a lot harder than it sounds," I said.

Once the kids were in bed, we went around downstairs, straightening things. When the back doorbell rang, we looked at each other and scrambled over to the front window. I expected to see flashing lights, three or four cruisers blocking the driveway. Instead, I saw the Talon. Meg told me to wait in the dining room. I followed her into the kitchen.

"What time is it?" I asked.

"He looks a little drunk," she said. "What's up?" she asked when she opened the door.

I saw Gregg lean to the side, trying to get a look at me in the kitchen around the side of Meg's head.

"Hey, Rich," he called to me.

I nodded.

"Mind if I come in for a sec?" he asked Meg.

"Not now. We've had a very eventful night around here."

"I'm all wired. I've got a bunch of new ideas I thought you and I could, you know, talk about."

I'm thinking, *This is so high school.* Next thing, I'm going to be outside punching him in the face. *You wanna go? Are we going? Let's go!* I wanted to climb into bed and wake up a different person, with a different life.

"Not now," she said with a tentative voice. "No. Give me a call tomorrow."

"A call," he said.

"The telephone? You remember."

"I see. You sure there isn't—"

"I'm sure, Gregg. This can wait until tomorrow."

"Really. You know that before you've even heard what—"

"Yeah, I know that," she said. "Okay?"

I'd heard her use this tone with telemarketers at the dinner hour.

"Fine. Did the Buffalo people mail you the—"

"Good night, Gregg," she said.

I leaned back against the stove, grinning. Go on, Gregg. Keep pushing. Keep it up. Keep digging deeper.

"Call you tomorrow."

"That sounds good. 'Night," she said, shutting the door in his face.

I smiled at her as she preceded me out of the kitchen, but she didn't smile back. She brought the envelope filled with money upstairs and placed it on her dresser. She didn't want to talk about it any more than I did. She wanted to spend one night thinking her life was going to turn out the way she'd hoped, without having to consider how we'd gotten here.

"Very impressive down there," I said.

"He has no sense of proportion. That's all."

"It was fun to watch. You put him in his place."

"I didn't do it for your amusement," she said, sitting on the bed. "I'm not feeling very entertained myself."

"We can get our lives back," I said.

"You think so?"

I sat beside her on the bed and put my arm around her shoulder, and she turned to me and just barely touched my lips with her own. I pulled her around and began to kiss her. She returned the kiss, wary at first, then with passion. She hadn't kissed me this way for months, a long kiss, pulling me down on top of her, and there was something desperate and sad in it.

When I came up for breath, I looked away from her long enough to take in the whole room. Everything seemed transformed. I felt the way a survivor must, like someone who has walked alive out of an airplane crash or an earthquake or a bombing. Everything in the room seemed different to me. There was something marvelous in the most ordinary things, the texture of a carpet, the way an armchair went bald in spots after a few years. I closed my eyes and imagined the peculiar scents of a home, the whole personal aroma, as if love, anger, and hope could soak deep into the fabric and paint, the woodwork and carpet.

We undressed together and got into bed, and she began kissing my chest and went lower, taking me into her mouth, and I sank what felt like miles into myself, into *her*, into the craving, everything in my world gone but the stroke of her tongue. After a while, she straightened up, locking her fingers behind my neck and then rocking backward, pulling me on top of her, bringing my lips down hard on hers. And then I was lost, my head and my heart completely given over to this one little feast, feeling myself come completely alive, cell by cell. Our sorrow synchronized us, in a way our moments of happiness never had.

Her skin seemed charged, the insides of her elbows, the hollows behind her knees, the back of her neck. Little sounds deep in our throats trapped behind closed lips, her fingers nuzzling the intersection of our bodies, stroking herself again, but then she stopped, didn't need it, and kept pumping her hips frantically, calling out my name, finally pressing her chin into the pillow to muffle her cries. It was like running into the heart of a dark wood, going far enough to forget your name, to forget everything you once knew. Then, as her eyes opened, seeing nothing, her breath caught, her face flushed, I joined her. As I groaned with relief, she puckered and gave a soft, muffled growl: *Oh Jesus.*

Later, after she fell asleep, and the rain started up again, I heard a siren start to wail at a great distance. It got louder, and the louder it got, the harder my heart pounded. It got closer and closer, and I was praying again as it passed our street and started to fade, and I stopped whispering when I realized I was safe, at least for the rest of the night.

I went to the window, and I could see out to the green light near the church, through all the bare trees. There were hardly any cars on the street as the light turned red. I saw one lone driver head toward the light, and I was certain he'd never stop. He had his left turn signal on already, which was a good sign, but as he approached the light he didn't seem to slow down. He wasn't going to stop, and I shut my eyes, knowing it would never happen. Yet, when I looked again, there he was, completely stopped, waiting for the light to change, sitting there with his turn signal winking. I whispered *Yes!* and gave him thumbs-up at the dark window, though he'd never see me, and I was sure I was the only one who cared enough to watch him.

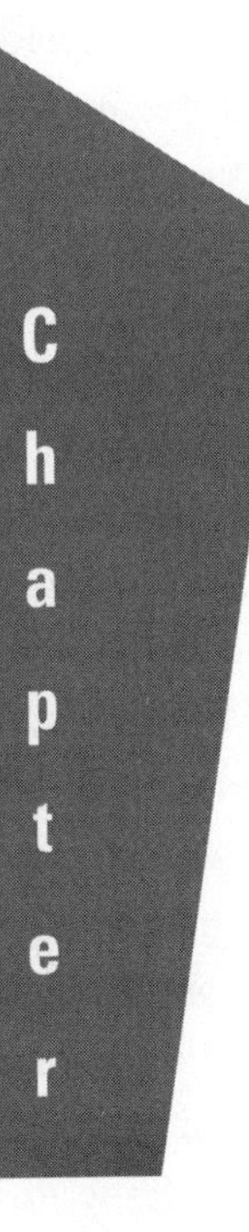

Chapter 17

They say you can control an elephant by roping him to a stake in the ground for weeks, and eventually, even if you merely tie the rope around his neck without fixing it anywhere, the elephant will never think to venture into open fields beyond the circus grounds. On my way home from the monastery and my conversation with Father Gregor, I realize I'm the elephant. My life has reduced itself to a circuit of time sheets, job jackets, job journals, Day-Timer entries, phone calls, input meetings, status meetings, creative reviews—an interminable lesson in how to endure grindingly boring hours of waiting punctuated by alarms and panic, for a minor pay hike every year, and maybe a bonus to cover half the Christmas expenses, like some carnival ride to shake you up and yet, when it's over, make you ready and eager to be abused again. And the elephant, eating straw, unshackled, stays put.

I had quite a ride at work after my night with GP and DeWitt and Paulette. It ignited something in me, a hot streak. Everything started to click. At work, they gave me the three-thousand raise, instead of the two, and I took it from there. I played chicken with them, and they flinched. I raised my worth in their eyes, forced them to see how much they wanted me on board, because they could see I genuinely didn't care what they would do to me, and they found my fearlessness curious, interesting, attractive. Word has gotten around about the raise—coupled with the promotion—and people look at me differently when I speak casually with them in the kitchen, and they choose their own words more carefully when they know I'm in the next room. I've landed three new accounts for us in the past two months. I'm bringing in eight million in capitalized billings in six months. I'm asking for another raise and getting it. And Jimmy's my star writer. They've worked out the numbers with Stringer and he's paying the stolen money back in installments, working in a lesser job, as if there's some kind of policy written somewhere on how to handle white-collar felonies without generating bad spin.

Yet none of it makes me happy. When I wake in the middle of the night, my cheek is moist, my tongue dry, and I'm itching to be where I've never been, a South Chicago blues bar, bottleneck licks in the air, the smell of cigarette smoke on my fingers, and yet I stay there in bed, alert in a dark room that seems more oppressive than whatever unpleasant dreams I've escaped. I've tasted life, real life, a dark and fertile and terrible streak of it, and I miss it. This doesn't compare, this treadmill. It doesn't pay as well either.

The night I came home after I did the job for GP, Meg and I woke simultaneously just before dawn and lay there, tossing, until we couldn't *not* talk about the money. So we talked about it, and without saying what I'd done to get it, we agreed that disposing of it in any way wouldn't make a difference. *Keeping the money won't make it any worse.* I pointed out again that if we turned in the money to Bogardus there was no telling what would happen. It would be foolish to admit having it. We convinced ourselves we were stuck with it.

For the first six months in the new house, it was a rush simply walking through the back door into that mud room at night, with the car engine ticking as it cooled in the garage. Then it came to seem—how can I put it?—slightly unpleasant to come home. Lately I've found myself driving through our old neighborhood, stalling on my way home from work. I drive past our old house, and it looks as if it's decaying from the inside out. The unmarried junior exec who moved in has accepted a stint in Japan and left the place furnished but uninhabited. No one goes in or out. The unfertilized lawn is getting bald in places, though somebody comes to mow in the summer. The hollies have grown all out of shape. Worst of all, he stripped all the ivy off the chimney and the stucco and hasn't bothered to paint over where the vines left their little roots, the varicose-vein shadows of their stems.

When I pull into our development, Sedgewick Estates, the guard nods to me and waves me on. I go directly into the house and place the money from my mother on the kitchen counter. Nobody's home: Meg's lunching with Corcoran and another developer, Dana's at a friend's house, and Alec had a sleepover with one of his Little League buddies. Meg left a note on the island in the kitchen: *Did you remember it's Father's Day? How'd you like to go out to dinner tonight?*

I meander through the house, feeling lonely. I start in Alec's bedroom, with his big windows looking out onto the grove of oaks, where shadows move across the lawn in the dusk. Alec has plenty of space now, plenty of room to dribble and dunk into the little plastic hoop on his door, because we haven't yet bought a new dresser for him. In her room, Dana has a classic psychedelic Beatles poster with a dove on Ringo's finger and a third eye staring out of George Harrison's palm. There isn't a single book anywhere in sight, and I don't know how she manages to keep up her grades, especially with the job she has in a check-out line. It's a zoo: CDs out of jewel boxes, the bed unmade, clothing on the floor, her script for *The Glass Menagerie* in loose pages over the dresser and beanbag chair.

I wander across the landing, which leads down a hall, toward the master bedroom. There's even a second-floor laundry room, which I pass along the way. Meg and I have a king-size bed, a new set of dressers. Meg likes to work in this room, with all her papers spread out on the comforter, putting together a pitch to another office-complex developer, hoping for another big hit, thinking it will give us enough money to complete Dana's college fund. Before she left, Meg cracked open one of the bathroom windows, and I can smell the swirl of cut grass and fresh air, and I can hear the spitting hiss of someone's sprinkler.

The phone rings.

"How'd it go?" Meg asks.

"Just fine. I've got the money. Now if I can just get Will to return my calls. I left another message on his mother's answering machine."

"I'm not sure I agree with you about this. We could use that money. But it's your call," she says. "Happy Father's Day."

"Some Father's Day. Nobody's even here to celebrate."

"Remember Alec's got Little League at four."

"Yeah, I'm coaching third," I say.

"And Dana's got that play tonight. She's subbing for that girl who got the role of Laura. Remember? We could go out to dinner before the play."

"That sounds fine."

"See you in about half an hour," Meg says. "Dana isn't home from work yet, is she?"

"Not yet," I say.

"Love you," she says.

"Love you, too."

On my way back to the kitchen, I pass my study with the gumwood bookshelves and the new computer. I go into the kitchen, with rows of copperware hanging from a wooden frame attached to the ceiling by chains, the little ceramic tiles on the walls above the stove with illustrations of rosemary, thyme, and chives. I love this house. So why do I feel so restless here?

The phone rings again. Probably Meg, remembering something. I pick up the cordless from the kitchen counter.

"Yeah?"

"Mr. Cahill? There's someone here at the gate for you," she says. It's the blond temp. She must have arrived only minutes ago. I love her voice, the way it rises at the end of almost every sentence. "He says he's a coworker."

It has to be Whit. He'd stopped by like this, unannounced, a couple weeks earlier.

"No problem. Send him in."

I head upstairs to change my shirt. When is Whit going to realize I have a life not entirely under his jurisdiction?

I don't see him immediately when I come down. But when I make a second trip through the family room, I spot something on the table: a photograph. I walk over and pick it up: it's a picture of me, in the front seat of the Range Rover, looking back at the camera. I spin around and see him sitting in the big reclining armchair I bought only two months ago, and he's wearing baggy warm-ups, seems to have a couple extra rings on his fingers, and he isn't wearing his sunglasses. He smiles faintly at me as I take a step back.

"Nice place here," he says, and I notice the beer in his hand. "Glad I could help you with all this."

What startles me more than anything is how much he seems to belong. He's got CNBC on the big screen, and he's watching a report about Thailand. He could sit here all afternoon watching the Bills in a playoff game, with a couple empties and a bowl of tortilla chips, and it wouldn't feel odd to me. Immediately, I wonder about Paulette. I find myself glancing around the room, aching to see how she looks, the way she moves through shadows on the hardwood floor, probably with even more assurance than she did in our little Tudor.

I realize it's a relief to see him. Many nights, waking up with a damp neck, I imagine this scene with GP, and each time some little whiff of fear within me turns, as I feel it, into yearning, as it does now. I'm hoping Meg will come home soon, find him here, be drawn into conversation with him, step inside his force field of benevolent self-assurance, see for herself what I keep telling her about what I remember of this man whenever I've had a few drinks. I drop the photograph on the table and move toward the kitchen.

"Coworker, huh?" I ask, going to the refrigerator for a beer of my own. I realize I'm trying to impress him with how casually I can take this. "How are you on that beer?"

I'm so steady, I'm amazed. I hope I'm amazing *him.* As I move out of the kitchen, I see my envelope filled with cash, the inheritance from my mother. I wonder if he can deliver it to Will for me. I know Will wouldn't accept anything from *me.* GP's presence in the house makes the money seem all the more like contraband, something suitable for his delivery channels.

"I'm fine," he says, clicking off the television. "I thought all you wanted was to get me out of your life. Last I heard, anyway. You don't look too upset to see me."

"I'm thinking maybe you can help me out," I say.

"I already *told* you I can help you out. You just pick up the phone."

"I got some money I want Will to have. For his tuition at Ignatius. I hear he's strapped," I say, picking up the envelope, walking into the family room, feeling all that space above me in the vaulted ceiling, watching the magnolias sway outside the windows, carrying the envelope over and dropping it into his lap. "It's about the same amount of money as you gave me."

"That wasn't no loan, if that's what you think," he says. "That was a wage."

"No. I just want Will to have it."

"I didn't come here to be your mule. I came here because Polette been on my ass to come here. I tell her she's free to come on her own. She seem to think otherwise."

My heart jumped at the sound of her name.

"So she's in town, too?" I asked.

"I can't help you with that money. Will don't have nothing to do with me now," he says, putting the envelope on the table beside him. "I got something I want to offer you, though."

"You know I'm not interested. Where's Paulette? Is she here?"

He motions toward the window. I get up and walk over to the glass and see Paulette sitting outside, on the deck, at the wrought-iron umbrella table, smoking a cigarette, looking off into the woods. She's wearing jeans and a sleeveless top, and she's done something different with her hair, but I can't, for the moment, remember what her hair looked like before. It couldn't have looked this good. What is it about her that generates the speed I feel, even at this distance, through the closed door? My heart's working, as if I'd just twisted the ignition for the first time in a year. I come back to sit across from GP.

"Polette plan to stay in town, sell airtime for the station I gone start up here I told you about."

"I thought that was a done deal last year," I say.

"Took a lot longer than we thought."

"Same kind of station?" I ask.

"Uh-huh."

"She ever done that before?" I ask.

"You don't think she could sell?"

I visualize her in a suit and low heels, that predator's smile, the way she presses her lips together, thinking about a passage of music or a sum of money or a man's body. She'd make a stunning account executive at any agency. It *was* a natural move for her, if they could get a station like that off the ground.

"Polette talk me into this," he says. "She wanted me to tell you what she wants."

"When has Paulette ever had trouble telling somebody what she wants?" I ask. "We had a deal. You were out of my life."

"You loved it," he says. "You know you did. You been missin' me. You been missin' Polette."

"This discussion's over, GP. I don't want to hear this."

"Polette want you to run this station," he says.

"What happened to DeWitt."

"DeWitt decided he wanted to divest himself of any business with me."

"What took so long?"

"Some guy Stein own the building out in Ontario County gave us a hard time at the negotiating table. Then we had the zoning. This country so fucked, man can't start his own business he don't grease some palm. And me, I got to get somebody else do all my negotiating. Then DeWitt took a powder. Me and my associates, we've got three others out in California didn't take half as long to start. Polette do all the legwork for you. But she don't want to run it. We need you, G."

"This is one of those little AM talk-radio things you told me about? The preachers come on all day."

"It's a license to print you own money. Preachers don't charge a penny. All you got to do, hang a bucket on the door for the advertisers to dump their cash in," he says. "*Big* bucket."

"And I'm just there to empty the bucket."

"Got the studio all set up. Take you out there right now, check it out, you like. This afternoon. Tomorrow. It's legit."

"I don't know that business," I say.

"But see, Polette don't want to run the thing. She like to be out on the road. Set her own hours."

"And what's your involvement?" I ask.

"Same as always. I get the profit. Brothers and sisters, they send money to the station. They just eat this shit up. They believe it. Me, all I want's the money. Same as always."

"Leaves a lot of room to play with the books, doesn't it?" I ask. "Donations. You could clean up a lot of money that way."

"You don't believe in that shit, do you?" he asks, studying me.

"What? The perfect tax dodge?"

"That preacher shit."

"Does it matter?" I ask.

He grinned, and looked at his fingernails.

"I know I can trust you. Got that picture over there say I can trust you."

"Aren't many people you can trust," I say.

"All I know is, I ain't nobody's nigger. Don't got to haul my sorry ass to some place every day that don't know me from Joe Six-Pack."

"I've been wanting a change," I say.

"There you go. Look like you and Polette need to talk. You two work it out, you got the job. Maybe she's right."

"About what."

"You not as dumb as you look."

"I don't know about that. You deliver this money to Will, we can talk."

"Get Polette to do it. It's *her* brother," he says.

He looks over toward the windows, where I want Paulette to come into view on the deck. But apparently she's keeping her seat at the table. He gets up and walks over to the sliding glass door and goes out onto the deck, and he disappears, without saying goodbye, without looking back, without giving me a phone number. I'm fighting the urge to walk after him, ask him for a number, but I stay where I am, watching the door. As always, he seems to go wherever he wants, do what he chooses. Then Paulette appears beyond the door and holds her hand up, a visor for her eyes, as she peers through the double-paned glass, until she sees me and smiles. She slides the door open.

After a year away from her, just seeing her I can feel my insides fold in on themselves, shrink and tighten and then go hard. Her shoulders are smooth and beautiful, and she smiles at me with her eyes, moving across the room, siting where GP did, and I feel a little twinge of resentment that she's absorbing the heat of *his* body, not mine, as she slides into those cushions. Idiotically, I imagine lowering myself into that chair, feeling the heat of her legs and her back after she's gone, and after only one beer I have a drunken man's certainty that this is precisely what's been missing from my life the past year, that leftover warmth of Paulette's skin against mine.

"How've you been?" I ask.

"Better than you, I bet."

I laugh, walk into the kitchen and get another beer. As I pass the table where GP sat, I see the envelope with my mother's money. As I close the refrigerator door and turn to place the beer on the sleek island, I nearly bump into her. She's a foot away from me, standing between me and the only convenient way out of the room. I can feel my hand trembling, the one holding the beer, and my legs go weak under me. She reaches for the beer, and I hand it to her, and I turn to get another one from the refrigerator, and as I curl my fingers around the cold can, I feel her hand on my back, slowly rising up my spine to my neck, where she lets her fingers rest, making little circles with her nails. I don't move, close my eyes, not wanting her to stop. Then I straighten up, and turn toward her. She steps closer, until her face is a foot away from mine, and she's looking up into my eyes, and she stands there, looking at me, glancing at my left eye and then my right as if one or the other of them might give her a better view inside me. Or through me.

I reach out and stroke her cheek with the backs of my fingers, once, twice, and she closes her eyes, leaning into it, and I reach around her as she pulls away, drawing her to me, feeling the length of her body against mine, the side of her face resting on my shoulder. She grabs onto me and squeezes, not hard, but firm, and we stay like that, and I can smell her scent rising off her bare shoulder, not Trésor anymore, a new one. Then we release each other and she turns away, slowly heading back out into the family room. I follow her to the door, and I see the envelope of money and pick it up on the way out of the kitchen, not quite sure what I'm going to ask her.

"Take a look at this," I say, handing the envelope to her.

She takes it and looks inside.

"What is it? GP give you this?" she asks.

"No. I want your brother to have it. You take it to him for me?"

"He won't take it from you," she says. "You know that."

"Why's he hate me so much?" I ask.

"Doesn't hate you. He resents you."

"Then I'm not even considering what GP's talking about."

"The station, you mean?"

"Yeah, the station," I say.

"Will could use this money," she says. "I see what you're saying. I could tell him it's from me."

"Whatever works."

"He *is* out of tuition money. The job he got at the Jamaican restaurant downtown pay minimum."

It's painful, just looking at her. My feeling whirls inside me, a little gyroscope, the flywheel revolving on its own, never losing momentum. I've learned how to talk, smile, balance a bank statement, make a tuna sandwich, commiserate with Meg about any number of things, and still the flywheel throbs, pivoting off-kilter, defying the gravity of all my responsibilities. I can kiss Meg, knowing I love her no less than I've ever loved her, and still, now, this feeling spins inside me, drawing everything into its orbit.

"Looks like a lot a money. You sure?"

"Just pay the school directly, if he won't take it."

"I'll take the money to him. You come work at the station. That's the deal," she says. "It's legit. It isn't like what you did before."

"How could you and I work together?"

"Seem to me, we work real well together."

"That's exactly the problem," I say.

I turn away and sit on one of the ladderback chairs along the wall. It's a hard, unyielding chair, a chair with firm convictions about posture, certainties built into the design about how a man is supposed to sit and stand. Nobody I know wants to sit in that chair, though. I imagine Meg and Corcoran having this sort of discussion, and I'm certain, at one point or another, they talked themselves through it toward a risky, working agreement. I'm sure neither of them sat in this sort of chair at the time.

"Sometimes I wake up and it's all I can do to crawl out of bed."

"I hate my life," Paulette says, gazing out the window. "This is my chance, Rich. But I can't do it alone. I want to do it with *you.* I need you there. I want to work for you."

"But he'd always be there. We'd always be answering to him."

"GP say anybody who run a big business be just like him, one way or another. They all like him. You end up working for GP no matter where you work."

I get up and go over to where she stands at the window and hand her the envelope. She hesitates, and then takes it.

"He doesn't have to know where it came from," I say. "You think he'd care?"

"He'll take it. But I think you makin' a big mistake. I wouldn't give away a penny of *my* money. I earned all of it," she says. "So did you."

"Yeah, well, I didn't earn *that* money. Not by a long shot."

"I got to go," she says, handing me a scrap of paper. "He'll be in town a couple days. You need to tell him soon."

The folded shred of paper has a phone number. Certain moments in life raise the hair on your arms, moments when it becomes clear how every day's like a good blues riff. Something new and unforeseen emerges, at least for a while, in the way it breaks free of a musical scale and yet keeps struggling to remain true to it.

"Don't tell me. The Hyatt again?"

"Call him," she says. "I be staying at home with Will, you want to call."

"Is he really out of it?" I ask. "GP, I mean. Is he out of the business? The *other* business."

"It's complicated."

Then she rises on her toes to kiss me on the cheek and I intercept her lips with my own, but she pulls away when she realizes what she's done. There's a seriousness, a restraint, here I don't remember from before. There are limits now. When she walks outside and around the house, I lean back against the wall and close my eyes.

When Meg comes home, I tell her the money's going to make its way to Will. She doesn't pursue it, but I can tell she wishes we were keeping it. We go through the motions, we finish the day as planned. I coach third for Alec's game. We sit through our daughter's performance of Tennessee Williams, and we come home and make popcorn and watch a rerun of *Parenthood.* Just like any other day.

When I wake up the next morning, I stay in bed waiting for some kind of insight into my life. The worlds I straddle seem to have fallen into perfect alignment, everything prepared, as if I've discovered the perfect way to put certain volatile powders together so they won't explode until just the right moment, presumably when I'm far enough away from everything I take for granted not to care about it. I know what I want to do, and I'm convinced it's what I need to do. But what would I say to Meg, to the kids? What would become of us? I know I would need to quit caring about these things and just make the leap, but I'm not jumping out of bed to do it. More than anything, I want to be able to say to myself, as I gaze up at a blank ceiling on a quiet Sunday morning: *Yes, this is it. This is what my life has been leading up to. Now I get it. Now it all makes sense.* But late into the morning, I haven't moved, still in bed, still waiting, still trying to decide whether or not to pick up the phone.

I hear a mockingbird singing outside for the first time in this neighborhood, a bird I never heard when we lived in our old house. I love the way it sounds, the way it feels to listen to it. It goes through its endless impersonation of other birds, car alarms, creaking tricycle wheels, television noises, conversation, lovemaking, sorrow, joy, as if it wants to reconcile everything into a single song. As if any common noise can sound beautiful if you sing it a certain way. He echoes everything around him, trying to convince himself he can become anything he wants to become. Just hearing him sing, you start to think so, too. You start to think there are no limits to freedom, that anything's possible. It's a wonderful thing to believe on a morning like this. At least until that gray bird flies away and his song is done and the actual day begins.